WRENCHED

LEGACY OF MAGIC
BOOK 5

LINDSAY BUROKER

1

"DO I... TOUCH ITS LEAVES, OR WHAT?" I PATTED THE AIR AROUND the magically-grown dragon-shaped topiary protecting the walkway leading to Val Thorvald's house. "They look prickly."

The eight-foot-tall shrub was one of four replacements for those that had been burned down by fireballs during the battle the week before. It loomed not only over me—at five-foot-one, *most* things loom over me—but over my enchanting instructor Santiago and the elven princess and part-time horticulturist Freysha.

"They are," Freysha said. "Per Lord Zavryd'nokquetal's request, the new topiaries are thorny, prickly, and the fire-retardant leaves seep a chemical residue similar to that of your stinging nettles."

"I can't believe you guys think *Sarrlevi* is the villain around here," I muttered.

Santiago arched his graying eyebrows, as if to say *he* didn't think that. Since Sarrlevi had given him a huge stack of gold coins to tutor me, Santiago might be more inclined to believe that my elf-assassin acquaintance was an okay guy.

Freysha's expression was more dubious. "He *is* an assassin," she pointed out.

"Zavryd is a dragon. I'm sure he's incinerated more *lesser* species, as he calls us, than Sarrlevi has been paid to kill."

"I don't know if that's true," she said. "The Stormforge Clan is generally considered to be law-abiding. Law-*enforcing*, in fact."

"*Dragon* law." Which I wasn't inclined to think much of, not when, the last I heard, the Dragon Justice Court was still debating if Sarrlevi should be whisked off for *punishment and rehabilitation.* I waved at the prickly leaves. "Do I *have* to touch them?" I'd only encountered stinging nettles a few times, since I kept my interactions with nature to a minimum, but I was familiar with the lingering lash of their kiss.

"It is easier to enchant what one is touching and manipulating —" Santiago pointed to the topiary, reminding me that he was here on Val's lawn solely for the sake of my education, "—but I have seen you use your power from a distance. It is certainly possible."

You did this in the vision I gave you, Sorka, the newly chatty sentience in my magical war hammer, pointed out.

Yeah, but that wasn't real, and that was more of a test *than a vision, wasn't it?*

When it comes to the way I am capable of influencing you, you may consider that not all visions are tests but all tests are visions.

Kinda like how not all fingers are thumbs but all thumbs are fingers, huh?

Your Earth-spawned humor is droll.

Yeah, I'm thinking of retiring from house flipping to become a comedian.

Aware of Santiago watching patiently—if he was ever impatient, he kept it to himself—I held my hands close to but not touching the leaves. I'd studied the enchantment on Dimitri's dragon door knocker, which spat flames at visitors if the proper passcode wasn't issued, and believed I could replicate it. Since Zavryd wanted to ensure his and Val's lair—had anyone else ever called a renovated Victorian house a lair?—was properly defended, the topiaries were supposed to spew fire at anyone who wasn't on their guest list.

Allowing access to some but not others was the challenging part. Even though I'd met everyone on the list Val had supplied, and was familiar with their auras, I struggled to imbue the knowledge into the topiary. It wasn't as if it had a *brain* and could remember things. Everything had to be woven in with magic.

I'd studied the other wards around the property, all designed to trigger in their own way at the approach of strangers, and thought I could make a metal contraption that did what they wanted, but the vegetation sneered at my attempts.

"Nothing's happening." I dropped my arms in frustration. "Are you sure dwarves—and half-dwarves—are capable of enchanting *bushes*?"

"I have not heard of it, actually," Freysha admitted, "but is it not a good test for you? A way for you to practice your burgeoning skills as an enchanter?"

"When I offered to help out, I was thinking of enchanting the mailbox." I pointed to the battered metal receptacle perched on a pole, the crooked red flag drooping sadly. "Maybe making an entirely new one, since that looks like it's been the target of local hoodlums driving by and playing mailbox baseball."

"I believe one of the assassins clubbed it with his elbow before hurling an axe at me on the porch." Val walked up to join us. She carried cans of flavored water and offered a drink to everyone. "You don't need to do anything more to help, Matti. The house is looking great." She waved to the repaired—and now enchanted for greater durability—porch, steps, and roof. "I *love* the new drainpipes. When it rains, they shoot the water all the way to the sidewalk. No chance of them clogging ever." She smirked. "I saw a chipmunk trying to stash nuts in them go flying earlier."

"I like fixing things." A true statement, but I was trying to fix everything in sight largely out of guilt. Though unintentionally, I'd brought those assassins to Val's doorstep. I'd already repaired and *upgraded* my sister's house for similar reasons, though I'd been careful to add only subtle enchantments there. The strictness of her homeowners' association made me certain that drainpipes spurting water, pine needles, and possibly chipmunks all the way to the street would result in fees and strongly worded notes of haughty disapproval.

"Even bushes?" Val asked.

"My instructor believes I should challenge myself." I nodded toward Santiago, then lifted my hands to try again.

"I *have* enchanted a cactus successfully before," Santiago said. "And one of my books from the dwarven home world discusses how to improve the algae and mushroom crops they farm in their tunnels by imbuing the rock underneath the substrate with growth-enhancing magic."

"I've seen those farms. The rock underneath, huh?" The words prompted me to use my senses to probe the ground around the roots of the topiaries. Rocks called to my dwarven blood far more than leaves.

Unfortunately, little but dirt comprised the ground, with the only rock anywhere near the surface being pebble-sized. Would enchanting *those* help? I didn't want the topiaries to simply grow better but to keep out strangers.

Hoping for the best, I willed my magic into the ground.

"Have you heard anything about Sarrlevi's mother?" Val asked Freysha while I worked.

"I know only that my father has ordered a guard to stand outside her home and ensure her safety," Freysha said. "He was unwilling to forbid a dwarven princess from visiting our people entirely, as such an ultimatum could end the period of peace and prosperity that dwarves and elves have enjoyed for the last few centuries, but if Barothla appears in our city, my father will know and keep an eye on her."

"I guess that's something," Val said. "Now that I know *why* Sarrlevi has been after Matti's mom, I want to club that princess."

I gritted my teeth, not at their conversation but at my struggle to get the pebbles in the ground to do anything. They were too small. They couldn't hold any useful enchantments. And the topiary kept resisting *everything* I offered it. Were I to bring out a watering can and gently saturate its roots, it would probably spit its stinging chemicals at me.

"It is unfortunate to have a family member working at odds with you." Freysha smiled sadly, probably thinking of her mother, the queen.

"Perhaps," Santiago said, resting a hand on my tense shoulder, "you should take a break from the topiary, work on the mailbox, and come back to this project later when you are fresh."

"I'm getting a mailbox enchantment?" Val asked. "Can you make it so I don't have to reaffix the box every time a villain takes his aggressions out on it?"

"Yes," I said through my gritted teeth, reluctant to give up on the topiary, however briefly. I *hated* to admit defeat. Especially when it came to crafting. This was my special skill, damn it. It was, at least going by my high-school grades, my *only* skill. Snarling, I poured more energy into my efforts.

Branches snapped, and the topiary burst into flame.

I stumbled back, jerking my arms down and withdrawing my power.

"Uhm," Val said.

Freysha stepped forward and conjured cooling magical water to flow over the flaming shrub.

"I'm sorry," I blurted, chagrined that I'd let my temper get the best of me.

"I didn't know you could do that," Val said.

My shoulders slumped. "I didn't either."

"Ms. Puletasi has demonstrated the ability to subconsciously affect that which she works on," Santiago said blandly.

"By causing it to burst into flames? Maybe I'll keep my mailbox the way it is." Val cast a worried look toward the drainpipes.

"*Metal* doesn't do that." I waved at the smoldering topiary.

Fortunately, Freysha quenched the fire before it did much damage. With a little pruning, the shrub would be fine.

"At least not at a heat point less than two thousand degrees Fahrenheit," Santiago murmured. "Roughly."

I grimaced, fairly certain fire got hotter than that. I would have to be careful with my temper going forward. Usually, I only punched walls or smashed posts with my hammer when I had a tantrum. This new awareness that I could light fires with my mind was alarming. Neither my grandparents nor my martial-arts instructor would approve.

You are attempting to enchant foliage? a familiar dry voice spoke into my mind.

Sarrlevi.

Grinning, I spun to look for him, though I hadn't sensed him and could only guess his location based on where his telepathic words had seemed to come from. *My instructor believes I should expand my horizons.*

You expanded the combustibility of that shrub. Sarrlevi dropped his magical camouflage and appeared on the sidewalk beyond the wards protecting the property.

Val and Freysha, no doubt sensing him, turned to look.

"I should have known that lovestruck grin wasn't for the ice-cream man," Val said.

I shook my head in denial of being *lovestruck* but waved and headed toward Sarrlevi instead of responding. A week had passed since he'd visited, and I missed him. It had been *days* since anyone tousled my hair, brought me cheese, or mocked my master-plumber certification, and the urge to hug him and kiss him came over me.

But as I jogged up, I noticed the scar on his cheek. *More* than a scar. The deep scratch that my aunt had given Sarrlevi when she'd clawed at him to escape had scabbed over but hadn't faded, not in the least. By now, it should have fully healed. *Especially* on an elf with magical blood that always repaired his injuries far more quickly than was normal for a mundane human. The scratches—I couldn't help thinking of them as *claw marks*—on the back of his hand were still there too.

I reached toward his cheek. "Why aren't these—"

Sarrlevi swept me into a hug, pulling me up on tiptoes to kiss me. Though startled, since he'd never kissed me in front of witnesses, my body responded as it always did to an intimate touch from him. My arms wrapped around his shoulders, and I enjoyed the hard warmth of his muscles under his shirt as I returned the kiss.

It was far more than a friendly *hello* kiss. There was a hungry, almost dangerous edge to him that didn't jibe with the amused greeting he'd given me. His magic flowed into me, scorching my nerves with the desire it aroused. My heart pounded as I envisioned him making a portal and taking me to one of his homes for the private passionate joining that we both wanted.

A growl escaped his throat, and he cupped my ass, pulling me hard against him. An image came to mind of him thrusting me against my parked truck and us *joining* right there. Was it one he shared? Or did my own mind conjure it? Either way, it and his magic were exhilarating and had me panting with such intense arousal that it took all of my willpower to raise an objection.

Uhm, Varlesh? I untwined my arms from the back of his neck to grip his shoulders and push him back. Or *try*. He resisted, keeping me close, his mouth hard against mine.

I didn't *fear* him, not exactly, since I'd long wanted to take our relationship in the same direction he did, but uncertainty sparked in me. Something was off. He wasn't himself.

Varlesh, I repeated, pushing more firmly on his shoulders.

His lips drew back, and he loosened his grip, but his gaze caught and held mine. The fiery intensity in his blue eyes made my breath catch, and I was tempted to suggest we go somewhere private and do exactly what he wanted. What my body had longed for since I met him. And what the rest of me now thought was a good idea too.

"I want you," Sarrlevi said, his words a raspy growl.

"I want you too, but not *here*." I looked over at Val, Santiago, and Freysha, not surprised to find them staring open-mouthed at us. Even the singed topiary was staring.

I squinted up at Sarrlevi. Before, *he'd* been the one to break off our impromptu romantic engagements, saying he didn't want me to have sex with him and then regret it, since he was still technically on Barothla's mission to kill my mother. He'd implied he was no longer considering doing that, but we had things to resolve when it came to her—and *his* mother.

"This isn't like you," I added quietly.

He'd been passionate with me before, and I'd even heard a growl, but we'd been alone on my bed then, and I'd rubbed his scalp and pointed ears, trying to use a bit of magic to increase his enjoyment. In that context, it had seemed *appropriate.*

Sarrlevi's arms loosened around me, and the soles of my feet returned to the ground. He tilted his face toward the sky and took a breath—a *steadying* breath?

"My desire for you has grown difficult to sublimate lately," he admitted.

"I'm flattered, but, uhm, *how* lately?"

"This past week."

I reached up to touch his cheek below the scar. "Why isn't this healing?"

"I don't know."

"Maybe we should figure that out."

2

SARRLEVI LEANED AGAINST MY TRUCK, HIS HANDS IN HIS POCKETS AS we talked. A couple of times, he'd lifted them toward me, as if to pull me close and return to kissing—or more—but he caught himself each time and jammed them back into his pockets. The gesture was as uncharacteristic as everything else about him.

Usually, he would stand calmly, perhaps with his hands clasped behind his back while speaking in his haughty erudite elven way. Oh, I'd glimpsed his passion a few times but always in private. Of late, he'd been more willing to let his guard down with me. But this was something different.

A dangerous tension radiated from him. I'd seen him angry before, and this wasn't entirely different from that, but it seemed more like barely restrained lust. I truly was flattered that he wanted to be with me—how long had we verbally sparred, him letting me know he had no interest in mongrels and me waking daily from erotic dreams of him?—but not like this. Not if something was *wrong* with him.

"It had to be her red fingernails." I recalled how we'd dragged Barothla away from her people to force her to drink a truth drug and recite the formula that could cure Sarrlevi's mother. "I remember wondering if it was nail polish or they were press-ons or what. When she first came to Earth, she didn't have anything on her nails. I don't think she wore makeup of any kind. But when I was led into the dwarven palace… she was armored and dressed, including those red nails, and waiting for me. Or maybe waiting for *you*?" I raised my eyebrows.

Sarrlevi eyed the scabbed wounds on the back of his wrist and hand. "I do remember noting her nails. It's possible the paint had an alchemical component and did something to affect my natural ability to heal wounds."

"I… think it might have done more than that."

"To what do you refer?" Sarrlevi looked at me, but his gaze dipped to my chest, lingering there for a long moment before he pulled it back up.

I pointed at him. "*That.*"

I had no doubt he was aware of my every curve—after all, he'd seen me naked—but he'd never ogled me before, not when I could see it anyway. It was possible he ogled me when he was stealthily checking in on me to make sure assassins hadn't killed me, but he was never brazen about his interest.

Sarrlevi pushed a hand through his short hair. Typically, it was as tidy as the rest of him, but it was unkempt, like he'd run his hands through it a *lot* that day. "To what end? Your aunt wants you dead, not sexually satisfied."

I snorted and was about to say this had to be a *side effect* rather than the main intent, but he turned a concerned expression on me.

"Or were you…" He glanced toward the yard, but Santiago had left and Val and Freysha had gone inside. Aside from cars occasionally driving past, we were alone. "Did it bother you that I'm more… that I'm less…" He flexed a hand in the air, groping for a term.

In control, was what came to my mind.

"Did *I* bother you?" he asked gravely.

"No." I'd been tempted to let him do exactly what that image had shown me, and I would have liked it. A *lot*. Maybe afterward, I would have been embarrassed at having had public sex, but when he'd been scorching my nerves with his magic, I'd never been so quickly aroused. I'd never wanted him more. "I am, however, concerned about the ramifications of you losing some of your control. *I'm* the one prone to temper tantrums." I waved to the singed topiary. "You're always calm and collected, even when you fight. Even when you're *mad,* you hold things together and don't lash out."

Sarrlevi didn't follow my gesture toward the topiary; his gaze remained on me. Maybe he was concerned that I wasn't telling him the truth? That lust-filled Varlesh would turn me off. Or… that he would hurt me and I wouldn't forgive him? Maybe that was it.

"She may wish to drive a right triangular prism between us." Sarrlevi tilted his head. "Is that the correct Earth expression?"

Was that a *wedge*?

I smiled. "Close enough."

"If we were no longer allied, she might believe I would come back and do her bidding without argument." His jaw tightened, that tension still present.

I stepped closer, though it felt like creeping toward a man-eating lion that had escaped its cage, and rested my hand on his shoulder. Too bad I couldn't ooze relaxation into him.

"She might only have been looking for ways to defend herself and take you out as an enemy," I said. "She threw down all those vials of things, remember? This has admittedly been more slow-acting. It wasn't designed to make you let her go in a fight. How long have you been feeling off?"

Sarrlevi shrugged. "A week, perhaps."

"Are you just feeling, uhm, randy, or is there more to it?"

A hint of his usual wry humor touched his eyes as he gave me a sidelong look.

"I'm not sure how to interpret that expression," I said.

"I'm frequently *randy*. That's not atypical."

"Really? At your age?"

"I am in my prime."

"You're three hundred years old, dude."

"Which is the prime of an elf's life."

"The randy prime."

"Yes." His humor waned as he studied the ground. "What has been different is that I feel less in control of it—of *myself*. I'm also having atypical flashes of irritation and urges to lash out." He glanced warily at me and didn't continue.

"I suppose elves don't get PMS, and I shouldn't ask if eating chocolate helps."

I had no trouble interpreting the blank look he gave me. Either elves didn't get that, or he, being male, was oblivious. Neither would surprise me. I'd never dated the kind of guy that I could send to the store to buy tampons for me, and I had a feeling that wasn't about to change. Though maybe less out of a familiarity with Earth culture than an unwillingness to be helpful. If I explained my needs, he would probably make something out of vines.

That thought made me laugh. Kind of a horrified laugh.

He arched his eyebrows.

Deciding not to explain, I said, "Maybe we should ask Zoltan to analyze a sample of your blood and see if there are any weird magical chemicals floating around in there."

"Whatever she did to me, my immune system will be able to handle it."

"Are you that certain?" It had been over a week. "Or is it that you're unwilling to let Zoltan poke a needle into you?"

"The vampire dislikes me, and I am disinclined to be close to alchemists right now. Allowing him access to my veins might be unwise."

"If he had access to your veins, he'd be more likely to fulfill his vampiric needs than attack you outright."

"That would also be unappealing."

"What if I stand next to him and threaten him with my hammer if he gets uppity?" I stepped closer, rested a hand on Sarrlevi's chest, and smiled encouragingly at him. I *really* wanted someone to check him out.

The smoldering intensity returned to his gaze as he met my eyes, and memories of the steamy kiss—and his vision—sprang back into my mind. Maybe I should have backed away, but it was all I could do not to move closer. It was *hot* when he looked at me like that. I couldn't help it.

Sarrlevi closed his eyes and swallowed. "It would not be wise for you to touch me, to be *close* to me, while I am… compromised."

Disappointment made my shoulders slump as I withdrew my hand and stepped back. He was right, of course, but some dumb part of me felt it as a rejection. No, it would only be a rejection if he refused to accept help.

"I have not been far away from you this past week," he whispered, his eyes still closed. "Even though I told the Assassins' Guild leader and all who escaped during the battle to let the other assassins know I will defend you, I do not trust them not to keep trying. You are still the prestige hunt, despite my attempt to get Nesheeva to change that. I dare not leave you alone. But I've been aware of my… control slipping and haven't trusted myself to get close." He opened his eyes, the heated desire lingering. "I don't want to hurt you," he whispered.

"You won't." I caught myself before reaching out to hold his hand. He'd told me *not* to, and I didn't want to make things harder on him. "Let's go see Zoltan. He's gathered some of the ingredients for the formula that could cure your mother's disease, and he's got a list of what he can't get here on Earth. Either you can go find the items, or *we* can go, if you think I could help. Then we can hunt down someone capable of creating the formula. Zoltan still doesn't think he can but believes a good elf alchemist would have the power."

"As we discussed, an *elf* alchemist will be unlikely to help me."

"Yeah, but *I'll* do the talking. Any elf would love to help me. I'm charming."

Sarrlevi looked toward the singed topiary.

"We won't mention to them that I light shrubs on fire." I stepped onto the walkway before realizing the wards that Zavryd had replaced would keep Sarrlevi from setting foot on the property. And it was broad daylight, so Zoltan wouldn't be able to come outside. Had Zavryd been there, I would have asked him to allow Sarrlevi on the property, but he wasn't around. "If I get a syringe, will you let me take a blood sample?"

"Yes. I have no fear of *you* molesting my veins."

"Yeah, it's other parts of you that excite me."

He managed one of his smug, knowing smiles. "I am aware."

Somewhere along the way, even those smiles had started appealing to me. I fought the urge to kiss him, instead pointing for him to stay there, and ran toward the backyard and the basement laboratory, hoping Zoltan would be able to figure out what Barothla had done to Sarrlevi—and how to heal him. Maybe he could create some kind of antidote for the poison, if that's what it was.

3

I TROTTED BACK TO THE FRONT YARD WITH TWO SYRINGES, RELIEVED to find Sarrlevi waiting. I had worried he would flee, not wanting to be tested—or would he think of it as being *experimented on?*—by Zoltan.

"Here's the list of ingredients he wasn't able to find." I held out a red sticky note with a bubbling and smoking cauldron in the corner, something that might have been custom printed for Zoltan. "He gave me instructions on how to draw blood and, in case I'm particularly dim and slow, per his words, a link to an instructional cartoon on the internet."

Though somewhat insulted, I *had* loaded the video. To show Sarrlevi, I held up my phone. Fortunately, it was working again, though the repair tech had price gouged as badly as Zoltan because I'd wanted it fixed *as soon as possible* so we could double-check my aunt's formula. I needn't have worried. Sarrlevi's memory was as perfect as he'd believed.

"Drawing blood doesn't look too complicated, but veins are apparently slippery little buggers, so I hope you'll be patient with me. My nursing experience doesn't go much beyond putting on bandages. Though I *did* cauterize the wound of one of Abbas's troll relatives who was assisting us once and got overly vigorous with the nail gun. It was a long trek to the clan shaman, and trolls can't stroll into the ER. I heated my hammer and used one of the heads." Another use Sorka might not have been pleased by. Since she'd started speaking with me, she'd made her feelings clear about being used to demo cabinets and tear down drywall.

"I trust *cauterization* will not be necessary after you draw my blood."

"I wouldn't think so. It's a little needle." I held up one of the syringes and smiled. "How many times can I miss?"

Was I babbling? This was making me nervous. Why couldn't Zavryd and Val give Sarrlevi access to their property? He was here as often as I was.

"Why are there two?" Sarrlevi asked.

"Zoltan suggested taking some blood from right around the wounds that won't heal too."

"Hm."

"Let me watch the video before we get started." I wiped my palm on my jeans. I *was* nervous. Why, I didn't know. It wasn't as if he wouldn't heal quickly if I screwed up. The needles didn't have alchemical nail polish on them.

He eyed my phone—was that a baleful look?—and drew one of his daggers. Before I could question him, he sliced open a cut on his forearm and held it out to me.

"I'm not sure someone with a compromised immune system should be cutting themselves, but I guess that works." Using the syringe, I drew a sample from the blood that welled out of the wound.

"My immune system is fine. And my *daggers* are not tainted with nefarious substances boiled up in a cauldron by a heinous dwarf *witch*." Irritation flashed in his eyes.

Witch probably wasn't the first word that had come to his

mind, but I couldn't remember Sarrlevi ever swearing, at least not in a language I could understand.

"I believe you." I capped the syringe. "I've seen how well your magical kerchief cleans things. Grandma is still mentioning to Grandpa and anyone who will listen about how well you detailed their truck. It even smells like nature inside. Christmas trees, is technically what she said."

"Their conveyance wasn't as in need of my kerchief as your sister's offspring transporter." Sarrlevi turned over his hand to offer me the inflamed scratches for a second blood sample.

"Children are messy. Even elven children, I'm sure. You must have made a mess running around your house and using your mother's paintbrushes as swords." I almost mentioned how he'd played with his sister that way in the memory his mother had shared with me but worried the reminder of the past would be painful for him.

"I cleaned up any messes I made quickly, lest there be repercussions."

I started to say that it was hard to imagine his mom beating him but realized he must have meant from his father. His father *had* beaten him. Probably for more reasons than messes, but maybe his fastidious streak had evolved back then out of a fear of leaving behind any excuses for his father to blow up.

Grimacing, I wished I hadn't brought up his past in any way.

Sarrlevi's voice softened as he gazed at me and said, "My mother told you we fought with her paintbrushes?"

"I don't know if she meant to, but she'd been speaking telepathically with me and shared the memory as she was dozing off." I tried a smile. "You were cute. Kind of goofy. Maybe because of the paint smeared on your cheek."

His eyelids drooped, though he didn't appear irked. If anything, a hint of humor entered his eyes.

"There are photographs of you as a child in your grandparents' house."

"That's true." I hadn't realized he'd gone inside when he'd gone up to carry luggage and escort Grandma and Grandpa to Val's house. "They're all over the place in there."

"You are missing teeth in some. I assumed from pugilistic tendencies—" that was *definitely* a glint of humor in his eyes, "—but your grandmother explained that human children lose baby teeth and grow adult teeth."

"That's right. My grandparents didn't usually ask me to pose for pictures when I had black eyes or puffy lips from fights."

"But those things occurred?" Sarrlevi hadn't completely lost that tension in his body, but he smirked and touched my cheek.

"They did. Before I started taking martial arts and learning to control my temper."

He looked toward the singed topiary.

"To control my temper *better*." After filling a second syringe with blood directly from the wound, I waved that I would take the samples to Zoltan, and offered Sarrlevi the list again. He'd glanced at it but not taken it. "Do you think you can get these? And find an elf alchemist for me to schmooze with my charm?" I hesitated, wondering if I should send him off by himself when he was compromised.

"I am disinclined to leave you alone while there are assassins after you." Apparently, Sarrlevi was as worried about *me* as I was about him.

Though that touched me, I wanted him to help his mother. "I won't be alone. Don't forget I have a roommate."

"The *goblinator* will not deter assassins."

"Tinja will be pleased that you remember the name of her weapon, even if you can't remember *her* name."

"My memory is excellent."

True. His memory wasn't the problem. Just a pompousness

that made him believe the names of lesser species weren't worth using. Maybe he would come around eventually. He never called me *mongrel* anymore except to tease me. Even then, it was rare.

"Do you want me to come with you?" I asked, though I had been, in between all my repairs, mulling over how to get in to see Kurt Hart in his technologically and *magically* secured lakeside mansion in Medina. I'd driven by it and knew it was not only fenced and gated but protected by a barrier even stronger than what Sorka could make to protect me. The fence and foliage had kept me from seeing any of the property from the street, and the barrier had kept me from sensing any magical beings or artifacts inside. I would be shocked, however, if they weren't there.

Willard had said Hart was in the country, and had promised to get in touch when she had more information, but I ached to get at the guy. He was the closest known link to the organization that had my mother and father. Since he'd hired assassins to go after me, he might even be one of the top-tier members.

"To hunt in the wilds of various worlds for ingredients?" Sarrlevi asked.

"Sure. Seattle couples forage for edible mushrooms in the woods. It's romantic." I imagined rain falling and mud squishing underfoot as one hunted around the bases of trees for grimy fungi. "Or at least a bonding experience. I know you enjoy bonding with me."

"I do." He smiled faintly and pushed a hand through my hair.

I was about to remind him that he'd suggested we keep space between us when a surge of magic came from the intersection.

"Portal." Sarrlevi shifted his hand from my head to his scabbards and drew his swords. "*Dragon* portal."

"It's probably Zavryd coming home to enjoy his mate's meat offerings." As the words came out, I realized that Zavryd usually opened his portals above the roof. Since the defensive wards didn't object to *his* presence, he could. What if this was his sister, his sister who thought Sarrlevi was a criminal and should be dragged before the Dragon Justice Court?

Judging by his grim expression, Sarrlevi believed that a possibility. He shifted to place himself between the silvery disc floating over the street and me.

I, being the stubborn and recalcitrant half-dwarf that I was, stepped up to his side to face the possible threat with him. After all, the dragons were more irked with Sarrlevi than me.

Neither a black-scaled dragon nor a lilac-scaled dragon came out of the portal. A green dragon I'd never seen before sailed from it, flapped his great wings, and flew in a wide circle over the neighborhood. His aura was as substantial as that of the other dragons I'd encountered, but he dipped and dove and did a barrel roll, antics I hadn't seen from Zavryd and definitely not from his stuffy relatives.

"That is not a Stormforge dragon," Sarrlevi said, as if reading my mind. He didn't lower his swords.

"Does that mean he's not here to arrest you?"

"I do not know."

A dwarf came out of the portal, flailing her arms and squawking in surprise, probably because it was five feet up in the air. As she came down with a clank on armored boots, I recognized her.

"Artie?"

Her male comrade, Hennehok, came out after her, emitting a similar sound of surprise. His magical hammer clunked against the pavement as he landed, gouging out a piece.

They grumbled to each other in their language—probably words about how *dwarves* knew how to make portals that came out a suitable height above the ground—before turning to face me. The dragon continued to circle lazily above the neighborhood, presumably visible only to those with magical blood. It was a sunny day with numerous people meandering along the lake path two blocks away, but no alarmed cries rang out.

"Matti." Artie walked toward me but stopped several paces away, gripping her weapon as she eyed Sarrlevi warily. "Elf."

"Dwarf," Sarrlevi said.

"You guys fought together," I pointed out. "Maybe you can be on a first-name basis now."

"Me being kidnapped *while I slept* and slung over the shoulder of a half-orc assassin to be used as bait in a trap isn't the same as *fighting together*," Artie said stiffly.

"Sure it is. We were all working to defeat the same assassins. Some of us in armor with weapons. Some barefoot in nightshirts with only our vitriol to unleash on our enemies."

"As I recall, you bit him," Artie said.

"Vitriolically, yes. I'm glad to see you were able to get your armor back."

"What we were able to get is an *ally*." Hennehok, who'd stopped farther back from Sarrlevi, spread an arm to wave grandiosely toward the dragon. "Last time, due to the interruption of the assassin, we weren't able to share our plans with you."

The front door opened, and Val and Freysha stepped onto the porch. As the green dragon soared low, skimming close enough to the roof to make a couple of Zavryd's wards screech and flash, they exchanged long looks with each other. Maybe they knew this dragon.

"If you've secured the assistance of a dragon, I'm impressed," I said, though Zavryd hadn't thus far been that helpful in locating the organization. He *had* helped Sarrlevi and me get into the military post to reach my father's prison, but since our mission had ultimately failed, it was hard to feel too chuffed about that.

"*I* have." Hennehok thumped a fist against his armored chest. "I built an advanced engineering marvel for the queen of the Starsinger Clan. In exchange, she sent her young but still capable offspring to help us find your mother. She agrees that the dwarf princess Barothla doesn't make for a restful existence and would prefer your mother be your grandfather's heir."

"What kind of engineering marvel could a dragon need?" Val asked, walking up with Freysha. "They live in caves or aeries on cliffs."

"It's for the queen's offspring who hatched last year," Hennehok said.

"It's a playpen," Artie said.

"It is *far* more sophisticated than that," Hennehok said, "and made with the needs of a winged and taloned creature in mind, not a dwarf or human."

"Playpen," Artie mouthed to me.

Hennehok squinted at her.

I looked at Sarrlevi, wondering if he knew anything about the dragon. He hadn't yet sheathed his swords. To my eyes, the dragon appeared full-grown, but if he was young, that might account for the playful flying.

Val was the one to speak. "That's Xilneth. I've met him." Something in her tone suggested that wasn't the best thing.

I am the great dragon Xilnethgarish of the Starsinger Clan, a voice boomed into our minds.

"Willard wants to see us later." Val showed me a text on her phone. "I think it's about your wealthy friend across the lake."

"Good." I nodded firmly. "I'm tired of messing around and not being able to find my parents. I feel so useless."

"Understandable. I wish I could do more to help."

Xilneth glided toward us and landed in the intersection, a wing knocking the mirror off a car parked on the far side. His tail flattened a tricycle left out in the yard across the street.

Val sighed. "Matti, this isn't the best dragon ally your dwarf acquaintances could have gotten."

"Your mate squishes things when he lands too," I pointed out. "I've seen it."

"*That's* not my objection to Xilneth. Not my main objection, anyway."

The green dragon—Xilneth—shape-shifted into a strikingly handsome young elf with piercing green eyes and smiled at her. *I see that the mate of the uptight Stormforge dragon Zavryd'nokquetal is as alluring as ever. Have your months enduring his tedious sanctimoniousness convinced you to join me in the nest for the most stimulating experience of your life?*

"*That's* my objection," Val said.

"I'm beginning to see it now," I said.

Artie blinked in surprise. Maybe Xilneth hadn't hit on her yet.

"Xilneth, I'm very happy with Zav," Val said, "and you know he'll challenge you to a duel if he hears you saying such things."

"Duel?" Xilneth asked, switching to the spoken word. "The members of my clan aren't preposterous, single-minded dragons who run around challenging others to battles to the death. We are poets and singers and romantics." He batted his eyelashes at her like a Hollywood starlet. "And *lovers.*"

"Uh huh. Have you met Matti?" Val patted me on the shoulder. "She's training to be an enchanter."

Sarrlevi stiffened as Xilneth's gaze shifted to me. I braced myself for dismissal from the dragon. Standing next to the six-foot-tall blonde half-elf Val didn't get me a lot of looks from guys, and I *especially* couldn't imagine a dragon having anything complimentary to say.

"An enchanter?" Xilneth purred at me, his elegant eyebrows rising. "Capable of infusing the male body with gloriously tingly magic?"

"Uh, Santiago hasn't covered that with me yet."

"Enchanters can be *most* stimulating lovers," Xilneth said.

Sarrlevi stepped closer to me, his arm brushing my shoulder as he glared. "Back away, dragon."

Xilneth's eyebrows flew up. "You will call me Lord Xilnethgarish!"

"This female is not available."

I don't need any male posturing, I said telepathically to Sarrlevi, surprised by his response. He'd always been supremely confident of his sex appeal and that I would choose him, even if I had other options, even if I was on a date *with* another option. *Especially not with a dragon.*

I could defeat this dullard in a duel.

Nobody needs to defeat anybody. This is a new ally. Apparently.

He covets you.

I get the impression that he covets anything with boobs.

"Surely, it is the female's *choice* as to whether she is available," Xilneth said. "Is that not the way on this world? She may wish to experience mating with a dragon."

"It is her choice," Sarrlevi agreed, "and she rejects you."

"She has *not* rejected me." Xilneth smiled at me. "And she is most voluminous. This is the word?"

"Voluptuous," Val said.

"Yes, she is that. A voluptuous enchanter is so rare!"

"I'm not interested," I told him. Then, because he seemed dim, I made it clearer. "I reject your offer."

"When I haven't even given you details? Or sung to you? My clan is known for its singing abilities."

"*How* exactly is your new dragon ally going to help you find Matti's mom?" Val asked the dwarves.

Artie, still gaping at Xilneth, didn't appear to know what to say.

"Assist us with finding the new lair of those who have her," Hennehok said. "He will examine the enchantment on the hammer Princess Rodarska made, then, with his powerful and precise dragon senses, seek out other items created by the same enchanter and follow them to the source."

"We think she's being insulated from those with the power to do that." I didn't know if Zavryd had tried what Hennehok had described, so I didn't mention him, but the dwarven priest Lankobar had. "Lord Xilneth, is there any chance you can heal scratches inflicted by an alchemist with fake nails?"

Sarrlevi frowned as I gestured at his cheek, and I sensed him wanting to reject the idea.

Dragons have powerful healing magic, right? I added silently to Sarrlevi as Xilneth peered at him. *It's worth a shot.*

He may ask you to have sex with him in exchange for his services.

Well, that would be a reversal for us, wouldn't it? I smirked at him.

An unappealing one.

My smirk widened as Xilneth stepped closer and examined Sarrlevi's face. I almost wished it would work out that way, if only because I'd had to watch him mate with those odious elven females in exchange for a favor for *me*. And, okay, maybe it would stroke my ego a bit too, to be wanted by a dragon. But something told me sex with Xilneth would leave me unsatisfied and him, three minutes after we began, smoking a Marlboro in bed. Besides, I didn't truly want to irk Sarrlevi or make him jealous. *He* was the one I wanted to be with.

Good, Sarrlevi told me, eyelids drooping as he focused on me—and reading my mind—while Xilneth studied him. *You are a wise plumber.*

Don't make me regret my choice.

He smiled. *I will not.*

Strange that this wound has not healed by itself, Xilneth said. *It is so minor. I will apply my curative magic, and the beauteous females present will admire my power and prowess.*

"Oh, undoubtedly," Val said.

"Does Zavryd call you beauteous?" I asked Val.

"No, he knows that would make me vomit."

"You're a classy lady."

"I am."

Whenever Sarrlevi healed me, it felt good, a tremendous relief, but his jaw clenched, the tendons standing out on his neck, as Xilneth used his magic on him. Holding my breath, I watched his cheek. The wound brightened slightly, almost glowing, and I hoped this would work. Dragon magic *had* to be greater than dwarf magic, right?

Odd. Xilneth drew back, and his magic faded. The wound returned to the same inflamed pink it had been before. *There is magic about it, something that prevents me from knitting the flesh back together and regenerating the scales.*

"Skin," Val said. "One hopes."

Skin, yes. I am unable to heal the wound. I do not know why.

"Sorry," I whispered to Sarrlevi and clasped his hand.

I am not surprised that fop cannot do anything.

We'll ask Zavryd to try when he gets back.

Sarrlevi's expression suggested he didn't think the result would be different, but he didn't reject the idea. He, too, had to want to be fixed.

More magic flared, another portal opening. This time, it appeared over the roof.

"That's Zav." Val pointed at Xilneth. "You might want to take a tour of the lake... in the next county over. You know how he feels about you."

"Zavryd'nokquetal invited me to your mating ceremony. He must adore me."

"He doesn't. He invited a *lot* of dragons to our wedding. And he hasn't forgotten that you also made passes at his sister."

"Ah, yes. The vivacious Zondia'qareshi." Xilneth clasped a hand to his chest. "She flexes her talons at me, but I believe she does not dislike me as much as she pretends."

Zavryd flew out of the portal, his violet eyes flaring with inner power as soon as he spotted Xilneth.

You! Feckless hippie of a dragon. You dare come to my lair? You are not singing for my mate, are you?

"Certainly not." Xilneth raised his hands and stepped back as Zavryd circled overhead. "I only spoke to her and asked if she was satisfied with an uptight Stormforge dragon in her nest."

Speaking of flexing talons...

I will slay you for your indolent, degenerate ways!

Xilneth, gaze catching on those talons as well, shifted back into his dragon form, then sprang into the air. Zavryd dove for him, looking like he meant to attack, but Xilneth flapped his wings hard, the wind they created knocking over a for-sale sign in a nearby yard, and Zavryd missed him, almost crashing into the street. At the last second, Zavryd spread his wings—there went the antennae on a car—and landed lightly on his taloned feet before leaping into the air again.

Xilneth was already flying south fast, toward the city. Zavryd sent a blast of fire after him, but Xilneth weaved left and right, speeding between the treetops, then diving low before flying up high again.

I imagined people eating lunch in the Space Needle, those with magical blood capable of seeing dragons, but most noshing obliviously as a battle took place outside the windows.

"Dwarf friends," Val told Artie and Hennehok, "I hate to tell you, but that's not the best dragon ally you could have found."

"He was the only one available and willing to work with dwarves," Hennehok said.

"We were a little surprised that his queen agreed to send him," Artie admitted.

"*I* was not surprised." Hennehok, maker of the dragon playpen, lifted his chin.

I rubbed the back of my neck and looked at Sarrlevi. As he

watched the dragons flying away, he appeared surlier than usual, but that didn't keep me from telling him, *You're my best ally, you know.*

He lowered his swords. *You agree that I'm superior to the roommate who shoots your kitchen appliances from her gun?*

She only shoots the blender blades and other sharp objects, but, yes, you're superior. You know that.

Yes. He managed a semblance of his cocky smile, but I struggled to appreciate it with that livid scar on his cheek.

I hoped Zoltan could find the answer—and solution—Sarrlevi needed.

4

AFTER DROPPING OFF THE BLOOD SAMPLES WITH ZOLTAN, I HOPPED into my truck with Sarrlevi and headed toward Willard's office.

Tools rattled in the back, and clumps of dirt and shreds of sawdust littered the seats. Earlier that week, I'd replaced several bushes and freshened up the garden beds that had been trampled during the battle at my sister's house. As I drove, I watched Sarrlevi out of the corner of my eye, expecting him to object to the entropy.

He shifted on the uncomfortable seat, the spring prodding him through the upholstery, but only brooded out the windshield at Val's black Jeep ahead of us. Willard wanted to see both of us. She hadn't mentioned Sarrlevi, but, since he'd appointed himself my bodyguard, he wasn't inclined to leave me alone.

Half of me was glad to have him close so I could keep an eye on him, but the other half wished he would leave to find an alchemist and hunt down the rest of the ingredients for his mother's formula. If we couldn't find someone to replicate it and cure her... we would have to deal with my evil aunt again.

The seat creaked as Sarrlevi shifted to remove his magical

kerchief and run it over the dashboard. A touch of magic flowed from him, and sawdust and dirt went up in tiny puffs of smoke.

"Thanks," I said, wondering if I could enchant the spring later so it wouldn't bother him. "I was getting worried."

"That the wood chips and grime would mobilize, rise up, and usurp your conveyance?" Sarrlevi scowled as he tidied.

"Worried about *you*. Because you weren't cleaning it."

"I'm not a maid," he snapped.

I opened my mouth but didn't respond right away. He never snapped at me. Usually, he acted unbothered or even amused when he tidied my messes.

"I know," I said. "Maids are a lot more customer-service oriented. They're not allowed to be grumpy with their clients."

"I am not grumpy."

A car on the opposite side of the street drove through a puddle as it passed us, and droplets spattered my windshield. Sarrlevi's scowl deepened, and with a whoosh of magic, he sent the moisture flying after the other car to spatter *its* windows.

"You don't think so, huh?" I asked.

He looked over at me, the scar on his cheek red.

We came to a light, and I reached over and clasped his hand. "Please don't feel compelled to clean my messes. Like I told you, this is my work truck, so it's always going to be dirty. I'm not going to take it through the car wash and vacuum it every evening."

Sarrlevi shifted again, making me feel I should install a new seat for his sake, but he could make portals and poof himself around if he wished.

"I have been more irritable," he admitted.

"And prone to challenge dragons to duels."

"I do *that* regardless."

I snorted. It was true. He'd done that to Zavryd long before Barothla's nails slashed him.

"If you ever retire from such dangerous work as challenging

dragons and assassinating powerful people and want to accept my offer to become my apprentice, Abbas and I would let you sweep and vacuum as well as hold our tools and make us coffee."

"Your generosity in such matters must send prospective job applicants flocking to your door."

"How do you think I got Tinja?"

"How *did* you end up with a goblin for a roommate?" Sarrlevi asked.

I almost said something flippant, but, thinking he might appreciate a distraction, I decided to share the story. "A year ago—no, closer to two years ago now—she came to the city to pursue her dream of getting an architecture degree. She wanted to design grand human projects that are built using materials superior to what goblins scrounge in the woods. She talks up the merits of structures that stand for centuries, not until the next windstorm.

"Tinja didn't have anywhere to stay and was living in a box by a dumpster behind the little strip mall where I get teriyaki takeout. I'd seen her once before and left an order of potstickers by her bedding. She was shy then, if you can believe it, and disappeared when I called out to her, but I noticed the inside of her box was covered in sketches—blueprints.

"One night, while I was inside ordering food, some teenage hoodlums with elven blood sensed my hammer and decided to break into my truck to get it. Since huge weapons being toted into restaurants can alarm the owners, I always left it in there. Tinja warned me of the threat by setting off goblin alarms—soda cans strung together with chimes—to make a bunch of noise. I ran out and thumped the teenagers appropriately since they'd broken one of my windows in addition to trying to steal my hammer. After they ran off, I invited Tinja to stay at my place until she found something more suitable than a box. She turned an old fish tank that a previous roommate had left behind into a side table for the couch, and she's been living with me ever since."

"I have seen that table," Sarrlevi said.

"There's a switch to make it light up and shine red and purple beams on the ceiling and walls."

"An important improvement for a domicile."

"Obviously."

I started to withdraw my hand since I'd been driving with only one, but he squeezed it and looked over at me. "I apologize for bristling. Grumpily."

"No problem. Zoltan will get to the bottom of your problem, and we'll fix you. Then you'll be back to *joyously* tidying my entropy."

"Assassins do not seek joy."

"That's depressing. You need to find something that makes you happy."

Sarrlevi slanted a smile toward me. "Like cheese?"

"That's what makes *me* happy. You need to find your own source of joy."

"I will consider this wise advice."

"Good." Nobody had *ever* called me or my advice wise, and I knew he was teasing me, but I was glad he could still joke.

As we turned onto the street where Willard's building was located, Sarrlevi fished around in his pack. I parked a couple of spots down from Val's Jeep.

"Earlier, I was distracted and forgot to give you this." He pulled out bricks of my favorite pink and blue cheeses to rest on the seat beside me, then also a pair of triangles wrapped in green foil, the labels handwritten in Dwarven. "Since your aunt did not give you a tour of the cheese caves in the capital, I acquired a popular Dwarven variety for you to try. It is flavored with the algae that you saw in the tunnels."

I gathered the bricks in my arms and smiled and sniffed them, though I hesitated to take the triangles from his hand. "Algae cheese? Is it good?"

"I bring you only the best. The alga is one of the rarer strains, and the Dwarven agronomists are extremely proud of having developed it over the centuries. It is *mostly* made from *higogrith* milk, the algae only adding… *tang.* I believe that is how the word would translate. Or tartness, perhaps."

My curiosity piqued, I accepted the foil-wrapped triangles and kissed him on the cheek. "Thank you. But you don't have to keep bringing me cheese, now that we're not… Well, I *hope* your goal has evolved and you're not still hoping I'll lead you to my mother."

Sarrlevi hadn't said that he absolutely would under no circumstances target her, but I knew he didn't want to do Barothla's bidding. He *had* said that he didn't know if he could go through with it anymore, essentially trading my mother's life for his mother's life. I did, however, want to make sure to get the formula to cure her before we came face to face with my mom. Just in case.

"The cheese is given with… What is your saying? No twine attached?"

"No strings attached." Curious if the cheese would glow green like the algae in the tunnel had, I peeled back a corner of the foil.

"Yes." Sarrlevi nodded, eyes crinkling. "And because you would be disappointed if I did not bring you joy."

"The self-help people say a person is supposed to be responsible for their *own* joy instead of depending on others for their mental well-being, but…" I grinned. The cheese *did* glow. Not all over, but the tiny dots of green in the creamy white cheese emanated a faint bioluminescent glow. Normally, I wouldn't get excited at the prospect of eating something that was possibly radioactive, but it smelled *amazing.* Salty, sweet, and, yes, tangy.

My mouth watered, and I nibbled on the corner. Oh, yes. That was divine.

"Okay, this *is* joyous." My eyes might have rolled back in my head as I chewed.

Sarrlevi watched me intently, his gaze dropping to my lips. I might have been self-conscious and wiped my mouth to make sure I didn't have cheese crumbs stuck anywhere, but his eyes weren't judgmental. They were interested. Sexually interested.

That knowledge sent a warm flush through me, one I tried to tamp down, reminding myself that he wasn't himself right now.

He lifted his thumb to brush my lips. "I like seeing you enjoy yourself."

"Thanks." I told myself to shift away from him, not lean closer, that this wasn't the time to enjoy his touch. It definitely wasn't the time to be turned on by his bedroom eyes. "I wouldn't mind seeing *you* enjoy yourself. Let me know if there's something I could bring *you* as a gift."

His eyes gleamed. "Just yourself."

I started to snort in dismissal, but he shared an image of us entwined and naked in a huge elven bed hanging from vines, the frame swaying with our vigorous movements. My breath caught as more heat flushed me, along with the desire to set all our problems aside for a time and to see just how much joy we could bring each other. Sarrlevi needed to be with someone who cared about him and didn't want to use him only for recreational sex or to show him off to make a mate jealous. He needed me.

"Yes," he murmured, sending more tingles of pleasure through me.

I had the desire to crawl into his lap, wrap my arms around him, and plaster myself to him. To kiss him passionately, to push his shirt off, to let my hands run down his hard abdomen to—

Val walked up to the passenger side and knocked on the window.

Sarrlevi gave her such a savage look that it startled me, but he grimaced, one cheek twitching, and got his face under control by the time she bent to peer inside. He lowered his hand from my mouth.

Val gestured for Sarrlevi to roll down the window. He either didn't know what the finger waving meant or was disinclined to obey.

After rearranging my cheese collection, I leaned across Sarrlevi's lap and reached for the handle to roll down the window. Awkwardly. The truck was decades too old to have automatic controls, and I didn't have the best angle, but I managed not to elbow Sarrlevi. Since he brushed his fingers through my hair before resting a hand on my back, he probably didn't mind having me sprawled across his lap.

"Am I interrupting something?" Val asked.

"Varlesh cleaned my truck and gave me cheese."

"And here I thought you fell for him because of his looks."

"His looks are okay. His cheese is *amazing*."

"*Okay*," Sarrlevi murmured. "Really."

"The garish cut on your cheek may be detracting from your elven beauty." Val pointed at it. "You might want to get that fixed up."

Usually, Sarrlevi would let an insult that didn't come from a dragon or other heinous enemy roll off his back, or offer some witty response, but his muscles tensed under me, and his face hardened.

"We'll be right out," I told Val, hurrying to roll up the window before Sarrlevi got grumpy with her. Not letting his frosty expression deter me, I kissed him on the cheek as I wiggled back into my seat. "Thanks for the cheese."

He recovered his equanimity and nodded solemnly at me, but before we could climb out of the truck, his head spun toward hedges fronting another office building across the street. He peered into them, his hand drifting to his swords.

I didn't sense anyone, but I *saw* a cloaked figure momentarily before he or she disappeared from view. The person didn't duck behind the hedges, instead applying magical cloaking.

Val must have noticed our stalker too, for she also looked

toward the hedges with her fingers wrapped around the tiger charm on her thong necklace. Since the camouflaging magic I knew about usually hid someone from sight as well as senses, I wondered if the person had *wanted* to be seen.

"Anyone you recognize?" I asked Sarrlevi.

"An assassin from the Guild. I telepathically told him to leave unless he wishes to contend with me."

"Did he say he agrees that you're very dangerous and not worth wrestling with, so he and all of his buddies will leave me alone?" I wished.

Sarrlevi hesitated. "He said I couldn't stay at your side forever."

"Shows what he knows. My side is magnetic." I grabbed my hammer and hopped out of the truck.

Val had already jogged through the front door. Belatedly, it occurred to me that, if the assassin had beaten us here, he might have threatened Willard. Or worse.

5

"Greetings, Plumber Puletasi," Gondo greeted me from the secretary's desk in Willard's outer office. He crouched on it, ignoring the chair, with one green finger pointing to an advertisement in a phone book. "Oh, and Lord Elf," he added, his voice surprisingly bright as he focused on Sarrlevi. "Perhaps *you* are who I need. Not an exterminator of rodentia."

"What?" I leaned through the open door to Willard's office to check on her.

Val was already inside and Willard appeared unharmed, though she was glowering out the window and pointing toward the street—or the hedges *across* the street? Had she also spotted the threat?

"Work Leader Willard said assassins were infesting the premises and that I should call an exterminator. Lord Elf, can you be hired to exterminate your own kind?"

"For the right price," Sarrlevi said.

"Is that more than—" Gondo looked at the ad in the phone book, "—a free consultation and a fifty-nine-ninety-nine introductory price for dwellings under twenty-five-hundred square feet?"

"Substantially more," Sarrlevi said. "Assassins are much more difficult to exterminate than *rodentia*."

"As I feared." Gondo shook his head sadly.

Sarrlevi and I joined Val in the other room. Willard stopped in the middle of a sentence to give me an exasperated look and Sarrlevi an even more exasperated one.

"Willard walked in on one of the members of your Assassins' Guild holding a dagger to her captain's throat and demanding to know everything in the Army's files about Matti," Val told Sarrlevi, though she also looked gravely at me.

"I am no longer a member of *my* Assassins' Guild," Sarrlevi said, "and could not be held accountable for the actions of those within regardless."

"Of course not," Willard muttered.

"How did you get rid of him?" I winced at the idea of more people being hurt because someone was after me. "Is your officer okay?"

"I kicked him in the balls."

"The assassin or your officer?" Val asked.

Willard gave her a flat look. It wasn't that different from her exasperated looks.

"Hey, it's a fair question," Val said. "You used to be a drill sergeant. Your disciplinary methods can be rather vigorous."

"It's the modern Army. You're not allowed to kick your subordinates in the balls or anywhere else."

"You see how wistful she looks when she says that," Val told me.

Ignoring that, Willard said, "I called you two here because I have information on Hart and got the full list of people who were at that meeting in the Dubai hotel."

I leaned forward, nodding eagerly. Hart, I was certain, was the key to finding the organization, my parents, and getting the assassins off my back.

"You, I didn't invite." Willard's lips pressed together in disapproval as she looked at Sarrlevi. Did she have top-secret information that she didn't want him to hear?

"While assassins hunt Mataalii, I will remain at her side." Sarrlevi looked at me. "It's magnetic."

"Guess that comes in handy when you can't find a refrigerator." Willard pointed at his face. "What happened to your cheek?"

His eyes narrowed. "I was wounded."

"Just now?" Willard waved toward the hedges.

"No."

"It's an unwelcome gift that my aunt gave him," I said. "We're working on it."

"Uh huh. Don't forget that the military *and* the police are looking for him. He might not be the best person to have at your side right now."

"He's *always* the best person," I said.

Sarrlevi didn't respond other than to give me a pleased nod.

Willard only scowled. She did that a lot.

"You said you have some news about Hart, ma'am?" I smiled encouragingly at her.

She grunted, let the Sarrlevi matter drop, and pulled a small stack of papers out of a desk drawer. The one on top held a list of names. Of the other super rich people who'd been at that meeting?

"As far as my research has revealed, all of these individuals were born on Earth and are full-blooded humans. Some are from families that have been very wealthy for generations, and some have built their wealth themselves through businesses they started. Four are in the energy industry."

I remembered that she'd believed the reactor my mother had made would be of particular interest to people in such fields.

"A mixture of energies, interestingly," Willard continued. "Two are oil barons. One is the owner of a private company that got in early and is well known for manufacturing onshore and offshore wind turbines. Another is the CEO and a major stakeholder in a network of natural gas pipelines."

"What other industries do those people represent?" Val asked. "Hart is a software guy, right?"

I shifted from foot to foot, impatient to figure out how to get to him and less interested in what he and his buddies did for a living. Their methodology for acquiring magical technology through *kidnapping* people made them all evil in my book.

"Tech, pharmaceuticals, banking, and investment and risk-management solutions," Willard said. "Some are reclusive and not well known, but some speak at global forums, advocating change in the world." She pointed at one name. "This one has a Malthusian streak and is always talking about the need to curb population growth."

Val tugged on her braid. "If they have one or more of these fancy magical reactors, and are planning to keep them for Earth instead of giving them back to the dwarves, wouldn't that mean they see a future with nearly limitless energy? Would growing enough food for a big population be a problem in that kind of situation?"

"I suppose it depends on who gets access to the reactors." Willard waved at the list. "These people are notorious for telling others to reduce their consumption to save the planet, while flying around on their private jets."

I lifted a finger. "I don't want to make this all about *me*, but my priority is finding my parents."

"Yes, I'm aware." Willard looked out the window again before returning to her desk and shifting another paper to the top of her stack. "You know Hart has been out of the country, right?"

I nodded. "That's why I didn't bash through his secured gate, ride into his compound like a vengeful Valkyrie, and send his soul to Valhalla." That and the magical barrier protecting the place...

Willard arched her eyebrows. "You're more educated than I would have guessed from your transcripts."

"You have my high-school transcripts?" I knew she'd been keeping an eye on me, but just how thorough *were* the Army's records?

"No wonder the assassin broke in," Val said. "He wants to know if Matti aced gym class and is a true danger."

"As I recall, she aced shop class and got Cs in P.E. Kind of surprising." Willard looked at my arms.

I folded them over my chest. "I didn't always excel in group activities, and I broke a light fixture when I got angry and smashed a pickleball into it."

"Speaking of smashing, how *is* the secured gate to your sister's neighborhood doing?" Willard asked.

I winced. Had there been camera footage of that?

"It had already been fixed when I went over to repair the damage to her house," I said.

"The residents there have to prioritize keeping the riffraff out," Val said.

"All right." Willard must have noticed there was steam coming out of my ears, more at her slowness to get to what I wanted to know than because of insults related to my transcripts. "It's good that you didn't try to mow down Hart's gate. From what I've learned, the barrier around his compound is impervious even to dragon magic."

I'd been afraid of that. "Sounds like the magic that protects the dwarven and elven capitals."

"If he's tied in with all that we believe," Willard said, "he does know a dwarf enchanter."

"He *kidnapped* a dwarf enchanter."

Willard lifted a hand. "It couldn't have been Hart. He would have been a teenager when your mother was kidnapped. Only some of the people on the list are old enough to have been involved with that, though, as I said, some of them have family wealth, and their predecessors could have masterminded a multi-generational plot. Whatever this organization is, it's possible it's been around for a long time."

"But Hart knows where my parents are," I said with certainty. "He hired the half-orc assassins. He might have been the one to pay the Guild to get *all* the assassins on my back." I looked at Sarrlevi, but he'd already shared all he knew about the person who'd brought the gold coins to the guild leader. It had been a minion.

"It is possible," Willard said. "Regardless, I've learned that he's returned home from his travels, and he's hosting a party next week. A shindig for the wealthy to show off a piece of rare artwork he acquired during his trip. It's not being publicized, of course, and is by invitation only, but I was able to find out that several of these people will be there." Willard waved at her list.

"Can you pull strings to get *us* invited?" Val pointed at herself, then me.

Sarrlevi arched his eyebrows at his lack of inclusion, but he didn't object further. Probably because he believed he could get in anywhere he wished. Though, if the magical barrier was strong enough to repel dragons, it could keep out elves as well.

"The *strings* I have access to don't go beyond the military," Willard said dryly. "If you want an invitation to a general's bash at the Officer's Club, I might be able to get you in."

"What's the plan then?" Val asked.

"You'll have to figure something out. Maybe someone on the list needs a date."

My lip curled.

Val's lip curled too. "I'm married. And you remember what a pest Zav was when I pretended to be Weber's girlfriend for a mission. That was before we were even officially a couple."

"Puletasi isn't married. Though with her lip stuck in that sneer position, she'll only attract certain types of guys." Willard glanced at Sarrlevi.

His expression was masked. He was too refined to outwardly curl a lip, but I wagered his inner lips were flexing madly.

I didn't attempt to manipulate my features into a more socially pleasing expression. This line of thinking sounded dumb. "What would I do? Knock on the doors of these billionaires, ask if any of them are hard up for women, and mention how much I like art?"

"Do you know anything about art?" Willard asked.

"The kind you carve with chisels and chainsaws, yes."

"There aren't a lot of pieces like that in the Louvre."

"Because the museums of this world were made by humans, not dwarves." I pointed at her list. "Those guys are probably all married."

"I'm not sure *that* precludes them dating other women," Willard said.

"Lovely. Anyway, they'd all be in houses as heavily secured as Hart's. It's not like I could walk up and knock on the door to flirt. I also doubt they spend their evenings surfing dating apps."

"If you have a better plan, I'm all ears."

"There is no need for Mataalii to *date* a guest at a party." Sarrlevi's emphasis on the word conveyed his opinion even if he wasn't a lip curler. "We will reconnoiter the dwelling together and find a way in. It will be a simple matter. I am accomplished at getting into secured residences."

"I don't doubt it," Willard murmured. "It's more of a compound than a dwelling, FYI. Twenty-thousand-square-feet plus outbuildings, according to my sources."

"It's important to have a lot of room for one's art collection," Val said.

"There are eleven bathrooms," Willard said.

"Maybe the lesser pieces go above the toilets."

"We will find a way in." Sarrlevi rested a hand on my shoulder.

"Such a *compound* will have many places for assassins—and craftswomen—to hide."

"Until we get an opportunity to leap out and thump Hart and interrogate him." I smacked a fist into my palm, more than ready to pound the guy who'd hired my assassins and wring his neck until he gave me the location of the secret base that held my parents.

"Since other guests who may be affiliated with the organization will be there," Willard said, "it might be more beneficial to spy on their conversations rather than leaping straight to thumping and interrogation."

"Such as might be made easy if one were the date of one guest and could wander about with arms linked with him all evening?" Val asked.

"Such as," Willard said.

I rolled my eyes. That plan *wasn't* going to work.

"This one is a widower and a real-estate mogul, Puletasi. Joseph Nakamura." Willard tapped a name toward the bottom of the list.

I'd heard of him and couldn't keep from curling my lip again. He sold books and courses and had probably made more money from that than from his real-estate deals.

Unfazed by my mobile lips, Willard said, "He might be right up your alley. Or, should I say, you might be right up *his*."

Sarrlevi sighed. It might have been a soft growl.

I doubted that me pretending to date a sixty-year-old real-estate mogul would bother him as much as a hot dragon in elf form wanting to experience my enchanting magic, but he favored similar tactics to mine. Thumping and interrogation.

"I'll think about it." I didn't like the date idea, but if we couldn't find another way in, I would have to keep it in mind. It *would* be ideal to be able to wander around the house and listen in on numerous conversations. Hart might be a kingpin and know a lot, but he also might not be. Just because he'd hired assassins to target me didn't mean he knew where my parents were.

"Don't think too long," Willard said. "The party is next week. It might take you time to use your allure to win over a new man."

"Probably true. My allure is known to be slow-acting." I looked at Sarrlevi. "Do you want to reconnoiter with me?"

Even though I had already driven by, I suspected he would be able to determine a lot more than I could, even from the outside.

"Yes," Sarrlevi said promptly, probably relieved that I was asking about *his* plan instead of doubling down on the date idea.

"How are you going to get close to the house?" Val asked.

"Perhaps a dragon could fly her over," Willard said.

Val grimaced. "Xilneth showed up, and Zav chased him to Portland."

"What's in Portland?"

"By now, Xilneth's singed backside."

"It's okay." Normally, despite my distaste for heights, I wouldn't have objected to an aerial ride for reconnaissance, but if someone in Hart's house could sense magical beings, circling the property on a dragon would be conspicuous. And *suspicious*. "I have another idea."

6

"This water conveyance is conspicuous," Sarrlevi said from behind me as we paddled along the shoreline away from Meydenbauer Bay Park and toward Groat Point. The sun sinking toward the Olympic Mountains gleamed yellowish-orange on the placid water.

"Not as conspicuous as a dragon," I said.

"Your target's security officers will notice us."

"It's a sunny evening on Lake Washington, and we're two of *many* people enjoying the water in a rented kayak."

"It is bright orange, and you are wearing a fluorescent-yellow vest."

"It's a life jacket, and the guy said it's required. It was rude of you to threaten to cut off his hand when he tried to give one to you."

"He *thrust* it at me and said in a condescending manner that I had to wear it. I am capable of swimming without a flotation aid."

"Are you sure? There's a lot of stuff in your backpack to weigh you down."

"I am certain." Sarrlevi clunked the paddle on the side of the kayak. "It would have been less noticeable to reconnoiter on a dragon."

"I don't think that's true. Besides, the only dragons we're on good terms with are busy lighting each other on fire. But if you want to camouflage us, I won't object." I'd already thought about suggesting that since someone with magical senses might notice us—Sarrlevi's powerful aura in particular—if we floated too close to the property, but I worried the kayak would be visible even if Sarrlevi and I camouflaged ourselves. That *would* be conspicuous. "Maybe you could *partially* camouflage us."

"The part that's orange and yellow?"

"Perfect." I grinned back at him and caught a dyspeptic expression on his face. Because elven assassins didn't deign to rent kayaks for their missions? Or because Barothla's fingernail gunk was making him surly? We hadn't heard back from Zoltan about that yet. "I think I *might* have camouflaged my motorcycle from the police when Val and I were riding to my sister's house, but I'm not positive. Santiago hasn't taught me how to do that."

"You do much that your instructor hasn't yet taught you."

"When you make observations like that, you're supposed to smile and beam approval at what a fast learner I am."

"I was thinking of the smoldering topiary at Thorvald's house."

"So... you don't approve?"

Sarrlevi managed a smile and rested his paddle across his lap to lean forward and reach for my shoulder. Maybe he meant to give me a pat or grip it, but the yellow life jacket may have repulsed him, for he instead rubbed the back of my neck.

That was much better than a shoulder pat. If not for the frame of the kayak keeping me in place, I would have leaned back into his lap.

"I approve of your assiduous study," Sarrlevi said. "Your half-dwarf instructor says you're doing well."

"His name is Santiago. Once you give someone a pile of gold, you should probably be on a first-name basis with him."

"Your progress is of more interest to me than his name. There may be assassins out here." Sarrlevi gazed left and right over the water as he massaged the back of my neck, nails occasionally drifting up to my scalp. That felt amazing.

"Of course. I hear they're big on recreational kayaking."

"One can see—and shoot—a long distance across the water. We are vulnerable to snipers."

"All I want is to paddle past Hart's house, hope we can see more than the satellite imagery offered, and come up with a plan to get in."

"If the magic is not too powerful, I can break through the defenses, and we can go in *tonight*. There is no need to wait for this party."

"Let's see what we can see then."

It didn't sound like the magic was *not too powerful,* but if we *could* get in, I would be tempted. Even if Willard's idea about spying on numerous conversations wasn't a bad one, yanking a pajama-clad man out of his bed and questioning him had some appeal. I liked the direct approach. Maybe I could buy more of Zoltan's truth drug to use on Hart.

"I will attempt to camouflage our auras and create an illusion that we are human tourists," Sarrlevi said.

"Thank you."

Since we'd stopped paddling, we were tourists in danger of floating into a log. Even though I enjoyed Sarrlevi's touch, I pointed the paddle to indicate the obstacle.

With a whisper of magic, Sarrlevi guided us around the log without pausing my neck rub. Warm tendrils of magic flowed into my body, distracting me from thoughts of reconnoitering—and everything else. Maybe I should have straightened and pulled away, but it was always hard to convince my body to move away from him instead of toward him.

The dragon was correct, Sarrlevi spoke into my mind.

"Which dragon? And about what?"

The Starsinger oaf. Enchanters, as well as other magic users, can use their power on their lovers to stimulate and arouse.

With water lapping at the kayak and the docks of the Groat Point residences not far ahead of us, this wasn't the right time for such a conversation, but I caught myself asking, *Like you're doing now?*

Like you did when you rubbed my head and ears. Sarrlevi shared his memory of us on my bed together, my hand on his head, massaging his scalp and stroking his pointed ears.

More than once, I'd wondered how that night would have gone if the trolls and Barothla hadn't shown up. I had no doubt it would have been stimulating and arousing.

I didn't realize that worked, I replied. *I wanted you to enjoy my touch and feel... well, to want to be with me.*

I did. As I do now.

I swallowed. Where was he going with this? We were on a mission, and he was always the one to point out that missions came first. *The life jacket is turning you on, huh?*

Removing *it would turn me on.*

We're almost there. Let's keep life-jacket removal in mind as an activity for later, okay? I made myself lean forward and dip my paddle back into the water.

Even though he'd been navigating us closer to the point with his magic, it was a way to say we needed to focus on the mission. When I glanced back to check on his reaction, his face was uncharacteristically emotive. He alternated between eyeing me with contemplative interest and jerking his gaze away, his cheek twitching, as if he had to fight to control his body.

Remind me not to wander around in a sexy dress until we get to the bottom of your wound problem, I said.

Unfortunately, my mind has no problem remembering what you look like without clothing. Sarrlevi withdrew his hand from my neck, took a deep breath, and nodded.

"It's that amazing memory of yours."

"Indeed." Sarrlevi joined me in paddling, perhaps needing to do something physical for a distraction. "More than one house on that shoreline has magical defenses."

"I suppose that's not that surprising. Hart's should be..." There it was. There hadn't been any real-estate photos online, but I knew his property from the size of the lot and the aerial image of the H-shaped dock. "That one."

"Hm. The magic of the barrier keeps me from sensing what's inside."

"Yeah."

"The barrier is made from *dwarven* magic."

His emphasis on the word made me examine the property with my senses as thoroughly as I could. Something about it was elusive though. I could sense that there *was* a magical barrier and see through it to the yard and huge three-story house, but a haziness about everything made me wonder how accurately my eyes pierced the veil.

"Is there an illusion?" I asked.

There was something familiar about the magic, but the haziness made me struggle to pinpoint what.

"Something like that, yes. The barrier is likely projected by an artifact inside the compound. It's more of a rectangular prism than the typical dome shape."

"Its border probably tracks the lot lines. In our cities, land is usually divided into rectangles."

"Yes," Sarrlevi said. "The barrier extends over the entire property and the nearby water and dock as well. If we tried to approach, we would bump against it. We might be zapped."

"Must be why there's no goose poop on that dock or beach."

"It's your mother's magic."

I blinked. "Are you sure? I can tell that it's familiar, but..."

"It scrambles the senses, yes, but it has her signature."

"You don't think there's any possibility *she's* being kept in there, do you?"

What if she'd been in the same city as me all this time? And I'd had no idea?

But, no, that didn't make sense. As large as that property was, there wasn't enough room to make magical helicopters.

"It's possible," Sarrlevi said, "but I would assume she simply made the artifact. Since the barrier obfuscates as well as protects, it will be difficult to plan an incursion."

"Presumably, once you're on the inside, you can see and sense everything, right?"

"Yes."

I nibbled on my lip as we paddled slowly past. As much as I wanted to linger and scrutinize the property, that would have been suspicious, even if Sarrlevi had managed to cast illusions on us.

A seagull squawked overhead. I dug out my phone to call Zadie.

"Looking to shop for a new house?" she answered.

"I'm at Groat Point in Medina."

"Unless you brought in some heavy-duty backers, that's a little outside your usual price range."

"Tell me about it. Will you look up an address for me? See when the house was built, last sold, and what buildings have been constructed on the property."

"Uh, all right."

I gave her the address that I'd memorized. "It's possible the satellite imagery for it isn't entirely correct."

"What are you up to, Matti?"

"Right now, I'm paddling in Lake Washington with a pointy-eared friend."

"Tinja?"

"A taller and less green pointy-eared friend."

Zadie snorted. "If you fantasize about him in bed at night, *friend* isn't the correct term."

"Ha ha." I might have chastised her further, especially since Sarrlevi could hear, but the clack of typing came over the phone. If she was running my search, I didn't want to interrupt.

Varlesh? I asked telepathically while I waited. *Do barriers like that usually extend down into the ground?*

Are you thinking of tunneling in? That would be a very dwarven thing to do.

While I'm sure it's in my genes to long to sap under the walls of an enemy stronghold, probably not. The water level here would be high enough that a tunnel would flood quickly.

It is easier to erect magical barriers in the air than through solid objects. Most that I've seen around cities do not extend more than a couple of feet below ground level. The dwarven capital uses other methods to strengthen the rock and earth on which their dwellings are constructed to ensure enemies cannot tunnel in.

Can you tell if such strengthening magic is in use here? We'd paddled past the property and around the point, but I would turn us around soon. After all, it was a normal thing for tourists to slowly meander past and admire the houses on the waterfront on the way to return their kayaks.

There's a lot of magic, but with the barrier obfuscating everything, it is difficult for me to tell what it does. Given the water-level threat you mentioned, the homeowner might not have deemed tunneling a likely concern. Do you have something else in mind?

Maybe. While I waited for Zadie to finish her search—the keystrokes had stopped, and she was mumbling to herself—I ran an internet search to see if the utilities map for the city was online. It was, including sewer and waterline maps. They were big .zip files so I would have to look at them later on my laptop. *I've successfully enchanted things from a distance a couple of times now. Okay, one time was in a vision, but my hammer said it counted.*

I looked warily back at Sarrlevi, expecting judgment.

Magical weapons know a lot about magic and what counts. He nodded to me. *My sword is certain of its wisdom.*

I'd forgotten that one of his weapons was also sentient and communicated with him.

You would have difficulty enchanting through the barrier from a distance, he said, *but perhaps you could do something to the ground under the house.*

That's what I'm thinking.

Sarrlevi stopped paddling, perhaps deciding we'd gone far enough and should turn back. Probably a good idea. The sun was setting, and we'd only booked the kayak for an hour.

With bags under his eyes, Sarrlevi looked atypically tired. The paddling wasn't that difficult, so it probably had to do with the emotional wrestling he was doing with himself.

That made me feel guilty. If he were alone, he wouldn't have to worry so much about holding himself together.

Depending on how well I can sense metal and what we can dig up on the water and sewer lines, I may have an idea.

My dear industrious mongrel, are you going to plumb *something?* Some of Sarrlevi's weariness faded from his eyes as he smiled.

It would be more sabotage than plumbing. If we got called in to fix it, then *I could plumb. While my assistant skulked around and spied on people.*

Sarrlevi touched his chest.

I was thinking of Val.

Thorvald doesn't look much like a plumber.

Neither do you, Lord Pretty and Sophisticated. There's probably no way you could contort yourself to reveal plumber's crack.

Plumber's what?

Never mind. I trust one could activate one's camouflaging magic once inside the barrier?

Sarrlevi considered his answer as we paddled. *The barrier shouldn't preclude it, but it's possible that other artifacts inside might nullify such magic. People whose only power is derived from their money tend to be paranoid.* He sneered disdainfully.

Dude, you had magical doohickeys all over your house too. I saw them.

To facilitate cleaning and the accommodation of my guests, not to prevent the use of magic. It's not my fault that a certain guest perceived them as weapons.

You're not going to bring up the soap dispenser again, are you? I really needed to make him another one. Maybe a whole fleet of them that floated around and spritzed people at random.

That is not necessary. I know you haven't forgotten.

That aside, I had better take an assistant who can legitimately pass as a plumber.

Your hulking half-troll laborer, perhaps.

My business partner *who's doing more work on our current project than I am? Yeah, he can pull off a good plumber's crack.*

Will I have to read your mind to find out what that term means?

You could, but you don't want to see the imagery that comes along with it. Trust me.

"Are you still there, Matti?" Zadie asked.

"Yes. Sarrlevi and I are discussing plumbers' cracks."

"Scintillating. I'll assume it's his *looks* that keep you interested, not his wit."

"His wit is wonderful. What'd you find?"

"Just that the house was built in 2010, after the previous home was torn down. It has a detached garage and a guest house, in case the twenty-thousand-square-foot main house isn't sufficient for the in-laws. There's a fancy boathouse that must have been grandfathered in from last century, because you can't build new ones there anymore. The house is on city water and sewer."

I clenched a fist. Perfect. That was what I'd wanted to know.

"It last sold for seven million," Zadie added. "You'd never get a property that size on the water for that now."

"I suppose all the magical gizmos keeping out intruders aren't described in the system."

"King County doesn't require those to be permitted or reported," Zadie said.

"Weird."

"No kidding. I'm sure magical security improves property values. They could charge more in taxes."

"Anything else interesting?"

"The owner filed and tried to get a permit to install a helicopter landing pad, but that was denied. It's tough being a billionaire. They're just not treated fairly by the county."

"Yes, people weep nights over their plight." I scratched my jaw, envisioning some of those huge cargo helicopters—magically *enchanted* cargo helicopters—cruising through the neighborhood. "Thanks for looking, Zadie."

"You're welcome. Since I'm assuming you'll use my services when you're ready to list the houses you're building, I won't charge you for my time."

"Those houses probably won't be ready until next year."

"I can be patient to get my commissions. Though we *can* list them for sale before they're completed. Keep that in mind."

"I want to wait until they're mostly done and assassins aren't dangling from the trees, thanks to someone's booby traps." I glanced back at Sarrlevi, but he was studying Hart's property again as we glided past it on the way back.

"From what I heard, *you* were the one dangling upside down from a tree," Zadie said.

"You can't trust everything Tinja says."

"Are you sure? She's pretty honest unless she's trying to sell you on a tiny home. FYI, a goblin's idea of copious closet storage is room for two pairs of shoes if you're a human."

"I know. I have to go." After saying goodbye, I joined Sarrlevi in scrutinizing the property once again, but I didn't spot anything more interesting than last time. I didn't even see the boathouse. It had either been removed or the dock area was also being fuzzed to our senses.

Twilight crept over the lake as we rounded the point and paddled toward the rental place in the park. This trip hadn't been as revealing as I'd hoped, but I had the inkling of an idea. It needed time to germinate, but if that party was a week away, I ought to have that time.

"I want to check on Tinja and Abbas," I said over my shoulder, "but then I'm available to go with you if you want to hunt for alchemical ingredients together."

Sarrlevi leaned forward and gripped my shoulder. *Neither of those is the gangly adolescent who rented us these water contraptions.*

Two shadowy figures lurked on the docks, docks that were dark and silent even though the boathouse should have remained open until the last kayaks returned.

They are elven half-bloods, Sarrlevi added. *I can sense them now. And their magical weapons.*

More assassins that are here for me?

Yes.

7

SARRLEVI ABANDONED THE ILLUSION HE'D KEPT AROUND OUR KAYAK and dropped his full camouflage over us, but the assassins probably already knew who we were. From the dock, the hooded half-elves peered straight in our direction.

After touching my shoulder lightly in warning, Sarrlevi climbed past me to crouch in the front of the kayak. With his fine elven balance, it barely rocked, but his weight made the nose drag. Using a whisper of magic, he kept the craft moving forward.

My hammer was with me, as usual, but I looked around for someplace to put my oar where it wouldn't splash into the water. I stuck it in the seat he'd left, but I didn't try to stand or crouch or do anything other than wrap my hand around Sorka's haft.

This placid boat tour may turn into a battle, she observed.

Yes, and it was an important reconnaissance mission, not a tour.

During which your suitor rubbed your neck.

Importantly. And he's not a suitor. He's... What, I wondered to myself. Not a lover yet. A boyfriend? Sorka wouldn't find that any more appealing. *He's... Sarrlevi.*

Hm.

With him crouching on the kayak in front of me, I could barely see the dock, much less the assassins, but I attempted to draw on Sorka's power and whispered, *Hygorotho,* in my mind to form a barrier.

A small flash of white came from the assassins, and a magical projectile zipped toward us. It splatted in the air in front of the kayak. Sarrlevi had also made a barrier.

Either through his magic or Sorka's, it melded with mine, fully protecting us and the craft. A good thing, for more white streaks came at us—more magical projectiles. They bounced off our barrier, either deflecting into the twilight sky or hitting the water with a splash and sizzle. A couple zipped past, missing us.

I itched to pound on the assassins. As we glided closer to the dock, the rain of attacks continuing, Sarrlevi whispered, *Brace yourself,* then sprang from the bow.

Even braced, I wasn't ready for the wild way the kayak not only rocked but surged backward. Clangs erupted on the dock as Sarrlevi struck at our enemies before his feet even touched down. Another time, I would have admired his speed, but I was too busy trying not to pitch into the water or lose my hammer.

Thankfully, Sorka wasn't easily distracted and kept her barrier around me. Two final white flashes showed projectiles striking it and bouncing off. After that, the assassins were too busy dealing with Sarrlevi to fire at me. Savage snarls sounded amid the clangs of swords striking, the battle noise ringing out over the water.

As I finally got the kayak to stop rocking, I realized Sarrlevi's enemies weren't making those snarls. *He* was. They grunted and cursed, but he sounded like a wild animal.

Something about that made the hair on the back of my neck rise.

Afraid he would lose control of his rational thoughts and be less effective at defending himself, I rose to my knees, wanting to spring out of the kayak. But my movement made it rock again, and I was too far away from the dock to climb free. Damn it.

I thought about slithering out and swimming, but that would be hard with my hammer. Frustrated, I jammed it between my knees, grabbed the paddle, and maneuvered toward a section of the dock far enough from the battle that the assassins wouldn't easily be able to reach me. Not that they had the time for side attacks right now. Even though these had to be skilled opponents, and their auras further suggested they were powerful, Sarrlevi pushed them back, his attacks overwhelming their defenses.

Finally, the kayak came alongside the dock and bumped against it. It rocked again as I stood to scramble out, but I made it, rolling onto the deck.

Something thumped down scant feet away, and I leaped up, hammer poised to defend. But the assassin—the assassin's *body*—lay unmoving in front of me, his aura already fading.

As I stepped over the body and toward Sarrlevi and his remaining opponent, he knocked the half-elf's blade away and swept one of his glowing swords toward—*through*—the assassin's neck.

I gaped, amazed that Sarrlevi had dispatched two trained killers so quickly. And ruthlessly. The head he cut off rolled past me and splashed into the water.

At the noise, Sarrlevi whirled toward me, his swords swinging. His savage eyes brimmed with battle lust, as if he was looking at a hated enemy rather than an ally.

"It's me!" I blurted, raising the hammer to defend myself as Sorka poured more power into my barrier.

It almost wasn't enough. With his blades glowing silver, highlighting his fearsome face with an unearthly hue, they sliced through my barrier. Its pop snapped at my senses, and I tensed to parry his powerful blows with my hammer.

His swords halted an inch away from the haft. He froze. We

both did. For a long second, we crouched in that tableau. Finally, he blinked several times, as if to clear his vision—or whatever enemy had taken over his mind?

Sarrlevi stepped back, lowering his swords, and bowed toward me. "I apologize."

When he lifted his face, it was back to usual, recognition in his eyes when his gaze met mine.

"No problem," I rasped, but my heart was pounding.

His earlier lust had been a little concerning, since it had hinted at a loss of control that was strange for him, but this... Having him turn into an enemy who didn't recognize me was terrifying. Even though I was a decent fighter and had won numerous trophies at tournaments when I'd been in school, he had centuries of experience battling not for points but for lives. If he ever wanted to kill me, I had little doubt he could.

Maybe he was thinking the same thing, for he released a deep slow breath and looked up at the darkening sky.

Sorka *harrumphed* into my mind. Because he'd gone crazy or because she hadn't been strong enough to deflect his magical weapons? That was another reminder that he could get through my defenses if he wanted.

No, *wanted* wasn't the right word. He didn't *want* this. I knew that.

My aunt Barothla might want this. I winced at the thought. Maybe her concoction hadn't been about driving a wedge between us after all. Maybe she'd foreseen this and wanted him to lose all control and kill me.

"Are you okay?" I thought so, but I also hadn't lowered my hammer yet. My body was too tense—too afraid—to let down its guard.

"I am now." His swords were still glowing, revealing not only the blood dripping from the blades but a tremor to his fingers as he shifted them to one hand and withdrew his magical kerchief.

Though I was well familiar with the adrenaline surge and shakes that came after a close call, I'd never seen *him* show signs of them. I couldn't keep from staring at his hands—at him—as he wiped off his swords. He took longer doing it than usual, a methodical aspect to the careful way he went over them, like he was using the ritual to steady himself.

It must have worked. The tremor in his hands stopped, and by the time he sheathed his swords, he appeared calm and collected again.

Arms tense, I forced myself to lower my hammer and tried not to think about the savage snarls he'd emitted. Or the look in his eyes as he, my ally who'd protected me faithfully these past months, had turned on me.

I rubbed a hand down my face, then took out my phone and texted Val.

Any updates from Zoltan? I didn't know if the vampire had worked during the day—his usual sleep time—but I couldn't help but hope.

Not yet, but I'll go down and check.

Thanks.

Sarrlevi watched, his face a mask.

I eyed the bodies and debated if we needed to do anything about them. Should I call Willard? They looked human—that must have been what their non-elven halves had been—and I didn't know if the Army made such people disappear or not. I sent her a text so she could decide, then waved for Sarrlevi to walk with me up the dock toward the parking lot.

The lights in the boathouse remained out, and I didn't see any security cameras, but they were probably there somewhere. Hopefully, they focused on the locked-up kayak inventory and building, not the dock. If nothing else, the twilight lighting should have kept them from seeing our faces well. I hoped.

The dimness hid the presence of more bodies until we were

even with the boathouse. I halted shy of stepping on a prone figure.

"The staff," Sarrlevi said, his eyes keener than mine in the dark.

I swore. That explained why the lights had gone out early.

"They're taking out everyone around me, including poor kids who are just trying to work an after-school job. I need to get rid of these assassins, Varlesh. "

That hadn't been phrased well, and I expected him to point out that he'd just gotten *rid of* a couple for me. But he rested a hand on my shoulder and said, "I know."

Before releasing me, he plucked at the life jacket and pointed at a rack where others hung, their fluorescent yellow making them visible even at night.

"There's nobody left to object if I don't return it," I muttered, unzipping it to hang with the others.

"*I* might object," Sarrlevi said, though there wasn't much humor in his tone.

When we reached the parking lot, my phone buzzed and lit up.

He doesn't have an answer yet, Val texted, *but he's been up all afternoon researching. He's got mounds of books stacked all around him and has an acquaintance bringing over more, specifically on chemical substances from other worlds. There's something in Sarrlevi's blood that isn't native to Earth.*

Yeah, I wouldn't have expected anything in my aunt's concoction to have come from here.

He says to remind you of his hourly rate, because this research is taking him a long time.

I dug into my pocket for my keys, barely resisting the urge to roll my eyes. Whatever it cost, I would pay it to have Sarrlevi back to normal. Still, I couldn't help but text, *What does Zoltan do with all his money? I've only seen him leave the basement a couple of times and never your property. I* know *he's not flying off to Las Vegas on the weekends.*

I think he hoards it in a vault somewhere and swims through it like Scrooge McDuck.

Thanks for the update. Let me know if he needs anything.

Will do.

I sighed and looked at Sarrlevi. He wasn't looking back at me but out toward the lake, his face pensive.

"Do you want to get some dinner before going to hunt for ingredients?" I wasn't in the mood to go out, not with a trail of bodies behind us, but maybe it would take his mind off everything. I assumed he could magically fuzz his face enough that any police officers dining at nearby tables wouldn't recognize him. "There's a fancy Brazilian steakhouse not far from here. Zadie has treated me a couple of times to celebrate closing deals. They have a huge salad bar. All you can eat fruits and vegetables to go with the skewers of meat." Never mind that the only fruit or vegetable that I loaded up on were the caramelized bananas. I'd heard from Zadie that the salads were great.

He turned his grave eyes toward me. "I believe... I will go alone to gather the ingredients."

"What about the assassins?" I didn't mind him leaving, but he'd been adamant about staying to protect me.

His voice grew soft. "Right now, I fear I am a greater threat to you than they are."

A tangle of emotions knotted in my gut. Denial. Disbelief. Rejection. And under it all... fear. Fear that he was right. Fear that he would get worse.

"You can keep control of yourself." I wanted to reassure him even if I wasn't positive it was true.

"I almost didn't."

"Varlesh." I didn't release my hammer, but I leaned in and wrapped my arms around him.

It might not have been wise, for that dangerous tension still radiated from him. I realized that he was, even in this quiet moment, struggling to keep control, but I needed him to know I cared. Tears welled in my eyes as I mashed my face against his shoulder. I needed… him.

Though he remained stiff, he rested a hand against the back of my head. "I will return as soon as I've gathered the ingredients, and I will hope your alchemist has identified what's wrong with me—and a solution. If not, I'll… have to return to her."

I scowled into his shoulder. "To strangle her and demand she fix you, right? Not to do her bidding because she's found another way to extort you."

Sarrlevi snorted softly. "Strangulation *would* be preferable."

That wasn't the answer I wanted. The thought that Barothla had done this to get rid of me and ensure Sarrlevi trotted back onto the proper path to kill my mother horrified me. And it made me hate her all the more.

Reluctantly, I made myself step back, aware that my chest was mashed against him and his lust was as difficult for him to control as his aggression. I didn't want to make things harder for him.

His hand tightened against my head, as if to keep me pressed against him, but, after a second, he released me and clasped his hands behind his back. Whenever he'd stood in that pose before, it had been a stance of calm patience. Now, it was more like he was clasping his hands to restrain himself.

"Will you remain at Thorvald's house or your house while I'm gone?" Sarrlevi gazed at me. "Or your sister's or grandparents'? Or your work site?"

Thanks to Zavryd's assistance, all of those places were magically protected now. I'd talked him out of putting in anything that spat flames or had glowing eyes, but we'd tested the defenses and found them adequate to fight off most enemies. Since a group of powerful assassins had gotten through the defenses of Val and

Zavryd's home, I knew none of those places were completely impervious, but they were safer than they had been.

"Probably the work site." I had the urge to bang nails into wood. Actually, I had the urge to pound my fists into a punching bag for an hour, but I would prefer to get work done while giving my body an outlet for its frustrations.

"Good. I wish you to remain protected while I'm gone. While I'm—" his face twisted with frustration of his own, "—unable to reliably protect you."

I wanted to hug him again but didn't. "Come back soon. I'm sure Zoltan will find an answer."

"Of course," Sarrlevi said, but the agreement didn't reach his eyes.

Zoltan wasn't a powerful enough alchemist to make the formula to cure his mother, so why would Sarrlevi believe the vampire could overcome Barothla's magic for this?

After making a portal, he sprang through and disappeared. I had to fight the urge to go after him. As badly as I wanted to keep an eye on him, and make sure he didn't deteriorate further while he was gone, I could do more good here. And he wouldn't have to worry about hurting me.

That didn't keep me from continuing to feel frustrated and wanting to put my fist through something. Hard.

8

AT THE JOB SITE, I WORKED THROUGH THE NIGHT, FIRST FINISHING the siding on Tinja's tiny home, then tackling the framing for the first of the three houses Abbas and I were building on the recently subdivided lot. We'd already completed the new flooring, siding, and roof—including repairing and enchanting the drainpipes—on the old house, and only the finish work remained. We'd talked about waiting so we could do the interiors of all four houses at once, but Zadie thought we could sell the remodeled home while working on the others and get some cash to buy the remaining materials we needed.

Abbas and Tinja surprised me by arriving before dawn, though Abbas took his mat to a private spot to pray before coming over to check on me.

"You finished the exterior of the tiny home." Tinja spun a pirouette after inspecting it. "And with enchanted nails and a roof too! That will protect it from even the worst Pacific Northwest storms, yes?"

I looked at the roof. *Had* I enchanted it? I knew about the nails, since those had been done under Santiago's tutelage, but the roof… Ah, yes, I did sense the magic. Another subconscious effort.

"Were you here all night?" Tinja asked. "When you did not return to the house, I assumed you were having vigorous sex with your virile assassin lover."

If only. I grimaced, thinking of Sarrlevi alone in a cave, scrounging *Fungi of Ferrous,* or one of the other ingredients, from the stone walls.

"This is so much *better* than sex." Tinja caressed the cedar-clad exterior.

Her plans hadn't called for siding, saying the aesthetic of treated plywood and corrugated metal was trendy, but my craftswoman blood had rejected the idea of leaving a home, even a tiny home on wheels, poorly protected from the elements. Or looking like a backyard tool shed.

"For you, maybe," I said wistfully.

It had been a long time since I'd had sex, and a *very* long time since I'd had *good* sex. Sarrlevi, I was certain, would make sure I was satisfied before contemplating his own pleasure. I'd gotten that sense from his head rubs and all those delicious tingles of magic. Those had been for *my* sake, not his, though I believed he drew some enjoyment from seeing *me* enjoy myself. Otherwise, he wouldn't keep bringing me such delicious cheeses.

A pang of loss went through me, but I shook my head. He *wasn't* lost. He would be fine, and he would come back, and Zoltan would know how to fix him. I had to believe that.

"Most certainly for me." Tinja patted my hand, drawing me from my brooding thoughts. "And I have a reward for you. Something else that's better than sex."

"Chocolate?" I asked, though I was positive Sarrlevi would be better than chocolate. Maybe even better than the glowing foil-wrapped cheese.

"*Blueprints.*" Tinja spun another pirouette, then ran to Abbas's truck and pulled them out. "I'm concerned that the houses you're building here aren't grandiose enough to bring in top dollar."

"It's not a grandiose kind of neighborhood." I waved toward the once-rural street that still held numerous old homes built in the fifties and sixties. Even the newer clumps of eight to ten houses jammed onto lots that had previously held one were fairly modest, at least compared to what builders put up these days.

"It will be that kind of neighborhood if *your* homes set the trend. Three-car garages instead of two, five-piece master bathrooms, spacious kitchens with islands and high-end appliances. Oh, and dual home offices for those who favor working from their dwelling. This is popular now, especially out here where the commute is farther."

"Those things are popular, yes, but most people can't afford them. And you have to build what makes sense for the neighborhood. There are chickens wandering around in the street, and, last night, a goat was noshing on the dogwoods out front."

"Does available food for foraging not add value to the neighborhood?"

It took me a moment to realize she was referring to the goats and chickens, not the dogwoods. "The kind of people who want dual home offices and a separate shower and tub in the master bath aren't going to take out shotguns to hunt the neighbor's livestock." I hoped there weren't *any* kinds of people who would do that, though I'd heard Abbas's troll kin had been known to make the pigs and goats in rural Maltby disappear.

"Matti." Tinja thrust her fists on her hips, her blueprints crinkling. "I do not feel you are fully committed to amassing great wealth."

"I'm not *opposed* to it, but I'd rather build houses that the average person can afford, okay? New construction is amazing, especially *our* new construction—" I waved to include all three of us, not feeling cocky for seeing our value, "—but most people who can afford to buy in the Seattle area get stuck in sixty-year-old homes without garages. Garages are nice in a rainy climate."

"You have a sixty-year-old home with a carport, and you are a *builder*." Tinja said that word as if it should convey great wealth, and I almost laughed. "You should have a grand house. *We* should have a grand house. With two home offices."

"If I built a home-office addition for our house, would you be able to keep your projects from swallowing the living-room furniture and dining-room table?" I admitted the furniture hadn't always been in view even before Tinja had moved in.

She touched a green finger to her lips in contemplation. "I could have *more* projects."

"That sounded like a no."

"When I am a wealthy entrepreneur and hire you to build a sanctuary for all urban goblins, I will design many home offices with worktables at the perfect height for my people."

"Good idea. Have you sold any tiny-home plans yet?"

"Not yet. I am waiting for the demo home to be completed before ramping up my marketing efforts." Tinja waved toward it and beamed a smile at me.

"Just don't add too many expensive things. Not only because I'm paying for everything but because the people who are going to build these won't be rich, and you can't get mortgages on them. I'm pretty sure they get treated—and financed—like RVs, not houses. No thirty-year low-interest-rate loans."

"The *demo* home can have high-end fixtures. I have already ordered granite for the countertops."

"Do you mean to say that *I've* already ordered granite?" I was positive my *intern* didn't have an account anywhere.

Tinja grinned. "It arrives tomorrow. Do not worry. The tiny home has tiny countertops. I got an end piece from the factory. People who build the homes can choose whatever materials they wish, but the model must look *amazing* for the promotional videos. I've already started the YouTube channel with tips from Zoltan."

"You should get *him* to star in them. Someone handsome." Someone not green, I thought but didn't say. Unless she wanted to promote these to the magical community. I supposed that was a possible market.

"Yes. Perhaps your elf assassin will stand beside the home and show it off. Once his garish wound heals, he will be beautiful again."

I imagined Sarrlevi next to the tiny home, wearing something sexy and waving his arms like the *Wheel of Fortune* lady. With his swords on his back.

"Let's see your blueprints." I didn't want Tinja to think I didn't appreciate her efforts, even if she had a luxury-home-builder mindset and Abbas and I were Middle America.

Beaming even more, she showed them to me.

"You do good design work," I said as I looked them over. There were a few elements we could add without raising costs too much.

"Naturally. I am gifted."

"And modest."

"Modest is a proper descriptor for rural goblins who excel only at scrounging substandard junk left alongside roads and making sheds instead of true dwellings."

"What's the proper descriptor for a city goblin who does her scrounging in her roommate's house and the yard next door?"

"Clever and resourceful."

During the night, I'd been mulling over my plans for getting into Kurt Hart's house, and seeing Tinja's drawings spurred an idea. "Could you make me a professional flyer for a local plumber? An actual, active plumber who has lots of five-star reviews online. But I'd need you to put a different number on it."

"Are you attempting to steal their business? Is this legal?"

"Only one client, and a client who, if I practice my

enchanting abilities enough to pull this off, will only briefly need the services of a plumber. I'll worry about that. You just use your design skills to make a professional flyer. I won't implicate you if I'm arrested."

Tinja rolled up her blueprints and used the end to scratch her head. "What goes on the flyer of a plumber?"

"When my grandfather had his own business, his flyers had a cartoon toilet with eyes on the tank and the lid partially up to look like it was smiling."

Tinja dropped her arm. "You wish me, a soon-to-be-licensed architect of great stature, to use the skills which I have laboriously honed over many years, to draw a *toilet*?"

"What's the problem? There are toilets all over your blueprints."

"Not *cartoon* toilets. With *eyes.* Matti, why don't you drive your wrench into my chest and tear out my heart?" Tinja flung her arm over her eyes, with much the same drama she'd used on her sickbed to convince me to build her tiny home.

Since she wasn't dying this time, I didn't give in to her theatrics. "I'm sure you can handle it. I need it as soon as possible, okay?"

"How much are you paying?"

"You're my intern. You're supposed to work for room and board and the opportunity to gain from my experience and wisdom."

"About cartoon toilets?"

"Most interns don't get room and board," I pointed out. "Here."

I pulled out some of the foil-wrapped cheese and, as much as I would have preferred to hoard it all for myself, allowed her to take a sample.

"Oh, that's good."

"I have more. Toilet?"

"Deal." She plucked up another sample.

Abbas finished praying and joined us, also sampling my

cheese. "That's amazing." He started to smile but faltered. "I should have asked if it's halal."

"What does Islamic law have to say about glowing algae?"

"I don't think it's covered." He nibbled on his lip, then took some more. "It reminds me of goat cheese, and that's allowed. It *must* be okay."

"Naturally."

Sarrlevi had better survive Barothla's machinations, not only because I cared about him but because, with such hungry business associates, I needed him around to restock my cheese supply regularly.

"Were you up all night? A lot got done since I left yesterday." Abbas scrutinized me. "And you look tired. And dirty."

"That is why I believed she had spent the night with the assassin," Tinja said.

"I wouldn't be *dirty* if I'd done that," I told her.

"No? Elves are into nature. He may enjoy mating on the ground among the pine needles."

"I've been to his house—*houses*. They have beds."

Tinja squinted at me. "Are trees, vines, or leaves involved in their construction?"

"Vines but not dirty vines." I shrugged at Abbas. "Yes, I was here all night. I've been feeling guilty about missing so much work due to assassins, elves, dragons, evil aunts, evil organizations of kidnappers, and I can't even remember what else." Admittedly, it had been more my frustration with the Sarrlevi situation that had driven me to work through the night. I'd tried to keep my mind as busy as my limbs in an attempt not to worry about him.

"Well, it looks good."

"Thanks. I'll let you take over for a couple of hours. I need to study some city plumbing maps."

"Are you still thinking of taking the existing house off the well and hooking it into the new line?" Abbas waved toward the street.

"Yes, but this isn't about our project. It's for a house in Medina, a house shrouded by magic and difficult to inspect. I need to learn as much as I can about the plumbing so I can sabotage it. Then arrange to be the plumber the homeowner calls for a problem I'm going to ensure comes up at an inopportune time." Such as when his hoity-toity party guests were arriving.

Abbas's mouth drooped open. Tinja tilted her head and frowned at me.

"I may call on you to drive the truck and look plumberly," I told Abbas, "but it won't be until next week."

"You don't have a plumbing business," he said. "Unless you've started a side hustle without telling me."

"No. I'm planning to advertise an existing business, change the phone number on the flyers to a temporary one that connects to mine, and hope I don't get caught and charged for anything fraudulent."

"And you'll be doing this because... why?"

"I don't want to make a wealthy real-estate mogul suspicious by showing up at his house and offering to be his date for a party," I said.

"That explained less than you might think," Abbas said.

Tinja nodded.

My phone buzzed with a text from Val.

Zoltan says he knows what the problem is. You better come over here so he can explain it. You and Sarrlevi.

He's not here, I replied. *Do you want me to come in person because it's super complicated or because... it's super bad, and you're going to offer me your shoulder to cry on?*

I'd meant the latter as a joke, at least I *hoped* it would turn out to be a joke, but the long pause before Val's reply came in worried me.

It's not good, was all it said.

BRT.

With fresh worry dropping like an anchor into my gut, I jammed my phone into my pocket.

"I'll give you more details about the plumbing scheme later." I waved at them and ran to the truck with more pressing matters on my mind.

9

By the time I arrived at Val's house, my eyes were gritty, I was yawning, and I regretted staying up all night. The work site hadn't been foggy, but her neighborhood was, the dense gray making it feel like dawn instead of almost nine a.m.

I sensed Zavryd's presence. If Sarrlevi returned to Earth soon, we could ask Zavryd to try to heal his wounds, but it was probably wishful thinking to believe he could do more than Xilneth in that area.

When I headed for the gate to the backyard, I intended to go straight down to the basement, but clangs announced a sword-fighting practice taking place, or perhaps a burglary being halted. No, I sensed Val's daughter as well as Val back there. A practice, it was.

They stopped when I came into their view. Val looked like she meant to pause only long enough to wave me toward Zoltan's stairs, but Amber, sweat dripping from her red face, staggered back and flopped onto a stone bench.

"Your friend is here, Val. She needs you. I can wait."

"We have fifteen more minutes left in our hour," Val said dryly.

"Your friend *desperately* needs you. I can tell. She's grimy and distraught."

Val eyed me. Since Abbas had said something similar, I probably did look like hell.

"No, I didn't spend the night on pine needles with Sarrlevi," I told her, lest she jump to the same conclusion that Tinja had.

"I was just going to ask if you're okay," Val said, still dry. "You look a little rough."

"I worked through the night while refining my plan to get into the Hart party."

"A plan that doesn't involve going as a billionaire's date?"

"Date?" Amber had been dabbing sweat from her face with a towel, but she lowered it and bounced over to me, visibly perked. "At a fancy party? Do you need help shopping for it?" She looked me over, lip curling. "Yes, you do. I'm available now if you want a fashion advisor. Don't take this the wrong way, but your style is as bad as Val's. Is that a men's Henley? I'm surprised you're not in overalls. You look like the *Grapes of Wrath.*"

"I didn't know you could look like a book." I eased away from her and toward the basement while giving Val a call-off-your-daughter-please look.

"Of course you can," Amber said. "You *need* an advisor."

"*You* have fifteen minutes more of your workout." Val gripped Amber's shoulder to keep her from following me down the steps and further critiquing my clothing choices. "And Matti has a vampire to see."

"Shh, *Val.* Don't say things like that so loudly. The neighbors will hear."

"The neighbors know about Zoltan. He's the reason we don't get invited to the block parties."

"As if there's only *one* reason," Amber muttered as I closed the outer door.

Even though I was careful not to let in any light, Zoltan gave me a cross look as I entered. True to Val's word, stacks of books loomed on the counter to either side of his work area, a microscope and other instruments I couldn't name framing a notebook with a pencil on it.

"This research is extremely extensive, my needy half-dwarf. To do your bidding, I rose well before my usual hour, and I am still up, well *past* a respectable vampire's bedtime." Zoltan looked toward the windows, though they had long ago been bricked in from the outside.

"Thank you for doing it for me. Val mentioned there would be fees." I sensed Zavryd shifting into a dragon out front and leaving the premises. To chase off Xilneth again? Or on some errand for his mother?

"Oh, *copious* fees. My rates go up whenever I must work during dreadful daylight hours."

"How can you even tell when it's daylight from down here?" I stopped close to the notebook, hoping to find something illuminating, but the dashes pointing to a capitalized double chain of letters were gobbledygook to me.

"Of *course* I can tell. You see the problem." Zoltan pointed to the notebook.

"Uh? Is that chemistry?" The letters were vaguely familiar, but it had been a long time since tenth-grade science. And what I mostly remembered from that class was fixing my lab partner's beater of a car in exchange for help balancing equations.

"Certainly, my simple pugilist, but some of these elements I cannot identify because they don't exist on Earth, or at least have not yet been discovered. Either way, they are not on the Periodic Table of Elements." He waved to spots on the chain with question marks instead of letters. "To add further complexity, the entire compound is magical."

"Is it what you found in Sarrlevi's blood?"

"*Not* in the blood that you presumably took from a random

vein in his body but from the sample at the wound site. You did *not*, I shall note, label the specimens. I had to deduce which was which."

"You only gave me the syringes."

"So your lack of thoughtfulness was my fault? Next time, I will send a label maker along with you."

"Just tell me what you found, please." I forced a smile, though he was making me want to grit my teeth—or maybe grab him by the neck. "You can insult me at the end while we haggle over your prices."

"Won't that be a delight?" Zoltan tapped the notebook. "As I said, this compound is *extremely* complex, making maitotoxin seem simple in comparison."

"And that is what?"

"A toxic polyether compound emitted by red-tide dinoflagellates and often cited for its complexity."

"Toxic?" I mouthed.

"Yes. This reminds me of it, but more because of its structure than its purpose. Its *purpose* I have been doing a great deal of research in an attempt to ascertain."

"Its purpose is making Sarrlevi lose his mind. No, his mind seems okay. But it's making him more... I'm not sure. Kind of animal-like. Less civilized."

"So you said. This compound is not in any of the texts I have consulted, and I believe it was custom-made by a master alchemist."

"She is that. So, it's not bacteria or a virus or anything biological? It's a foreign substance in his blood? Like a drug?"

"It is a *magical* chemical compound, but, interestingly, it does act in many ways like a living organism. It is capable of using the organic material in the body to replicate itself through something akin to binary fission. In that way, it is *like* bacteria."

That didn't sound good. "Does that mean Sarrlevi is going to get worse because it's reproducing?"

"It is likely that he will grow more compromised, yes. I have isolated the compound and attempted to break the bonds using the typical methods of applying heat or electrical energy, but it is hardy and impervious."

I swallowed. "So you can't destroy it?"

"Not *yet*, but I am doing experiments. Since it is magical, it is likely that a magical solution will be required." Zoltan waved toward a row of Petri dishes. "Currently, I am observing how it replicates and which organic materials it prefers. That may give me more clues about how to destroy it, or at least inhibit its growth, which could keep the effects created by its presence in the body from getting worse."

I didn't want Sarrlevi to simply not *get worse*. I wanted him to be healthy and in control. Back to his usual self. I cared about his usual self. Maybe I even *loved* his usual self.

That was something I'd been hesitant to admit, even to myself, both because of our conflict of interests and because he'd made it clear that he didn't expect to stick around on Earth. I hadn't wanted to let myself fall in love with him. But as the letters and question marks grew blurry before my eyes, emotion making it hard to swallow, I realized how devastated I would be if he went crazy or *died*. It would be hard enough losing him because he left Earth and returned to his normal life, but if he died, there would be no chance of seeing him again.

The door opened, and Val stepped in. I drew a shaky breath and wiped moisture from my eyes. Val wouldn't care, but I didn't want to weep in front of Zoltan.

"So far, I've determined that blood alone doesn't interest the compound. It was not present in large quantities near the wound site." Zoltan wasn't paying attention to my moist eyes nor did he do more than glance at Val when she walked in, thankfully without her fashion advisor. "Originally, it surprised me that the assassin could be affected so strongly by something that doesn't appear to be that pervasive in his body, but I considered that it might have traveled to more preferential areas. Normally, I wouldn't assign an intelligence to a chemical compound or believe it could *have* preferences, but, as I said, magic imbues this and makes it more than some inert substance. Fascinating, don't you think?"

I shook my head mutely, not trusting my voice—and not *fascinated* in the least. Horrified, maybe.

"Since," Zoltan continued, "I keep brains, spinal cords, nerves, and various organs in my lab, I was able to place the compound into dishes with samples from them."

"We pretend it's not disturbing that he has those things down here," Val told me.

"The compound did show some propensity to be drawn to the organs, but it is *feasting* on the brain matter." Zoltan, sounding more excited by than horrified at that, picked up a Petri dish to show us. "I know what you are thinking. How can a chemical compound feast on something?"

"Not exactly," Val murmured.

I didn't comment, only wanting to hear about how we could get this out of Sarrlevi's body.

"It is drawn to and breaking down the lipids in the brain—as you may know, fatty acids are highly concentrated there—to use for replication. They are, of course, crucial to the brain's function. It is also possible that certain select parts of the brain are being targeted over others. The orbital and dorsolateral prefrontal cortical areas, for example, are known to be linked with aggression."

"And you think this chemical is in Sarrlevi's brain?" Val asked. "Can it pass through—what's that membrane called?"

"The blood-brain barrier," Zoltan said dryly. "Yes, my erudite robber, I believe it was handcrafted to do exactly that. To zip past the brain's defenses to get inside and replicate. I would like to do an MRI of our elf assassin."

"I'm pretty sure you don't have an MRI machine down here." Val looked around.

"I do not. Is there any chance you can order him to report to an imaging specialist for a scan and have the results sent to me?"

"I doubt we're going to be able to do that," Val said. "An imaging specialist might notice his ears are pointed."

Zoltan waved dismissively. "If not, I can only guess what it's doing to his brain based on what's happening in my Petri dish. I did, however, find a similar and more studied chemical compound that I believe this might have been based on." He opened one of the thick tomes to a bookmarked page. The text was in Dwarven, but there were diagrams of compounds not that different from the one he'd drawn in his notebook. "It is something the dwarves of Dun Kroth found deep in their tunnels, emitted in gray puffs from creatures indigenous to the subterranean rocks. The scientists who studied it believed it a defense mechanism that the creatures used in an attempt to protect their habitat. The miners who inhaled it soon developed symptoms of traumatic brain injury, including confusion, agitation, and aggression. Eventually, they lost their ability to reason and even speak."

I straightened with interest. Sarrlevi could speak and wasn't yet confused about anything, but the other symptoms fit.

"The compound caused decreased function in the orbital and dorsolateral prefrontal cortical regions that I mentioned and also inhibited the cerebral cortex, which is, of course, responsible for high-level functions such as reasoning, memory, and language. One of the researchers wrote that it seemed like the subjects were reverting from civilized dwarves to their savage ancestors who had evolved from a lesser and more aggressive species that lived in the lava tunnels of their world hundreds of thousands of years ago."

"Were they able to reverse it?" Val asked.

"Yes." I gripped Zoltan's arm. "Did the dwarves return to normal after a time when they didn't get any more doses? Or did the scientists find a way to counter it?"

Zoltan glanced at my hand but surprisingly didn't make a snippy comment about it. "According to the notes, the subjects continued to deteriorate and became too aggressive for the safety of the scientists doing the experiments. They were locked up for their own good, in the hope that a solution could eventually be found, but one then escaped and killed several people working on the experiment. After that, the rest of the subjects were terminated for the safety of everyone else."

"*Terminated*?" I stared at him and then at the book. "You mean killed?"

"That is the meaning of that word, yes."

"Why the hell were the scientists dumb enough to get themselves killed? Why couldn't they keep the affected people locked up? Did the families of the miners give permission for their kin to be *terminated*? Did the king?" I closed the book to look at the cover, but there weren't any names on it.

"This is what you seek," Zoltan said, flipping to a table of contents and a particular entry, "and, because I'd encountered their names before, I was able to translate them. One of the scientists involved was Princess Barothla Ironhelm."

I rocked back, though I shouldn't have been surprised. Of *course* Barothla had been on the team. That was how she'd known about the compound and what it did in the first place. Then she'd magically tinkered with it to make it worse. Or maybe just to make it so she could put it in her *nail polish* like a crazy woman and slash people with it.

Shaking with anger, I stalked away from the book.

"Dear robber," Zoltan said, grabbing beakers off a counter near me as he addressed Val, "do keep an eye on your guest, will you?

The way she's flexing her hands into fists is most alarming to the many breakable objects in my laboratory."

I couldn't help it. The desire to pound my fist into the brick foundation for the fireplace upstairs surged through me. Only with great effort did I force open my fingers and stop myself. I couldn't destroy Val's house because I was in a bad mood. A *very* bad mood.

"Can you counteract the poison, Zoltan?" Val asked. "The compound?"

"When it's self-replicating, magically protected, and likely snuggled deep in the assassin's brain? Since it's not a bacteria or virus, it wouldn't be as simple as finding an antibiotic or antiviral medication. I have no idea how to destroy it, and... even if I did, brain damage doesn't tend to be reversible."

"In humans." Val gave me a concerned look as I stopped to gape at them, the implications sinking in. "Elves are magical beings who can heal wounds that no human ever could, and they live hundreds of years. Maybe damage to their brains does heal."

"I would have to do more research to determine that," Zoltan said.

Taking a deep breath, I attempted to summon calm, rational thinking. "What about the other scientists who worked on the compound? Would they have more of an idea of how to counteract this?" I refused to accept that permanent brain damage was inevitable.

"According to the paper, they did not find a solution in time to save the dwarves," Zoltan said, "but it's possible they continued to study it after it was written. At the least, they have more experience working with the original compound than I. One of them may even have engineered the altered version."

"I'll bet."

Val looked at me. "You think your aunt made it?"

"I wouldn't be surprised. Somehow, I don't think her *career* choice is the reason her people aren't that into her." I thought about the cages in her laboratory and wished I'd been able to free all the creatures inside, especially the goblins she'd held captive. "Can you give me the names of the other scientists who worked on this? Were they dwarves?"

"The other three were elves."

I grimaced, thinking of Sarrlevi's certainty that his people wouldn't help him, not when he'd been exiled and was a known assassin. When we'd only sought to heal his mother, I had thought we might talk an elf into helping us—it wasn't as if *she* was an exiled assassin. But this? This would be purely to heal him. The elven scientists might prefer to see him die.

My fingers curled into fists again. It wasn't fair. He never should have been exiled. He wasn't a criminal, damn it. His *father* had been. *He* was the one who should have been kicked off their world.

"One is a microbiologist," Zoltan murmured, reading from the book, "and two are renowned alchemists."

"Could you write down the names of the second two for me? Val, would you ask Zavryd if he can give me a ride to the elf world?" I looked at Zoltan. "I assume they live there?"

"Their addresses are not published along with their biographies and contributions," Zoltan said.

"Zav just went back home to do some work for his family," Val said, "but I can ask when he gets back."

"Is there any chance he would like to collect Barothla and force her to do the right thing and fix all the people she's screwed over?" I asked. "Aren't dragons supposed to be the just rulers over the realms?"

"They think they are, but, from what I've observed, they mostly want to keep the lesser species in line to make sure they don't combine forces and rise up against their kind. Zav is a good guy, for a dragon, but he won't go against his mother, and she's...

prickly. I also don't think they're going to lift a talon to help Sarrlevi." Val shrugged apologetically.

I clenched my jaw and stalked around.

"Dear robber, the breakables." Zoltan shifted in front of a display case to block me from getting close to it. "Please don't instigate the hammer-wielding half-dwarf."

"I'll go see the alchemists as soon as someone can give me a ride." I ground my teeth, hating that I had to depend on others for that. I longed to learn to make portals of my own, whether I had the aptitude and power for it or not. Somehow, I would find a way to *build* a portal generator if I had to. "I needed to talk to an elven alchemist about making the formula for Sarrlevi's mother's disease anyway."

Val nodded. "I don't think Zav will be gone that long. When he gets back, I'll call you. Why don't you get some rest, Matti? You look rough."

"Like the *Grapes of Wrath*?"

"Maybe so."

I headed for the door, but I doubted I would find any rest. Not when I was imagining Sarrlevi searching for ingredients in some remote jungle while he slowly descended into madness.

10

RAIN FELL OUTSIDE MY WINDOW AS I LAY IN BED, ATTEMPTING TO manipulate the pipes in my neighbor's house with my mind. Already, I'd managed to manipulate the ones in my kitchen from the bedroom. That was promising, but if I wanted to force the Hart household to make a last-minute call for a plumber during the party, I needed to be able to do something from farther away. And it had to be to the pipes underground so the barrier around the property wouldn't impede me. Further, my magical touch would have to be subtle in case he had staff with the ability to sense such tinkering.

"Subtle is *not* my strong point," I muttered, glancing at the window, beads of rain running down the glass.

Soon, it would be dark out, and I hadn't yet heard from Val. That meant Zavryd hadn't returned.

Earlier, I'd managed to doze for a couple of hours, but I'd had unsettling dreams. In them, Sarrlevi had turned into a wild animal, ripping off his clothes and running through the wilds, attacking everyone he encountered. Before this, whenever I'd dreamed of him naked, it had been in a much more pleasing context. These had been nightmares.

I wished I hadn't let him leave Earth without me. He shouldn't be out there alone. He needed someone—*me*—to keep an eye out for him.

The names of the two elven alchemists were on a sticky note on my bedside table, the hammer leaning against it. Too bad Sorka couldn't make portals. I'd asked earlier. She'd said only that she wasn't aware of any weapons that had been given that power. Maybe magical hammers weren't encouraged to whisk themselves off to other worlds to look for new wielders.

Reminding myself that finding my parents needed to be as much a priority as helping Sarrlevi, I made myself focus on the pipes again. I attempted to send my power flowing underground between the two houses to ultimately form a barrier across one heading up to a toilet. My temporary impediment wouldn't do anything unless someone flushed at that moment. Even then, it would only delay the filling of the tank. I would have to do something more dramatic to ensure Hart's people would call a plumber, but I had time to practice.

"Got nothing *but* time." I held the barrier in place for a minute, then dropped it. When I'd done this in my own house for the kitchen sink, I'd been able to confirm that the water had been cut off, but I refused to run over and knock on Mrs. Ming's door and ask to use her bathroom to verify things.

Your mother never did this, Sorka spoke into my mind.

Oh? Do you think she would be disappointed that I'm going to use the power I inherited from her to sabotage my enemy's toilets?

Probably not. She always wanted to protect her people, ideally without hurting others. She might even approve.

Since the words warmed my heart, I didn't mention that I might end up wringing some necks once my plumber ruse gained me access to the house. It occurred to me that Sorka might have known—might *know*—my mother well.

How long has it been since she crafted you? I asked. *Were you two together long?*

I am not certain what mortals consider long, *and I do not track the passing of years. Time is largely insignificant to a weapon.*

A weapon that doesn't rust or develop a patina, anyway, huh?

Those afflictions only affect weak metal unaltered by magic. I did go on numerous diplomatic trips and occasionally into battle with your mother. She made me some time before coming to this world. Living here was not something she longed to do, but, as you know, she was forced to flee her home to avoid the assassin—the assassin you now spend time with.

I winced, wondering if the hammer had been judging me all along for more reasons than my using her to demo cabinets. *He's going to help me get her. He regrets his choice to work for Barothla.*

We shall see. Your mother and those who accompanied her to this world sought first to establish diplomatic relations with the natives. When that did not work, they looked for a secret place to build a colony where refugees could stay. They attempted to build where they believed no claims on the land had been made, but we learned that on this strange wild world all *land is claimed. She didn't know that then.*

Yeah, the governments own whatever isn't privately held. People can often use government land for recreation, but I don't know about setting up colonies.

*She led the building of a colony in tunnels they hollowed out in a mountainside outside of this city, an area that was unused by humans. Now and then, she came to the urban area to invite in other dwarves that were refugees here. They used magic, as much as could be summoned on this anemic world, to make the colony a pleasant place for them to stay. The humans here eventually found out about it, however, and questioned her about the project. They were ignorant and unaware *that she was a dwarven princess—they hadn't heard of Dun Kroth at all. Even the belligerent orcs are more respectful toward dwarves than these people were. At first, the humans shunned her and the other dwarves. But, when she invited some of them to the colony, hoping to be amenable and show them that creating a place to live was all her people wanted to do, they saw what her magic could do. And they wanted her power for themselves.*

The Army did? Or was it always this organization? I stared at the ceiling in the darkening room, listening raptly, realizing I should have asked for Mom's background as soon as Sorka had spoken to me. Of course, I'd been busy fending off a dozen dwarves and my aunt at the time.

Your government and military deemed the dwarves a threat. They originally captured your mother to question her.

And that's when she met my dad.

Sorka paused. At first, I thought it was because she hadn't approved of him—a lowly human—for my mother, but what she said was, *Presumably. I was separated from her for a time, locked in a box that dulled my powers and cut me off from the outside world.*

Some kind of insulating metal to thwart magic? I wonder how the soldiers knew to do that.

It has been millennia since this wild world was first discovered and other races made portals to visit it. Some *of your people were aware of dwarves, elves, dragons, and the like.*

I guess that makes sense. Lord of the Rings *and Dungeons and Dragons and all those old mythologies had to be based on something.*

I'm certain your military found someone to consult who had at least some *knowledge of the Cosmic Realms. From what your mother told me when we rejoined, I know they questioned her and were trying to coerce her to make power generators for them.*

Like the one that was under the park in Bellevue? I asked.

Yes. The man who became her human mate was the one to free her from the military and also retrieve me.

My father.

Yes. Once she was free of the restraints they used, she used her powers of camouflage to hide them so they could sneak out of the facility. The years after that were tedious for me.

You mean when they were enjoying being a couple and eventually having me?

Tedious.

Not enough battles?

Occasionally, the military and the organization that had learned of Rodarska found them. They usually ran, but she also dusted me off for a couple of battles. Largely, however, she fornicated copiously with her human mate and performed domestic duties unbefitting a female of her rank and station.

Like what? Begging in the streets? I had no memories of missed meals or our family being impoverished, but I'd also been too young to remember much. We'd lived in an apartment though, not a box next to a goblin under a bridge.

Cleaning waste from the sodden undergarments of her squalling offspring.

Oh. That was me.

I'm aware.

I suppose dwarf princesses usually have servants to change diapers? I supposed *most* princesses did, at least on Earth, but I'd never imagined dwarves, for whom hard work seemed wired into their DNA, foisting off duties. My firsthand experience with my mother's people was admittedly limited though. My vision of dwarven females chiseling ore from tunnels while their babies were strapped to their backs in carriers was probably not accurate.

One such as your mother would at least *have a maid to assist with such mindless duties. When Rodarska was with her people, everyone agreed that her time was better spent working on forging and enchanting great weapons such as myself and other tools and machines that could be used for the good of many people.*

I supposed, given the choice, I would rather craft things that would live on beyond me and be appreciated by others than change a diaper, though I couldn't imagine hiring a maid. Maybe if one was royal and lived in a palace, maids simply came with the place.

When she was captured again, you got a battle, I said.

Yes.

How did you keep from being captured along with my mother and father the last night they were free and together? I didn't think anything of it as a kid, but I've recently come to wonder how you ended up in my grandparents' umbrella rack.

Rodarska and I battled until the building caught fire and soldiers surged all around us. Some were the same soldiers that had once imprisoned her, but there were also men from another organization, men who had magical weapons capable of hurting her. When they added their might to that of the soldiers, Rodarska knew she couldn't win and couldn't escape. All she wanted was to buy time for her human mate to get away with you and his other offspring.

Penina.

After her family escaped the building, and as the attackers attempted to swarm Rodarska and steal me, she flung me across the room and brought the structure down around us. I know she worried about harming innocent people and hoped the other apartment inhabitants had run at the sounds of battle, but the building was already weakened and would have fallen regardless. She knew that. She used its collapse and her own magic to hide me under the rubble. She also asked me not to let myself be found unless an ally came. She didn't want those who were kidnapping her to have the key.

The key? You?

Yes. After she was gone, men came several times to look for me, but her magic and my own hid me. They looked at me without seeing me. Only when someone familiar to me came did I reveal myself. Sorka shared an image of a dark-skinned man with black hair.

It took me a moment to realize it was my grandfather. I couldn't remember a time when he'd had fully black hair, but that was his gruff face picking through the rubble. He must have come to see if any of our belongings had survived, anything that his son would want saved in case he was ever released from the military prison.

I have not seen Rodarska since that night, Sorka continued, *though I have called out to her with my magic. She has remained either far away, perhaps on another world, or well insulated from magic on this one. A prisoner this entire time, I believe. You must find her.*

Trust me, that's still my goal.

You seem distracted. Sorka shared an image of Sarrlevi.

I grimaced. The hammer wasn't wrong that my attention was divided, especially now, but I refused to feel guilty. *Everything I'm doing with him is to make sure he won't attack my mother when we do find her.*

Everything. Really. Apparently, magical hammers had no trouble grasping and using sarcasm, for the next image she shared was one of us kissing on my bed.

I blushed. *I've come to care about him too, I admit.*

Maybe the next time Sarrlevi and I got involved in anything, I would leave the hammer outside the bedroom...

As if the conversation had made him appear, I sensed Sarrlevi on the front stoop.

You are waiting for me exactly where I imagined you being, he spoke into my mind.

In bed?

Yes. He shared imagery of us writhing on it, naked, bathed in sweat, and clearly enjoying ourselves. *May I come in?*

The graphic vision didn't surprise me, now that I knew about the chemical compound munching on his brain, but it rattled me. Before, if he'd thought of such things, he hadn't thrust them into my head by way of a greeting, and I wasn't sure how to respond.

Had he already finished collecting ingredients for his mother's formula? Or had he put that on pause to check on me and make sure assassins hadn't gotten me? Maybe, as the imagery suggested, he'd simply gotten horny and decided to pop in for a quickie.

I've learned that my hammer doesn't like you, I said, deciding to ignore the naked writhing.

Sarrlevi paused. *I suppose that makes sense. It—she—would be loyal to your mother and was with her when I hunted her.*

Even though the word *hunted* sent a chill through me, his thoughtful response relieved me because he sounded more like his normal self. At the least, he didn't come across as a savage wild animal. Not yet. The lusty bedroom imagery promised he wasn't himself, but he didn't seem any further gone than before. And the lust concerned me a lot less than the fury and lack of recognition that had taken over his eyes when he'd sliced through my barrier on the docks. Maybe the lust even titillated me a little, the thought that *I* inspired it. I was tempted to take off my clothes and greet him as naked as I'd been in his vision.

But—I glanced at the note with the scientists' names—we had other priorities. It would be better if we stayed out of my bedroom so he—*we*—wouldn't be tempted to engage in something distracting. Besides, I would rather Sarrlevi be in his right mind when we had sex. I didn't want there to be any doubt that he was choosing me because he *wanted* me, not because weird magical chemicals in his brain were making him horny. Right now, he might jump into bed with anything female.

The thought made me pause in the middle of swinging my legs to the floor. *Would* he, in his compromised state, join with some random other woman if I didn't make myself available to him?

I shook my head again and told myself not to think about that. I hoped it wouldn't be the case, but it wasn't a reason to sleep with him, regardless.

Maybe you should start bringing my hammer gifts. I stuffed my feet into my shoes and tossed some clothes in the hamper, though I intended to meet him in the living room, not invite him back to my bedroom.

What gift would win the affection of a hammer?

Hell if I know, and, yes, you can come in. I realized he still stood on the stoop. *Sorka doesn't feel affection for me yet either. Given your past, the best you might be able to hope for is indifference.*

What gift would win the indifference *of a hammer?*

Maybe some nice weapons-cleaning oil? Or a cozy sheath? I've been thinking of making a sling so it's easier to carry the hammer on my back.

I stepped out of my room, intending to meet Sarrlevi at the front door, but he'd already entered the hall. I halted and stared at him—more specifically at his *chest.*

Usually, if he wore shirts with buttons or laces, they were fully fastened, and his sleeves were always down. Tonight, his shirt wasn't buttoned, leaving his muscled chest and abdomen on display, and his sleeves were rolled to his elbows. Every muscle was taut, radiating tension, the same dangerous tension that he had exuded the last time I'd seen him. Maybe more.

The scratches on the back of his hand and his cheek remained, a reminder of what afflicted him, and a few new narrow abrasions marred his forearms and pecs. It looked like he'd decided crawling through thorn bushes with his shirt half off had been a good idea, but I couldn't help but remember the elf ex-princess and how she liked to use her nails on him when they had sex.

Thorn bushes, I told myself. Those were from thorn bushes. He hadn't been out sating himself on random people. He was on a quest to save his mother. He wouldn't have shirked that duty, no matter what.

I lifted my gaze from his chest to his eyes, hoping I was right. But he was looking *me* up and down.

"You're not wearing my favorite garment," he said, his roaming gaze pausing on my chest.

That heated look made me flush.

"The robe?" The memory of his warm callused hand slipping inside it to stroke my breast sprang to mind.

Smirking, Sarrlevi walked down the hall toward me, his hands lifting. "The robe."

"Because we've got a mission." I raised my own hand to stop him. It came to rest on his bare chest, the hard swell of his pectoral under my palm, the heat of his skin warm against mine.

Sarrlevi pressed his hand over mine, then bent to kiss my neck. Delicious zings of pleasure shot through me, making me hyper aware of my body—and his. Logical thoughts fell out of my mind as I realized how amazing it would be to give in to this, to pull him to my bed and push his shirt the rest of the way off.

"I need to tell you what I learned from Zoltan," I said even as my head fell back, giving him permission to kiss his way up my throat, to nip at my skin, then nibble on my earlobe. His teeth roused such exquisite sensations that I gasped, my hips shifting toward him of their own accord. "Did you... get the ingredients for the formula?" I managed to ask as I gripped his shoulders.

I've longed for your company. Sarrlevi breathed in my scent, as if I were the most enticing thing in the world, and wrapped an arm around me to pull me closer. His body pressed against me, hot and hard. *To have you with me on the hunt, to thrust you against a tree every time I grew taut with need and have you, my beautiful and loyal and sexy female.*

"My fantasies usually involve beds instead of trees," I whispered, though the words excited me. I'd longed for him to believe I was all those things—to want me—and I caught myself rising on tiptoes to kiss his neck, his warm skin salty from his day's efforts.

He growled and pushed me against the wall, a roughness to his touch that had never been there before.

A frisson of uncertainty went through me. This wasn't Sarrlevi, not entirely, and I didn't know what to expect. I was tough, but he had the power to hurt me.

I was in the wilds, and trees are suitably sturdy for what I had in mind. When he telepathically shared exactly *what* he'd been fantasizing about, my uncertainty shifted to lust. I would enjoy being with him in any state. My body knew that.

I tried to wrap my arms around his shoulders, but my knuckles smashed against his sword hilts. He wore his pack as well. Because he was on a mission. A mission he'd forgotten about because of his desire.

Even though I wanted to be with him, I couldn't let him forget that his and his mother's lives were both at stake. He might regret it if he cast aside his mission, even for a night.

"Varlesh," I whispered. "We should wait. This is important."

Yes, it is. He growled again and slid his hand under my shirt, magic flowing from his fingers. It aroused me even more than his touch. *I need you. Now.*

Though I didn't want it to, my body responded. Eagerly. I caught myself arching against him, rubbing him and excited by the pants of desire that my actions elicited from him. My fingers tightened around his shoulders. I wanted to push aside his shirt, his weapons, everything. I wanted—

No.

"We need to talk to a couple of elven alchemists about your problem," I blurted, looking away. Damn. With him making me crazy with his magic, my lust was almost as hard to control as his.

Sarrlevi growled again, this time more with irritation than desire, and I knew he didn't want to talk about *alchemists.* He had me pinned against the wall, and his grip tightened around me, promising I wouldn't escape if he didn't want me to.

"Maybe at the same time, we can see if they can help your mother," I said, hoping that mentioning her would quench his lust and remind him of his mission. To help, I shared my memory of her with him, of her lying in bed and ill.

His next growl was one of frustration, and he pulled back, putting space between us, though he braced his hands against the wall to either side of my head, the corded muscles of his forearms in my peripheral vision. *You're thinking of my mother* now?

"We have to. *You* have to. I don't know how much time we have. Did you get the ingredients?"

"Yes," he rasped, finally answering the question. He jerked his head back toward his pack.

"Good. I'll get the names of the alchemists. We can go visit them now."

Sarrlevi stared at me, his hands still against the wall, his taut muscles almost quivering to either side of my head. Even though he was looking at me, I sensed him battling within himself, fighting the desire to continue what we'd been doing. My body also wanted that, and I had to keep wrestling with the urge to fling my arms back around him, to believe that maybe having sex would help him relax for a time, sand off that dangerous edge.

"I'll get the names of the alchemists," I said again, afraid to let my mind wander down that path. Remembering the list was on my bedside table, I ducked under his arm to get it.

His hand shifted with startling speed, catching me by the shoulder, and I froze. Would he *let* me go?

I swallowed. "Varlesh..."

His fingers loosened, and, almost as if he'd been stung, he jerked his hand back. It thumped against the wall, and he stared at the spot where I'd been as he continued to struggle to get control of himself.

I ran into the bedroom to grab my hammer and the list. The idea of going off alone with him to see alchemists—or anyone—on another world when he was like this scared me, and I wondered if I should ask Val to come along. Val and *Zavryd*.

With the list in hand, I started to turn, but I sensed Sarrlevi behind me and jumped, almost dropping the paper. His arms came around me in a hug, and I froze, afraid I would have to conjure the memory of his mother again—and more afraid that it wouldn't work twice.

But all he did was kiss the top of my head. "Thank you," he whispered, that raspiness still in his voice. "For caring."

"You're welcome."

I'd never had someone hug me with his entire body tense, but I stood and let him, realizing he needed a lifeline.

What did the alchemist say? Zoltan?

Though I hated to give him more bad news, I shared my memories of the meeting with him.

He sighed. *We had better hurry then. I may not have much time left to save her before I'm too insane to do anything. Too dangerous to be around you.*

"That won't happen." I hoped. "But I agree that we should hurry."

Yes. Stop me again with that memory if I lose... If I try to...

I will.

He bent to rest his cheek beside mine. *I want you to enjoy being with me, not be pawed over by an animal absorbed by his own lust.*

I was positive I would have enjoyed being with him no matter what, but I appreciated that he cared. *Okay. Do you know where on the elven home world either of these alchemists lives?*

I know where they both live. I've already visited them and asked for their help.

Oh. They said no?

They said no. That's why I came back. For your help in case— You mentioned using your dwarven charm.

Damn straight, I will. I hefted my hammer inasmuch as I could with his arms still locked around me.

Careful. It arouses me when you swing your weapon at things.

Maybe I'll just talk to the elves.

A good idea.

11

We came out of Sarrlevi's portal by a lake in a lush temperate forest, unfamiliar birds chirping and what might have been an insect making a distinct *jhirrrrup* sound out over the water. The leaves were rich shades of green, not the pink that had infused the forest when I'd visited Veleshna Var with Zavryd and Val.

Clouds hung in what felt like an afternoon sky, but the towering trees made it hard to guess the sun's position and the time of day. It wasn't as if I knew which way was west or even if the sun set in the west here.

Along the shoreline in the distance, a few dozen platforms and houses were built into the trees, a settlement much smaller than the capital city. It was warmer here than it had been there, and I wondered how many miles away it was. Though I didn't sense anything similar to the barrier that encompassed and defended the capital, numerous tree houses emanated magic. Protections?

Something with a powerful aura stirred out in the lake. The surface didn't so much as ripple, but visions of the Loch Ness monster came to mind.

Beside me, Sarrlevi inhaled deeply, holding his breath for a moment before letting it trickle out through his nose. The air smelled of damp earth and vegetation with floral scents, nothing quite like I'd experienced back home, but there was a comforting familiarity about the forest. Maybe he thought so too for he seemed to relax an iota. He walked to a thick tree growing near the water, placed a hand on the trunk, and rested his forehead against it.

Home, I realized. This was home for him, a home he'd been denied access to for centuries.

That reminded me that he was still in exile and wasn't supposed to be here. If he'd already spoken to the alchemists, he'd broken that exile once and survived, but did his people now know he had visited? Were they lying in wait in case he returned?

Wary, I looked toward the village. My senses picked up the auras of elves, though most weren't as significant as whatever lived in the lake. There were a few hundred citizens, I decided, instead of the tens of thousands in their capital city.

That didn't mean there couldn't be dozens of armed warriors ready to pounce on an intruder. Hand in my pocket, I fingered the camouflaging charm, wondering if I should activate it. Sarrlevi hadn't yet hidden himself.

Still leaning against the tree, he turned his face toward me and smiled. He continued to look like hell—his shirt hung open, showing the scratches all over his chest, bags haunted his eyes, and a clump of moss now dangled into his tousled hair. Even so, he managed to be achingly handsome. Especially when he looked at me and smiled.

"Good to be home?" I asked.

"I hadn't realized how much I missed the sights and scents and —" Sarrlevi patted the tree as he looked up, a bird chattering in the branches, "—*syllen.* That is the word our people use. I don't think you have an equivalent. Presence of the forest." He ran a loving hand down the trunk.

"Do you want to be alone with that tree for a minute?"

He slanted me an I-know-you're-teasing-me look.

"I could wait over on that beach there." I pointed to the pebbly shoreline. "Where the creature living in the lake can have easy access to me if it enjoys munching on half-dwarves."

"That is not necessary. I already took a moment to *shaysor zee* when I came earlier." Sarrlevi pressed a clump of moss to his bare chest. "Forest bathe."

I imagined him rolling around in the dirt, rubbing his armpits and everything else with pine needles and moss.

His eyebrows quirked. Reading my mind?

"It's not *quite* like that." Sarrlevi stepped back and extended a hand toward me. "Imagine standing under moisture dripping from the moss hanging from the branches. It is not so much a thorough washing as anointing oneself with the presence of the forest."

"I *knew* moss was involved." I was hesitant to get close, lest I stir up his lust—or more worrisome aggressions—but this place seemed to be clearing his mind a bit, so maybe it would be all right. With my hammer in one hand, I clasped his with the other. "Are you going to forest-bathe me?"

"It requires nudity, so it might not be a good idea right now." His smile grew a touch darker, an acknowledgment that the compound continued to affect him and he might not trust his control. "But if I live and escape this—" he pointed at his temple, "—I will happily bathe you."

"You're going to live."

"If I do not..." Sarrlevi looked toward the lake. "I would prefer to die here in the home of my ancestors, the home of my youth."

"You're not going to die, dude. That's why we're here. Show me to the alchemist so I can work my charms."

His gaze shifted to my hammer.

"I'm not going to hit anything. Just talk to him."

"Her. The second name on your list, Hyslara Broadleaf, is female and eccentric."

"She's female and you couldn't convince her to help you?" I waved at his chest, wondering if his shirt had been half-off at the time.

"She's an *odd* female."

"If she didn't want you, that's clearly true."

"It's possible I'm not at my most appealing right now."

"I'm afraid not." I stepped forward and buttoned and tucked in his shirt.

"I grew warm earlier," he explained but didn't stop me.

"You can strip naked later and jump in the lake if you want, but let's look our best for her, eh?"

"I will send you in while I wait nearby. Last time, when I attempted to convince her to help, she didn't summon the guards. She only called the *dashar* on me. I deem her our best bet."

"And that is what?"

"The lake guardian." Sarrlevi waved toward the presence I'd felt. "It looks over Menlolee—this village."

"I *knew* there was a Loch Ness monster."

"It is not a monster but a long-lived, magical herbivore that grows large in lakes rich with forests of aquatic plants rooted in the bottom. My people have long had a symbiotic relationship with them and feed them the blue cones of one of the trees that grows in the forest—a rare treat for the *dashar* since they cannot go out on land to retrieve them and must otherwise hope for them to fall from branches into the water. In exchange for the treats, they help protect our lakeside villages from strangers with their magic—and their teeth."

"Herbivore teeth?"

"They are large and capable of snapping a log—or an elf—in

half." Sarrlevi showed me an image of a finned creature with a long neck and tail. The neck and tail *did* remind me of artists' concepts of Loch Ness, but the rest of the body was more whale-like.

Still holding my hand, Sarrlevi led me toward a path that followed the lake toward the tree houses. His magic wrapped around me, camouflaging us.

It didn't take long to pass the first elves, two females out on a fishing boat, drawing up nets. Others were foraging in the woods—or maybe those berry bushes were cultivated—and someone was singing as they wove on the balcony of one of the elevated homes. I wondered how quickly everyone's serenity would shatter if Sarrlevi revealed himself.

We crossed a bridge made from roots and vines that grew out of the banks on either side of a small river. Two elves worked upstream at a mill, dumping something like acorns into a trough to be ground into flour.

It is a community of artists and scientists, Sarrlevi told me, switching to telepathy as the path led us into the village. *There isn't a guard compound, and those with an interest in more martial endeavors head to one of the larger cities for training.*

Meaning it'll take a while for the police to get here if they're summoned?

Not that long. You had better speak quickly and convincingly. Since I came before, she'll know right away that I'm either back and nearby or that I sent you. I should have brought you here the first time, but I didn't want to risk— Sarrlevi glanced at me, *—what almost happened in your house. Or worse.*

What almost happened is sex. It wouldn't have been a big deal. I squeezed his hand, not wanting him to feel guilty or conflicted about what was happening to him. As long as he didn't kill me, I would survive.

Sarrlevi shook his head. *I was not present with you, not caring about you. All I could feel was lust. If you had told me to stop—* He looked away, his eyes bleak. *I do not know if I would have heard you then. Or understood.*

I did ask you to stop, and you did. Albeit imagery of his sick mother had been what got through to him. *And I only asked you to stop because we're pressed for time, and I'd rather be with sane you than crazy you.*

Yes. Precisely.

But I'd be okay with crazy you too, all right? I didn't mention how tempted I'd been to give in and have sex with him, against the wall or a tree or whatever he wanted. My body had craved his touch since we'd met, even before I'd known I *liked* him, and it made me feel hot and desirable that he wanted me, both in his sane and crazy moments.

I'm not certain that's true, and I *would not be* okay *with it.*

Whatever you need, Varlesh, I want to give it to you. I care about you. I almost said I loved him, but something clattered in a nearby tree house, and two elven voices rose in a discussion. That reminded me that we weren't alone. And we were on a mission.

No female—no person—should be rewarded for caring by being pawed over—by being hurt*—by a savage monster.*

Sarrlevi stopped, released my hand, touched my cheek, then stepped back. We'd reached the base of a tree growing scant feet from the lake, its trunk more than twenty feet wide with a ramp that circled it, climbing to a platform fifty feet overhead. It was the first ramp I'd seen. I'd assumed the elves levitated themselves up with their magic or rode their giant birds to reach their tree houses, but maybe for a scientist having large cargos delivered, a ramp was easier.

A rivulet of water ran down the trunk, forming a puddle at the bottom. Runoff from the earlier rain? Elsewhere, leaves and branches kept rainwater from stagnating around the base of the trees. Maybe the alchemist had a leak in her house. Other than the quirky amenities in Sarrlevi's guest room, I hadn't seen many examples of elven kitchen and bathroom fixtures yet.

He extended a single finger toward the air above the ramp, and a zap of energy buzzed at my senses. The whole tree was protected, I realized. It wasn't quite a barrier like Sorka could make, and his finger had gone through it, but it seemed to exist to deter people from entering.

She does not care for visitors, Sarrlevi said.

I reached out to touch the barrier. Its zap wasn't pleasant, but it did appear that we could walk through it. Fish were carved into posts that supported the ramp to either side, and I rested a hand on one, admiring the craftsmanship.

It throbbed under my palm, and a female voice spoke into my mind. *Appointments are required to intrude upon the research laboratory and home of Lady Broadleaf.*

It reminded me of the AI voice on my phone, and I half expected it to ask if I wanted it to search for answers for me. It did not. If anything, the angry buzz that followed sounded dismissive.

I would like to make an appointment, I replied telepathically, assuming the fish didn't know English. *I'm Matti Puletasi, an emissary from Earth.*

The first availability is on Leaf Day the Third, Year 872.

I turned a questioning look toward Sarrlevi, who stood protectively close to me, as if he worried the ramp would attack me.

Approximately three years from now, he informed me. *On a Tuesday.*

Addressing the fish again, I said, *I'd like to see Lady Broadleaf now about an experiment she did and that was written up in—* I tried to remember the name of the text but didn't think Zoltan had translated it for me, *—a book,* I finished.

Lady Broadleaf's research has been in many *books,* the voice replied tartly. *Are you a student?*

I am currently a student, yes. A student of enchanting, not alchemy, but the fish hadn't asked that. *It would be a great honor to speak with such an esteemed elf working in the alchemy field.*

Sarrlevi arched an eyebrow, maybe not thinking my attempt to suck up was any more *charming* than when I clubbed things with my hammer. He was probably right. This wasn't my forte.

A decent student would know the name of the book and article that she was citing.

I squinted at the fish. If the craftsmanship hadn't been so fine, I might have been tempted to smash it and send it flying into the lake where the *dashar* could decide if it was as tasty as blue pine cones. But I had a feeling I was communicating with Lady Broadleaf herself, so I resisted the urge to even give it the middle finger.

The article was on research done on dwarves who went crazy because of a substance they encountered deep in their mines. I need to know if Lady Broadleaf and her colleagues ever found a cure of it.

They did not. The dwarves all died.

I hadn't mentioned that to Sarrlevi when I'd explained Zoltan's findings, but he didn't look surprised. His already grim expression didn't change.

The tunnels where they were attacked and afflicted, Broadleaf continued, *were collapsed and erased from dwarven maps to ensure their people would not chance upon the creatures again. The elven scientists who studied it were asked to leave. I do not know if the dwarven alchemist continued to work on it.*

Princess Barothla did.

How do you know this? Indignation entered the previously calm voice. *Has she published more work independently? Did she give me credit? I was crucial in identifying the pathway through which the chemical compound absorbed nutrients from the body to self-proliferate.*

She not only continued working on it, but she refined it and is using it on people. On elves.

A long pause followed before Broadleaf said, *So that is what happened to that crazy degenerate. I* thought *he was unhinged even for an assassin.*

Sarrlevi's expression grew even bleaker, and I wondered what had happened between them. Had he threatened Broadleaf? Lost his temper? And had I screwed up and inadvertently let her know I was working with him?

It's not the only time the princess has experimented on your people. Hoping to take Broadleaf's mind off Sarrlevi, I summarized Barothla's role in causing his mother to develop *Shiserathi* Disease. I was vague and didn't mention her name specifically, again not wanting to bring Sarrlevi to mind, but I worried my story didn't sound that truthful without that detail.

She is an attention heterotroph and an exothermic reaction waiting to happen, came the response.

It *sounded* like Broadleaf didn't like my aunt, but that was too many vocabulary words for me, and I looked at Sarrlevi for confirmation. Or maybe a translation.

He managed a faint smile, though that tension in his face made it more of a grimace. *I believe you would say unstable heinous bitch.*

Good. That's what I thought that translated to. Focusing on the fish again, I said, *I managed to get the recipe for a formula from her that could cure, uhm, any elves afflicted by that disease, but I need a great alchemist, one equal in power to Barothla, to create it. An infusion of magic is required in addition to the ingredients. Which we— which* I *have with me.* Damn it, I kept screwing this up. An emissary or diplomat, I was not.

Who did you say you are?

Matti Puletasi. I'm half-human, but my mother is a dwarf, Princess Rodarska.

Isn't she dead?

No, she's not. She was forced to leave her home. Do you want the formula?

How did you acquire it? Theft? I cannot author a paper on something that was stolen from another alchemist's lab.

My brow furrowed. I wanted Broadleaf to *cure* people, not publish papers. Was she implying she would only help if she could get credit?

"Your aunt isn't the only attention heterotroph around," Sarrlevi murmured.

"Are you sure that word doesn't mean whore instead of bitch?"

He snorted. "It refers to organisms that can't produce their own food from the sun and have to consume other organisms. It's a bit of an insult among elves, even though *we* qualify. Plants are considered superior lifeforms."

"No wonder you bathe in them."

"Just the dew-kissed moss."

I cannot help you, Lady Broadleaf responded. *The dwarf princess is vengeful and poisoned the lake near the home of Lord Wildworm after they had an academic disagreement. She said it was an accident, but we all know the truth. Chemicals do not* accidentally *fall into lakes in quantities large enough to slay all the fish and even the* dashar *living within. Not on this world. The elves had to leave. Decades have passed, and the lake has not recovered.*

Don't you want to cure your people? I'll make sure *you get credit. And I'll talk to King Ironhelm and tell him not to let his daughter bother you.* I bit my lip, afraid I didn't have the power to make good on what I was promising.

A hiss came from the rivulet of water—of what I'd *thought* was water—running down the tree. Another hiss sounded when whatever it was landed in the puddle, and smoke wafted up before fading.

And, uh, I'll fix your leak. I'm a plumber.

Sarrlevi's eyebrows went up again. I expected him to point out that it was hypocritical of me to be affronted when he called me that and then claim it as my profession to a stranger.

A master plumber, I added with a defiant chin tilt that was more for him than the unseen Lady Broadleaf.

He smirked.

A mongrel master plumber? Lady Broadleaf asked.

Yes. Mongrels have to be resourceful since we have so little magical power. I use Earth inventions called wrenches.

"Your method of charming people is unique," Sarrlevi murmured.

"Because *I'm* unique."

"You are," he agreed.

This leak has *been vexing me. I worry that it's damaging the roots. Come up, and repair it, and I will look at your formula.*

The buzz of energy around the tree faded, and the fish pulsed in invitation.

Wait here, I told Sarrlevi and stepped onto the ramp.

But he stepped onto it right behind me, sticking close. His camouflage was wrapped around him, and I barely sensed him, but I worried Broadleaf would change her mind if she realized he was with me.

She's quirky and an academic, but she's powerful and has a temper, Sarrlevi told me, nodding that he would go up with me. *When she called the* dashar *to attack me, she tried to hold me in place with her power to make it easy for it to bite me in half. She almost succeeded.*

People don't sic lake monsters on their plumbers, Varlesh.

You will find elven plumbing *to be different from what you're familiar with. If you can't fix her problem, she may not be pleased.*

At least wait outside her laboratory.

I will. To guard against the dashar *and watch for troops.*

We were halfway up the ramp when Lady Broadleaf spoke into my mind. *I practice strict hygiene practices in my laboratory, and you have many germs on you from another world. You will allow me to run a sanitizer over you before stepping onto my platform?*

Uh. Okay.

I imagined having to step into a decontamination chamber spitting strange gases all over us. But she shared an image of two floating cylinders that reminded me of Sarrlevi's soap dispensers. In her vision, they spritzed the air all over the ramp. The process looked innocuous enough.

That's fine, I said, continuing up. To Sarrlevi, I added, *At least she* warns *people before having her devices spray them down.*

My soap dispensers were programmed to assume that a person standing naked in front of the bathing basin wishes to be spritzed.

I'm lucky I didn't get pelted by dew-kissed clumps of moss.

I'll ensure those are available at my chalet when you join me there.

I can't wait.

As we neared the top, four of the floating sanitizers wafted toward me. Since Sarrlevi remained camouflaged, I assumed they would only target me.

To prove I was an amenable and polite guest who would comply, I stopped and held my arms out. The imagery hadn't shown me naked, so I hoped that wasn't required.

Sanitizer won't bother you, will it, Sorka? I asked the hammer, belatedly wondering if I should have tossed it ahead. It was hard to imagine anything disturbing the nearly indestructible magical alloy, but I'd never been sanitized by an elf scientist before. The air smelled like vinegar.

No. Assuming that's all this is.

A little chill went through me at the words. *What* else *would it be?*

I don't know, but two of those canisters are dispensing something different from the others.

Behind me, Sarrlevi sucked in a startled breath and drew his swords. Two of the canisters had flown back to spritz him, even though they—Broadleaf—shouldn't have known he was there.

"Look out," he barked to me as he swept a sword through one canister, slicing it in half.

The broken pieces sent viscous liquid spattering everywhere, and I ran up the ramp to avoid the droplets. The other dispensers, spraying a much finer mist, trailed after me. I held my breath and batted at the air, then lunged at one canister with my hammer. It connected, sending the dispenser ricocheting off the tree. Sarrlevi took out the other one that had targeted him and wiped his face.

The fourth zipped back up to the platform and disappeared.

Sarrlevi looked at the spatters on his hand and swore. Then *roared.* Startling me, he lashed out with his swords, striking at the ramp railings. I backed farther from him.

"This isn't charming," I warned. Though I was worried about him—what did that stuff do?—he was breaking Broadleaf's railings. "She's not going to be happy with you."

His face twisted with fury that he couldn't restrain, and he whirled toward me with his swords raised. Seething. He didn't take a step toward me, but this was so unlike the looks he usually gave me—even the looks he usually gave his enemies—that fear crept into me.

His aura, his *power,* also seethed. I sensed him preparing a magical attack but not for me. He looked up at a bespectacled female elf peering over the railing. I hadn't realized Broadleaf had come out of her laboratory.

Sarrlevi thrust his swords in the air, and an orange beam shot from the tip of one.

"No!" I sprang toward him and grabbed his arm.

Lady Broadleaf conjured a powerful shield around herself, and the beam didn't get through.

"Stop, Varlesh," I whispered harshly. "We need her help."

Sarrlevi roared his response in Elven, as if he'd forgotten English. Even his Elven words sounded slurred.

He staggered, surprising me, and almost pitched backward off the ramp. I tightened my grip on his arm to keep him steady. The railings he'd broken would do nothing to keep either of us from falling.

His tense arms slackened, his swords drooping. The orange beam cut off.

"Varlesh?" I whispered.

His face also grew slack, the fury leaving his eyes. *Awareness* leaving his eyes. They grew glazed.

"What did you do to him?" I called up before remembering to speak telepathically.

Broadleaf merely gazed down from the platform, her nose crinkling distastefully as Sarrlevi staggered again. His eyes rolled back in his head, and he collapsed.

12

WHAT DID YOU DO TO HIM? I REPEATED TO THE BESPECTACLED alchemist as I knelt on the ramp beside Sarrlevi. With a shaking hand, I reached for his throat to check his pulse.

I didn't *think* an elf would murder another elf, even an exiled assassin, but what did I truly know about their people? Maybe exiles were fair game. If Sarrlevi had scared Broadleaf earlier, maybe she felt justified.

He will not loom threateningly behind you for now.

He was protective, *not threatening.* I couldn't deny the looming part. He'd been doing that all night, standing closer than he usually did, but I knew why.

His face kept twitching, and he reached for the back of your neck twice as you climbed. You cannot be unaware of the threat that he represents.

I'm sure he was reaching for my head, not my neck. He likes to... I caught myself before saying *rub my head*, not wanting to explain our relationship to a stranger, especially one who wouldn't approve. *My hair is soft. Elves can't help themselves.*

That earned another distasteful nose crinkle from Broadleaf. I trusted *she* wouldn't be drawn to rub my head.

At least she'd said *for now*. That meant Sarrlevi was only knocked out temporarily, right?

His heart beat steadily under my fingers. That was a relief, but what was I supposed to do? Leave him on the ramp and go up and speak with Broadleaf? What if the elven guards came by?

My gaze jerked back to her as that possibility sank in. She'd rendered a criminal unconscious. Why *wouldn't* she call the guards? Or that lake monster?

Broadleaf waved for me to climb up. *Come and fix my* shraydilar, *and show me the formula.*

"I hope that means toilet or something else I'm vaguely knowledgeable about," I muttered as she disappeared from my view and headed back into her laboratory, trusting I would follow.

Unwilling to leave Sarrlevi in the open and vulnerable, I positioned myself to grab him by one wrist, then crouched and pulled him over my shoulder in a fireman's carry. He didn't stir.

"You're heavier than you look, Varlesh," I grumbled and climbed the rest of the ramp with six-plus-feet of solid elven muscle draped over my shoulder.

Something large stirred under the surface of the lake, my increasing elevation giving me a good view of the water. That made me glad I hadn't left Sarrlevi behind. The guard creature might be an herbivore, but it sounded like it chomped on people regularly.

When I reached the platform, Broadleaf stood in the doorway, watching me. Since she'd repelled Sarrlevi's magical attack, I knew she had the power to levitate him, but she didn't assist me in any way. She probably wanted to levitate him into the middle of the lake for the creature.

If I had any doubts about your claims to a dwarven heritage, this would have assuaged them, Broadleaf said as I rolled the limp Sarrlevi off my shoulder to lean against the wall near her door.

She'd held up a hand when I'd walked toward her, not wanting me to bring him inside. At least here, he was close enough for me to keep an eye on. And my *senses* on. When he'd fallen unconscious, his camouflage had slipped. That worried me. Every elf in the village had to be able to sense him now. I could only hope that few recognized him or paid much attention to their alchemist's guests.

He's not that heavy, I said, even though I'd noticed his solid heft. *No more than two bags of cement mix.*

It was wrong of him to come here.

He needs your help. He's not himself right now, and that's not normal. That magical chemical thing is making him aggressive.

I assumed that when you were explaining it. Why are you helping him? Our people consider him a criminal and exiled him long ago. It would be best to let him die to ensure he kills no more.

He's been an ally to me, and your people were wrong to exile him. I couldn't argue that Sarrlevi had only ever killed those who deserved it, so, as usual, I didn't address that objection.

This time, Broadleaf wrinkled her nose *and* pursed her lips. As I looked around the interior of a one-room laboratory carved out of the core of the trunk, winding stairs leading to upper and lower levels, I wondered how the trees survived having huge holes in them. The wooden walls emanated magic, so I supposed that was the answer.

A soft scraping sensation inside my skull made me scowl at Broadleaf. Another magical being who thought nothing of reading other people's minds.

If you're trying to get the formula, I have it and all the instructions on my phone. I showed her the device, though I would have to read everything and hope she understood Dwarven, since I'd been spelling the ingredients phonetically. *If you're trying to tell why I'm helping Sarrlevi and his mother, it's a long story and involves me wanting to protect my* own *mother.*

And you find him sexually appealing when he's shirtless.

I scowled at her but refused to be embarrassed. *I find him sexually appealing* all *the time, okay? Here's the formula. Don't you want to cure your people?*

Broadleaf pursed her lips again, but she came over and used her magic to float my phone out of my grip.

"Uh." I assumed she wouldn't know what to do with it or how to read what I'd written with English letters in the Notes app, and my fingers twitched to grab it back, but I decided to let her look.

She took it to a wooden counter built into the tree—built *from* the tree—and opened what I might have called a breadbox. It contained a couple of quirky gadgets that looked like things Tinja would make from recycled junkyard parts and… I blinked. Was that another phone? And a laptop? From Earth? They appeared to be plugged into the wood of the tree wall via vines. They couldn't possibly be charging the devices, could they?

Broadleaf patted her Earth items, as well as a globe that emanated strong dwarven magic, and pulled out a spare vine and pressed it against the port for my phone.

That's not necessary. The charge is fine.

The screen not only lit up but projected my Notes app into the air.

"Uh," I said again. "I didn't know there was a hologram setting."

The English words scrambled before my eyes, rearranging and turning into clumps of unfamiliar symbols. They weren't Dwarven runes but might have been Elven. I wasn't that familiar with their language.

The shraydilar *is downstairs. I will study this formula while you repair my leak. The acid is eating through the tree like a liquid fungal rot and causing damage. It is unacceptable.*

The ingredients are in his pack. Do you want them?

He has acquired them all? Some are quite difficult—and dangerous—to get.

Yeah. Didn't you talk to him? He should have told you that when he came.

He broke through my tree's security barrier, stood glaring at me with clenched fists, and ordered me to cure an elven disease known to have no cure. When I recognized him, I feared for my life and called the dashar *to chase him away.*

Like I said, he's not himself. He's usually articulate and logical and haughty. Like the rest of you elves. I'll get the ingredients.

Since I'd never presumed to lift the lid of Sarrlevi's magical backpack, I hoped I *could* get the ingredients. Also that he'd long since disposed of the heads of those werewolves that he'd once stuck in there.

I knelt beside Sarrlevi, touched his cheek, then awkwardly maneuvered the straps off his shoulders. The swords had to come off for me to remove the pack, and I worried he would leap up, enraged because someone was touching his weapons, and throttle me. But whatever Broadleaf had sprayed him with had been effective.

Once I had the backpack, I opened it and patted around inside. My heart dropped into the pit of my stomach. It was empty.

"What the hell?"

Broadleaf leaned through the doorway. *You must envision what you want a magical bag of enhanced storage to give you before it can remove the item from the dimension in which it exists.*

My shoulders slumped. I hadn't seen Sarrlevi collect the ingredients and had no idea what the mumbo jumbo I'd written down looked like or even was. I'd been copying the Dwarven terms. Would we have to wait for Sarrlevi to wake up?

With my hand inside, I tried envisioning a bag of vague lumpy ingredients and hoped the backpack would understand. If he'd stuffed the items in there individually, there might be no hope. Unless Broadleaf knew what all the things looked like and could do it. I was about to ask when something hard poofed into the bag, brushing my knuckles. I pulled out a mesh sack of tubers and held them up to Broadleaf.

That looks like a random collection of wild root vegetables that he foraged for a stew, she said.

Root vegetables. Had he foraged them for *me*? Maybe he'd come across the equivalent of a potato patch while he'd been out scavenging.

I need the other *bag of ingredients,* I told the backpack. I was about to thrust it at Broadleaf to try when another bulge formed inside. I pulled out a net that held such strange gems as the taloned purple foot of something similar to a chicken, two glass vials of blue powders, a fungal nodule, a green bristly flower head, dried herbs, and a miniature pink banana that smelled like rotten eggs.

That is they. Broadleaf held out her hand.

I gave the ingredients to her and returned the root vegetables to the backpack. They disappeared from view, leaving the interior empty once again.

"Anything else interesting in there?" I still had the cheese Sarrlevi had given me, and was sure he hadn't had time to get more, but I did wonder what else lurked inside his pack.

Reminded that he kept the decapitated heads of enemies in there, at least some of the time, I decided I didn't want it to conjure anything else for me, but as I drew my hand out, my fingers brushed against paper. An envelope?

I pulled it out, and my breath caught. My full name was written on the front of the envelope in the same handwriting that had been on a gift he'd once had delivered to me. *His* handwriting.

For some reason, my fingers trembled as I held it. Should I... open it?

If he'd meant me to have it, he would have already given it to me. When had he written it? Yesterday? Three weeks ago?

I glanced at the door, afraid I would catch Broadleaf watching me and shaking her head, but she'd taken the ingredients inside.

"Can I read this, Varlesh?" I whispered. "Since you can read my mind, you'll know right away if I did. But you wouldn't blame me, would you? I'm a curious sort. You know this, right? And it's not *my* fault your backpack so easily gave up its secrets. What if I'd been a robber? Would it have spat your fine china out at me at a simple request for valuables?"

Sarrlevi didn't stir. I hadn't expected him to, but I found myself missing what doubtless would have been a snarky response.

"There could be something mission critical in here," I finally decided, breaking the wax seal. "Like the secret to defeating obnoxiously vile dwarf aunts and siphoning cures for horrible diseases—and brain-altering chemicals—out of their heads."

I drew a single piece of stationery out and read.

Mataalii, if you are reading this, it is likely that I am dead, or I've gone insane and flung my backpack at you before running off into the wilds to live like an animal.

I halted, staring at the sentence. Hell, was this his will?

I shouldn't read it. But I couldn't stop.

I've just woken after a day of scrounging for ingredients on three different worlds, and I'm feeling more lucid than yesterday, than the last two days. It's likely the calm before the storm, as I am aware of the caged animal within me, struggling to get out, and I know my body hasn't fought off Barothla's spell. Nonetheless, in this moment, I want to get these words down, words I couldn't say when I was with you, and the animal within rose up, thinking only of sex, thinking of you only as a female to be claimed, pleasure to be obtained. I'm terrified that will be your last impression of me. I need you to know that you mean much more to me than that.

Tears welled in my eyes, and I had to pause to wipe them and take a breath before continuing on.

I've already told you that it means much to me that you've been loyal and defended me to others, even when you shouldn't have, and how rare that's been in my life. I do not think I've admitted that you are also worth defending and being loyal to. I hope my actions have said that even when my tongue hasn't managed it. I perhaps enjoy teasing you too much, because you glower at me in the most adorable and appealing manner, but I know that you are hardworking, as befitting a dwarf, and have clearly spent the time necessary to bring out your talents, for they are many. I am certain that your mother, once you meet her again, will be proud of the woman you have become. It has been a pleasure to know you and come to love you. That is not an emotion I thought I would ever feel again. In truth, I'm not certain I have ever felt it before, not in the romantic sense. Since I was very young, I've been presented with enemies, not allies, and when everyone comes at you either with weapons openly displayed or secreted on their person, you learn to harden your heart and build barriers around yourself. You learn not to let yourself care. Thank you for encouraging me to feel.

You owe me nothing, but in the event that I fail to get the formula made that can help my mother, I hope you will be able to succeed and take it to her. I know you would do that whether I made this request or not, because that is the kind of person you are, but I will write the words, regardless, in the desire... Well, perhaps you will share some of this with her so she knows that her son cared. I hope that you are able to find your parents and that they also know that you cared.

With love, Varlesh.

"I love you too, Varlesh," I whispered and hugged him and kissed him on the neck.

I was tempted to stay there, snuggled close to him with my face buried, but Broadleaf stirred in her laboratory. *My plumbing is not repairing itself.*

"On it," I muttered, kissing Sarrlevi again before releasing him.

Carefully, I folded the letter, returned it to the envelope, and tucked it into my pocket.

I hoped this alchemist was the answer to our problems. I would do what Sarrlevi had requested in his letter, but there was no way I was going to let him die *or* turn into a wild animal.

13

The problem with the *shraydilar*, which presumably meant *automatic mixing machine and vat for storing chemicals*, was that it had been made by a goblin or maybe a gnome. I hadn't met many gnomes but knew that many of them were also inventors and tinkerers. That alone wouldn't have been problematic, but Broadleaf, or maybe some local elven plumber, had used hollow vines and twine and whatever that silver *glitter* was to connect the machine to the wall and pipe the contents to what I'd learned were four more levels of the laboratory. If she had a bed and actual living chambers within the tree, I had no idea. It seemed entirely possible that she slept on the counters among her experiments.

The vines were leaking a magical acid and defied patching—the elven equivalent of duct tape was stuck all over them. The liquid ate through it. Why Broadleaf needed such a caustic substance I didn't know, and I definitely didn't know how to repair *vines*.

"Talk about things that weren't covered on my plumbing certification test." An altered version of one of the exam questions popped into my mind: *Vines are an acceptable means of joining materials of different types, true or false?* "Definitely false."

Deciding the vines needed to be replaced with something resistant to acid—glass came to mind—I hunted around for components I could use. The bottommost level of the lab housed all manner of empty vials, beakers, and parts I couldn't identify. Tinja would have been in heaven scrounging for materials there.

I gathered armfuls of beakers with the thought of turning them into glass tubing. Thus far, I'd mostly enchanted metal, but I *had* enhanced Val's wooden porch steps, so I knew I could work my magic on other materials. There was enough glass for me to experiment, but the crafting turned out to be more difficult than the enchanting.

Metal, I soon decided, was much easier. Metal never exploded when I heated it.

"Glass melts," I grumbled, tugging shards out of my cheek. "I know it does." Maybe I had to heat it more slowly and uniformly.

Are you plumbing or destroying my laboratory? Broadleaf asked.

I'm being creative. Neither dwarves nor humans plumb with vines *so I'm not that experienced with them.*

A vine *is not what I heard explode, I am certain.*

Just give me a few more minutes.

As I worked, slowly figuring out how I could use magic to melt and reshape the glass into the pipes I needed, I swept upward with my senses to check on Sarrlevi. It worried me that he'd been out for so long. Maybe that was exactly as Broadleaf had intended, but I knew sedative medicines could be dangerous if the amounts given weren't right, and I was positive those spritzers hadn't delivered precisely measured dosages.

Sarrlevi was in the same spot on the platform, but I noticed the auras of two elves at the base of the ramp. Friends or colleagues arriving to visit Broadleaf? Would they recognize Sarrlevi and report him?

The elves made no move to come up the ramp. Maybe it was a popular spot for the local kids to come and smoke, but I doubted it.

Two more elves arrived, joining the others. They didn't have auras as significant as Broadleaf's or Sarrlevi's, but they weren't *in*significant. From deep within the windowless tree trunk, I couldn't tell if they were armed, but I knew with certainty that I didn't have a lot of time. I hurried to finish replacing the vines with glass pipes, then headed for the stairs.

The elves on the ground hadn't yet started up the ramp, but I sensed more of their kind approaching from the sky. Riding some of those giant birds? They were arrowing toward Broadleaf's tree.

On the platform, I sensed Sarrlevi stir. He brushed my mind with a telepathic touch but didn't form any words. Maybe he was reassuring himself that I was still there? Was he hung over and groggy from Broadleaf's concoction? He had to be.

I'm coming, I told him. *I think some fighters might be too. Can you camouflage yourself and hide?*

Was it too late for that?

I dug my camouflaging charm out of my pocket, intending to hide him myself if he hadn't regained full consciousness. I ran up the stairs and started for the door leading out onto the platform.

Broadleaf stepped into my path, her hand out. I would have bowled her over, but she halted me not with her palm but with magic. Since it appeared at the last second, I smacked nose-first into it.

Outside, visible through the open doorway, the great birds flew close. Elves leaped from the saddles, drawing swords as they landed on the platform.

"Sarrlevi! Look out!" I couldn't see around the doorframe to where I'd left him. I sensed him out there and was sure he'd seen the warriors coming, but I *wasn't* sure his head was clear enough for a fight.

Elven shouts of triumph came from the warriors as they charged toward Sarrlevi. Excited to get a chance to kill him? The bloodthirsty bastards.

Snarling, I tried to go around Broadleaf and her barrier. I was able to get past her, but her magic extended farther, blocking the doorway. I smacked into it again.

"Damn it." As a sword clanged on the platform, I hefted my hammer and swung at the barrier, willing Sorka to break through.

It had worked when I'd battled Barothla, and I needed it to work now. Badly.

The hammer glowed silver-blue and smacked into the magical obstacle. A shimmer of light rippled through it, but it didn't break.

Steps away, Broadleaf's power swelled and flowed into the barrier, reinforcing it as I swung again. Against a lesser opponent, Sorka would have won—I was sure of it—but Broadleaf's aura promised she was no pushover.

Let me help him! I cried at her, swinging again and again.

Each time, the barrier deflected my hammer. I told myself to back off and try something else, but my surging fear and frustration made it difficult to think of anything but bashing down what stood between me and the vulnerable Sarrlevi.

More clangs sounded, a battle engaged. At least that meant he'd gotten to his feet and was defending himself, but six elven warriors had reached the platform, and those down below were charging up the ramp now. Even Sarrlevi couldn't win against so many.

If you attack and harm elves, Broadleaf replied, watching me calmly as I beat at her barrier, *I will not make the formula.*

You have to. It's to help your *people.* With my entire body shaking, I backed from the barrier and glowered at her.

Protected behind her magic, she wasn't a target I could hit. But the barrier didn't extend over the entire laboratory. My gaze whipped about as I sought another way out—why didn't elven houses have *windows*?

I could use some assistance, Sarrlevi spoke into my mind. *I'm struggling to clear my body of this drug, and—* His words broke off with a rapid flurry of clangs.

The elves had him backed against the wall and were trying to push him toward the railing.

Out in the lake, the powerful aura of the *dashar* moved closer. What, were the elves going to keep their hands free of blood by ordering *it* to kill him?

"Cowards!" I yelled.

My gaze caught on Broadleaf's devices and my phone, the Elven runes still floating over it. If I took it, she wouldn't be able to complete the formula, but it didn't sound like she would do that anyway. We would have to escape and find another alchemist.

I ran over and snatched my phone from the vine, then raised the hammer over the laptop and the dwarven globe.

Let me out, or I'll destroy your stuff.

Her eyes widened, and her barrier shifted toward me.

"*Hygorotho*, Sorka," I barked, hoping her barrier could encompass the devices as well as me and keep Broadleaf from reaching them.

A startled shout came from the platform. Wood snapped. The railing?

I couldn't see the *dashar,* but I sensed it right beside the tree, its long neck and head rising up from the lake.

Let me out! I repeated, waving my hammer above my head, poised to smash it down.

Sparks flew, and the air buzzed angrily as Broadleaf's barrier clashed with Sorka's, trying to knock it back. My hammer might not have been able to smash through the elf's barrier, but hers wasn't strong enough to push mine aside.

Broadleaf lifted her chin defiantly. *You will not battle against my people.*

More elves on birds approached, and I heard the twang of bowstrings. An arrow ricocheted off something—a barrier?—and sped past the doorway. They were unloading everything they had on Sarrlevi.

Mataalii? he whispered urgently into my mind.

Certain that smashing the laptop wouldn't do anything except irk Broadleaf, I brought the hammer down on the sphere, willing Sorka to crush it.

It was more like hitting a rock than glass, and it didn't shatter the way I'd envisioned, but a deep crack split it in half. Tremendous energy blasted from it, knocking me into Broadleaf's barrier. I bounced off and flew across the laboratory.

Her barrier fell under the wave of power, and she cried out, stumbling back. I slammed into a counter, beakers flying and breaking as they crashed down around me. Though it hurt, I forced myself to my feet and sprinted out the now-unblocked doorway.

As I burst onto the platform, a loud splash came from the water below. The huge head of the creature that Sarrlevi had earlier shared telepathically with me dropped out of view below the elves and the railing—the *broken* railing. A large gap had been knocked in it.

Elves crouched all over the platform with their weapons raised, but I didn't see Sarrlevi. Or sense him. No, I *did* sense him. Down below.

"No!" I shouted, realizing they'd knocked him over the edge—or the creature had attacked him from behind. I sprinted to the railing.

My fear of heights and falling warned me to stay back since part of the platform had broken away—or been bitten and *torn* away. But I ran to the very edge anyway and peered down.

The whale-like topside of the creature was visible, but much of its neck and head were underwater. Its body jerked and dipped lower, as if it were lunging at something down there—or snapping at Sarrlevi?

"No you don't." I hefted my hammer.

When I'd run to the railing, the elves hadn't stopped me, but they surged forward now, shouting in their language.

Ignoring them, I bellowed, "*Hyrek!*" and threw the hammer.

It sped away an instant before several sets of hands gripped me.

A wet *thud* sounded as my weapon hit the creature, but the elves hauled me back, and I didn't see what happened after that. A pitiful keening screech came from the water. I would have felt bad about attacking an animal, but it was trying to *kill* Sarrlevi.

I bucked and twisted, shouting, "*Vishgronik!*" and trying to free myself so I could catch the hammer and throw it again.

Magic flowed from the elven hands holding me, giving their grips the power of steel. A band of magic wrapped around my body and held me in place.

Still glowing silver-blue, the hammer floated into view and toward me. I managed to kick one of my attackers, making him grunt and bend over, and twisted my arm out of someone else's grip. I lifted my hand, willing the hammer to reach me. Then I could make a barrier and knock these guys back.

But a stern-faced elf stepped in front of me and intercepted the hammer, catching it.

Sorka! Don't let him keep you!

The elf was the one to answer, not the hammer. *Cease your struggles, mongrel.*

I spat at him. *Let me help Sarrlevi.*

There's nobody left to help. That was Broadleaf. She stood at the broken railing and was looking down.

The elves fell silent, and I heard the water rippling as the *dashar* moved away from the area. With a sick lurch of dread, I realized I didn't sense Sarrlevi anymore. Was his dead body floating on the water?

The elf with my hammer joined Broadleaf at the railing. They conferred in Elven. A debate?

Maybe it was foolish, but that gave me hope. If Sarrlevi's body had been floating in view, there wouldn't have been anything to discuss. He might have hurt the *dashar* enough to convince it to leave. Or maybe he'd evaded it and camouflaged himself.

He is dead. The elf with my hammer turned back to me. *You sought to assist an exile and known assassin. Were you one of our citizens, you would be taken before the local magistrate for a justice hearing.*

"Wouldn't that be fun." I tried to pull away from the rest of the elves, but they wouldn't release me. The one I'd kicked glowered and gripped me extra hard. *Are you going to give me back my hammer?*

Orange light flashed inside the laboratory, and something hissed and clicked. The sphere I'd smashed. Broken beakers and equipment were visible on the floor. Broadleaf scowled at the mess, then at me and stretched out a hand.

Magic flowed from her fingers, and I thought she would choke me to death. Instead, a portal formed in front of me.

You will leave our world, go home, and not come back. Broadleaf scraped at my mind, digging into my thoughts. For what? Reassurance that I wouldn't return? *You are not welcome here.*

I can't go, not yet. I have to— I stopped myself before saying *search for Sarrlevi,* since they would never let me stick around to do that, *—finish what I promised him I'd do, find someone to make a formula to cure his mother. To cure* all *elves afflicted with that disease.*

If that was truly your goal, you shouldn't have brought a murderer here with you. Nobody will help you now.

It's not about helping me. *This is for the good of your people, damn it.* I struggled again and ordered, *Let me go,* trying to put some magic into the command, willing them to release me. If I could get away long enough to camouflage myself, I might be able to escape, to run down there and search the lake.

Even if Sarrlevi had managed to get away and hide himself, I was certain he was injured. He needed my help. He'd *asked* for it when he'd never asked for it before. And I'd failed to give it to him.

Using magic and brawn, the elves shoved me toward the portal. I fought, but they merely hefted me from my feet and carried me in the air, head-first toward it.

Surprisingly, the stern-faced elf with my hammer thrust the weapon into my grip. I hadn't expected him to return it, but they were about to kick me off their world, so I didn't feel that grateful.

Wait, I blurted, looking at Broadleaf. Her face didn't invite me to say anything else. I'd brought Sarrlevi, and I'd messed up her lab. She hated me. *At least if you complete the formula,* I tried anyway, *tell Princess Freysha. She'll make sure... She knows who needs it.*

Broadleaf's face remained rigid and cold, and she didn't respond as the elves thrust me through the portal.

14

PORTAL TRAVEL WAS DISORIENTING ENOUGH THAT I DIDN'T HAVE TIME to collect myself and get my feet under me when I came out. My shoulder struck unyielding cement with a painful jolt, and I flopped onto my back like a dead fish. As I stared up at the sky, not certain where I'd come out, four green faces peered down at me.

For a bewildered moment, I thought the elves had sent me to the goblin home world, but two of the faces were familiar, and I sensed the magical wards of my own property nearby. I was on the sidewalk in front of my house.

"Plumber Puletasi?" Gondo lifted a screwdriver and used the tip to scratch his ear. "Are you here to celebrate Tinja's victory? We brought many ten-pound cakes. There should be enough for a half-dwarf with a hearty appetite."

"Victory?" I mumbled, my heart feeling like *it* weighed ten pounds and was pinning me to the ground. Sarrlevi. If he hadn't been dead when the elves had forced me through the portal, he could be by now.

"Work Leader Tinja has sold a tiny-house plan!" another goblin proclaimed. Was that frosting on his lips? And hanging from his pointed ear? It was oddly thick, more like toothpaste than a confection.

"That's good." I thought about getting up. At the least, I should check my phone and see if any messages had come in while I was gone.

"Matti?" Tinja knelt to touch my shoulder. "Are you all right? Where did you come from?"

"Elf Land. *Haughty* and *uptight* Elf Land."

"Veleshna Var." Gondo nodded firmly. "That is how it translates in our language too. Cake?"

He waved forward a goblin carrying a covered tray so heavy the porter had to use both arms and spread his legs to keep it up. Gondo removed a wrench-shaped frosted doorstop, or so I deemed it when he rested it in my open palm.

"Thanks." Though it was hard with the hammer in one hand and the heavy cake in the other, I managed to sit up. "Congratulations on your home-plan sale, Tinja," I made myself say, though celebrating was far from my mind. "Do you know if Zavryd is around? Here, hold this, please." I gave her the cake, wiped the thick, sludgy frosting on my pants, and pulled out my phone.

One of the goblins pointed at my house, or maybe the vines and leaves covering the damage. Seeing Sarrlevi's work only made my gut twist with fresh pain. He'd intended the magical foliage to act as temporary patches, so I wouldn't have to worry about fixing my home until I found my parents, but if I never saw him again, I would leave those vines up forever. Building codes be damned.

There was a message from Val on my phone, and I pounced on it. Zavryd had returned.

Hands shaking, I called her. Maybe it wasn't too late. Maybe he could take me to that lake, and we could thoroughly search the area. Maybe he could light Broadleaf and the guards on fire at the same time.

"Hey, Matti," Val said. "Sorry, you missed Zav. He and

Xilneth got into another pissing match. Xilneth said Zav wasn't an effective hunter since he hadn't found the missing dwarf princess yet, and Zav said he'd had more important things to do, even though we both know he *has* been trying. He would never admit that to Xilneth. Xilneth said *he* would find the missing princess and prove he's the superior hunter—and *dragon*. Naturally, Zav can't allow Xilneth to outdo him, so he's back on the hunt. About an hour ago, they both took off with your two dwarf friends."

"Damn it." I rubbed my face. As much as I wanted them to find the organization and my parents, I needed to return to search for Sarrlevi. "They're on Earth, right? Can you reach Zavryd and ask him to make a portal for me? It's important."

"They're actually *not* on Earth. They're exploring a hypothesis that the reason the organization has been so effective at staying hidden is that they're on another world. Apparently, when the dwarves and Xilneth were searching that cave the organization used as a base and to hide the artifacts they stole from Willard, they found some magical residue that suggested they'd been making portals there and coming and going."

"Do you know when they'll be back? I need—" My throat tightened, and the words wouldn't come out.

"Ten-pound cake?" Gondo offered me another one, or maybe the same one. I wasn't paying attention. "They're delicious. My rural cousins make them from acorn flour and lard. They're wonderful with coffee. If you dunk the cake, it can soak up half the cup."

"Is it truly lard if the rendered fat comes from random roadkill animals?" Tinja asked. "Does not the human word refer specifically to pork?"

"It refers to things that are *delicious,*" Gondo said.

"Are you okay, Matti?" Val asked.

"No." I sighed. "Let me know if the dragons come back, please.

Or if Freysha visits." I hung up without waiting for an answer. I was about to lose it and needed to be alone.

But the lights were on in the house, and bangs and clanks emanating from within announced the presence of more goblin guests. I hoped those weren't the sounds of my appliances being disassembled.

Ignoring the lard-roadkill discussion, I shambled away from the goblins and into the backyard. Needing privacy, I sat alone in my tool shed with the door closed and the lawn mower jabbing me in the back. Tears trickled down my cheeks, and I let them.

The walls did little to insulate me from the noise of the house, and I was tempted to walk to the park, but, with my luck, assassins were lurking in the area and would take advantage of my distraction to pounce. Sarrlevi wasn't here to watch out for me. He might never be again.

I let the hammer clunk to the cement floor and buried my face in my hands.

The loss of an ally is always regrettable, Sorka offered, reminding me that I wasn't entirely alone.

I didn't want to talk and only mumbled, "Yeah."

At least she hadn't said *good riddance.*

Tinja came out, and I wiped my eyes, but she only walked to the door of the tool shed, then turned around and went back into the house.

Some time later, Val arrived in her Jeep. Had I sounded so wrecked on the phone that she'd come to check on me? Or did she have news about the Hart party and want to help me plan? I *should* shift to thinking about that again, but I didn't think I could tonight.

Zavryd wasn't with her. By the time someone capable of making a portal showed up, I feared it would be far too late to help Sarrlevi. Maybe it already was.

Val knocked on the shed door. "Matti?"

"Yeah?" I croaked.

"Mind if I come in?"

"There's not much room."

"There's not much room in your house either. I'd say your neighbors might call the police, on account of that many goblins in one house exceeding the maximum-occupancy rating for a residence, but I suppose a party is tame compared to what usually happens around here."

"Lately, anyway. My life used to be normal. Ish." I pushed open the door and scooted off the floor to sit on the lawn mower.

The door creaked open, and Val stepped in. She found the chain for the light bulb dangling from the ceiling and turned it on. I blinked and sneered at the odious brightness but didn't tell her to turn it off. She was carrying something. *Two* somethings. One was the dubious ten-pound cake that was following me around like a stray dog. The other was a colorful piece of paper.

"I believe these are for you." Val offered the paper but not the cake. Maybe she knew I didn't want it. Or maybe she planned to keep it for a few sets of biceps curls.

The paper was the flyer I'd requested from Tinja. It featured a beautiful and one might even say tasteful cartoon toilet with a smiling plumber leaning against it holding a wrench. The temporary number I'd signed up for was hand drawn under the toilet, with the name of a local plumbing business along the top, as well as quotes from customer reviews, each including a line of five stars. I smiled, imagining her tiny-house-plan videos overlaid with rows of stars and testimonials. She was learning the ropes of marketing in the human world.

"Yes." I set the flyer on my worktable, careful not to rest it on anything grimy. Even though I didn't intend to mass distribute it, I would make extra copies in case anything went wrong. I snorted. In case *everything* went wrong. That was the story of my life these days. "Thank you."

A breeze pushed at the door, making it creak again, but Val didn't shut it. Maybe it would have been too claustrophobic with the two of us closed up inside. Or maybe she worried the goblin party would flow out of the house and threaten her Jeep, and she wanted to be able to hear what was going on out there.

"Did something happen with you and Sarrlevi?" Val looked around, then perched on the half-buried canister vacuum for cleaning out the truck—Sarrlevi would have been shocked to know I owned such a thing. Of course, it had been a year since it had moved from that corner of the tool shed. "You sounded choked up on the phone."

"Something happened *to* him." I took a breath so I could get through the story without breaking into tears again and told her everything.

"If you didn't see his body, he might still be alive," Val said in the end. "He could have made a portal or camouflaged himself."

I was certain I—and the elves—would have sensed it if he'd made a portal, and I didn't know if one could even do that underwater. The thought made me envision a lake's worth of water flowing through a portal and into my yard. But I'd had the thought about camouflage myself.

"Don't give up on him yet," Val added.

"I won't. That's why I want to go back to look for him. If those elf warriors have any doubt about whether or not he died... they're probably there searching for him, wanting to finish the job. They didn't care that he was one of their kind. They wanted him dead."

Val grimaced. "I'm sure. They're not very forgiving when it comes to elves who don't comply with their ideals. Even Freysha gets a hard time for studying goblin engineering and being a little quirky."

My hand strayed to the pocket where I'd tucked Sarrlevi's letter. Earlier, I'd felt guilty about reading it when he was right there and hadn't given me permission to poke through his pack and take it. Now, I was glad I had.

Though Val glanced at my hand, she didn't ask why I was fondling my pocket. "Do you think the alchemist will create the formula? If you could help Sarrlevi's mother..." Val spread a hand but didn't voice the rest of the thought. That Sarrlevi would have wished it?

I had no doubt that he would, alive or dead.

"No. Broadleaf wasn't that interested to start with, and then I busted up her laboratory to escape when she trapped me inside. I shouldn't have, I guess, not when it ultimately didn't matter. I wasn't in time to—" Damn it, there went my throat tightening up again. "I wasn't in time."

"What about the other alchemist? Zoltan gave you names of a couple of people who worked on that research paper, right? Though I guess that was for the crazy-maker chemical and not the disease-curing formula."

"All the ingredients for the formula are at Broadleaf's place. I guess I do still have the recipe." I waved to my phone. "If I could find someone knowledgeable about the Cosmic Realms to help me, I could go out there and collect another batch of ingredients." Broadleaf's mention that some of the items were hard to get—*dangerous* to get—came to mind, but I didn't care. More than ever, I wanted to cure Sarrlevi's mother. "And then hunt around until I can find someone who can make it. Or, when I find my parents, maybe my mother and I can go back to Dun Kroth, and she can throttle her sister and make *her* make it. Sisters are allowed to do that to each other, right? Throttling."

"I was an only child until very recently, but I've heard that's true." Val smiled. "You've got an older sister. Did she ever throttle you?"

"Penina was always too good to descend to fighting with me.

The only time I managed to piss her off enough for that, she bit me in the leg."

"Because you throttled her?"

"I think I pulled her hair because she got cupcakes for good grades and I didn't."

"Look how far you've come since then. Now, you have your very own goblin ten-pound cake." Val waved to it where it rested, seeping lard—or whatever—into my workbench.

"Yes, my life is complete." I rose, grabbed paper towels from the holder, and set the cake on the floor to prop open the still-creaking door. It was as effective a doorstop as I'd envisioned.

"What's next?" Val considered me with a little wariness, probably afraid I would be incapable of doing anything but pining or scheming ways to get back to Veleshna Var for the next week, but I couldn't do anything for now, not about whatever was going on—or not—there.

"Getting into that party and finding out where my parents are," I said.

"Do you have a plan? You didn't seem keen on Willard's date idea." Her gaze shifted to the flyer.

"I do have a plan. Would you be willing to pose as a plumber with me?" Originally, I'd envisioned taking Abbas since he looked the part a lot more than Val did, but... I couldn't afford to screw up this opportunity. I needed another strong warrior at my side, not someone with pacifist tendencies. If we needed to fight magical bad guys, or beat the snot out of Hart to make him talk, I wanted someone who would help me do it.

Val arched her eyebrows. "How much about plumbing would I need to know?"

"Nothing. You can be my assistant who's new to the job and training for a career change."

"So, I'd get to hold your coffee?"

"See, you know about assistants already. I wouldn't have to

train you. When I described the job duties to Sarrlevi, he was flummoxed." I started to smile before remembering I might have lost him.

"You have to carefully explain things to people from other worlds. Not that they always listen. Feel free to ask Zav about the time he experimented with one of my razors."

"Ah, I probably won't."

"Wise." Val stood and thumped me on the shoulder. "I'll help with the plumbing scheme. Get me a uniform or whatever we'll need to wear."

"I would offer to lend you some of my overalls, but the cuffs would be at your knees."

"I'd say Amber would mock me for that, but she would mock me for wearing anything from the *overalls* category, whether they fit or not." Val shook her head ruefully. "I guess I should be happy she's spending time with me at all."

"Is everything okay?" Maybe I should have asked Val about her life more often. Since I'd met her, I'd constantly been in trouble and in survival mode. It had me asking for help left and right, which I hated, and thinking more about my own woes than those of others.

"Yeah, she just told me she's too busy for sword practice again. It's about the only time I see her. But since Thad won't buy her everything she wants whenever she asks—if you can imagine that —she's determined to get a part-time job. Apparently, her attempt to start a social-media video channel and become an influencer who gets big brands to give her tons of stuff for free hasn't been fruitful. Probably because she doesn't want to spend hours editing the videos. I offered to get Zoltan to give her tips, but she's disinclined to spend time with my basement roommate."

"She probably values her veins."

Val nodded. "She's finding it difficult to get what she wants, a high-paying fashion-industry job—or even one in retail—with her limited two hours a day and four on weekends. That's all Thad will give her. He's torn between thinking it would be good for her to get some work experience and not wanting her grades to fall. *I* think sword-fighting skills are more valuable to her than learning how to make slushies in the food court at the mall, but, since I'm unwilling to pay her to practice defending herself, she won't prioritize it."

"You know what's really useful?" I held up the flyer. "Learning a trade. Even if you don't want to go into a career in the field, if you know enough, you can save lots of money doing your own home repairs. At the least, you'll never be taken advantage of by disreputable service people."

"Are you offering to teach my daughter to renovate houses?"

"Er." I hadn't been *offering* anything. I would take Sarrlevi, even in his chemically altered state, over a teenager who would highlight the deficiencies of my wardrobe every time she came to work. If Amber's ideal job was in the fashion business, I couldn't imagine her hauling around bags of cement and putting up drywall.

Val arched her eyebrows. Hell, was she seriously asking?

"Would she *want* to work for me?" I asked dubiously.

"No. But it would be good for her, and I could probably talk Thad into financing it."

"Financing it? Like your ex-husband would pay me to hire your daughter? That's an odd arrangement."

"I believe it falls under nepotism, which makes it perfectly normal in a capitalist society. Thad has offered to hire her to help in *his* business, but she doesn't have any interest in programming and also doesn't want to email his clients and be his lackey, as she calls it. Too menial and not enriching enough."

That sounded like a direct quote.

"Val, I don't think your daughter understands the concept of work."

Val smirked. "Of course she doesn't. She's a teenager."

"Tell her work is a service you do for others to earn your place in society." I snorted, realizing I was quoting my grandpa. I could imagine how he would have reacted to a fashion-forward teenager who didn't want to be a *lackey* showing up for work on one of his job sites. "Besides, entry-level jobs are supposed to be skill- and character-building, not enriching."

Val's smirk only deepened. "She expects twenty-five dollars an hour too. Since she's only got a few hours a week, she must be well compensated."

"I compensate Tinja with free room and board."

"Do you want Amber to move into your house?"

"There aren't any available rooms. She would have to sleep in the tool shed."

"That *would* be character-building."

"Well, I don't think being paid by someone's dad to employ them sounds right, but if she can carry heavy stuff around and hold things, I could find a use for her. At minimum wage until she proves herself worth more." I wasn't excited by the idea of hiring someone who didn't want to be there and didn't have any relevant skills, but I owed Val numerous favors by now and didn't feel I could refuse. Maybe Amber would be handier than she looked. She was tall and a quarter elven, so she ought to be stronger and more agile than normal. "Maybe, after I've resolved my assassin problem—" *all* of my problems, "—she could come by the work site and see if she would be interested. It's very *Grapes of Wrath* out there."

"Hilarious. I'll mention it to her." Val waved and headed out.

I wished I could find amusement, but as my hand strayed again to my pocket, all I could think about was that I was here chitchatting while Sarrlevi might be dying and in need of my help. He'd *asked* for my help, and I hadn't been able to give it. If he hadn't made it, that would eat me up forever.

15

THREE DAYS PASSED BEFORE I SENSED A DRAGON. IN BETWEEN worrying about Sarrlevi and practicing distance-plumbing enchanting, I'd been at the job site, distracting myself with work.

Today, I was carving a few trophy pieces for the house Abbas and I were almost done renovating. I enjoyed putting my touch on the homes we worked on, and Zadie always said the buyers loved my custom pieces. The new front door, a replacement for the one a magical arrow had split, lay across sawhorses as I carved my artwork into the front.

Soon, Zadie would be by to take photos of the house and list it. Per her suggestion, we were going to sell it to buy the remaining materials for the other three homes. I'd been in the business long enough to have a number of backers happy to lend me money, but interest rates had been heading up, and I preferred not to carry more debt than necessary. This was a more involved—and expensive—project than we'd taken on before, and I wanted to be conservative.

Plumber Puletasi, came Zavryd's voice from the north. He seemed to be flying past the area instead of toward me.

Uhm, yes, Lord Zavryd? You don't need to call me plumber, *by the way. Puletasi or Matti is fine.*

It is what the goblins call you, is it not?

Gondo does.

I believe all *the goblins refer to you this way now. Plumber Puletasi, the assistant to Work Leader Tinja.*

I lifted my chisel and shot a dirty look toward the tiny house. Too bad Tinja was inside decorating and couldn't see my glare. I'd finished its interior, including installing the granite she'd ordered for the little kitchen and bathroom, without complaint since she'd drawn my flyer. I'd since had copies made as well as a matching giant vinyl decal for my truck. Though a van would have been a more believable plumber's vehicle, I had enough boxes and racks installed on it that it looked like the work vehicle it was. It ought to pass muster.

My mate said you wish to see me about a journey to Veleshna Var and are prepared to provide nourishment for the trip.

That's right. There's a barbecue place that delivers out here. I hadn't mentioned nourishment when I'd spoken to Val, but if Zavryd would take me to look for Sarrlevi, I would buy him an entire pig.

I only wished he'd returned to Earth sooner. After three days, any chance of finding Sarrlevi might be long past. I'd kept hoping he would show up here on his own, letting me know he'd outsmarted the *dashar* and the elves, but as more time passed, I worried he truly had died. My dreams of him had turned to nightmares in which I kept witnessing his horrible end. I much preferred my earlier erotic dreams of him and hoped my subconscious mind wasn't trying to tell me the truth.

Excellent. Princess Freysha has arrived at our lair, and I must meet her and my mate, but I shall return.

Okay. Please tell Freysha I'd like to see her. Maybe it was vain to hope that she'd heard anything about Sarrlevi, but, if nothing else, she probably knew exactly where that lakeside village was and could direct Zavryd where to open his portal.

Inform the goblin that I have temporarily lowered the wards at the front of your property, so that her guests may walk to her wheeled domicile, but that they remain up along the sides and the back. Further, the ones out front will return in one of your Earth hours. You must remain protected from assassins.

Guests? Wards? I looked around. Did he mean *here?*

Brakes squealed on the damp pavement in the street, a large bus pulling to a stop in front of the property, and I missed Zavryd's reply.

The door opened, and middle-aged Asian men and women filed out of the bus, led by a male goblin in a suit. My jaw dropped as the goblin led them up the driveway, then veered off onto the dirt and toward the tiny house. Dozens of people passed by, a few pausing to take pictures of me and the door I was carving. They all had phones or tablets out for photos and chatted excitedly in their language as they pointed around.

Abbas stuck his head out of the house, a paintbrush in hand. "Zadie hasn't listed this place yet, has she?"

"No, and I don't think those are prospective buyers." I raised my voice. "Uhm, Tinja? You've got... guests."

A lot of the visitors had faint auras, suggesting half- or quarter-magical blood, but many of them were normal people. Normal... tourists? That's what they looked like as they snapped photos, but we were a long way from the Space Needle and other popular Seattle destinations.

The goblin leading the visitors called out in another language—that one I recognized as goblin since I'd heard Tinja curse in it under her breath enough times. She hopped out of the tiny house, grinned, and threw up her arms in excitement, not appearing surprised by this development.

The male goblin greeted her with a hearty handshake, then

explained something in the language he'd been using with the humans. They streamed forward and took photos of Tinja and the tiny house and then her posing in front of the tiny house.

"Huh." Abbas scratched his jaw and went back inside.

I might have walked over and asked for an explanation, but Zavryd's aura came back on my radar. This time, Freysha was with him as well, riding on his back. Surprisingly, I didn't sense Val with them.

Freysha and Zavryd, I said, attempting to project my thoughts to them from a mile away. *If you're coming here, please camouflage yourselves. There are a bunch of tourists here, and some of them have magical blood.*

Tourists? Freysha asked in surprise.

Yeah, I'll explain it when you get here. Uhm, actually, I can't *explain it, but I need to talk to you, so please come anyway.*

Certainly, Freysha replied. *I have news for you.*

I swallowed. *Good news or bad news?*

Mm, some of each.

My insides knotted. The only bad news I could imagine coming from Veleshna Var was a confirmation of Sarrlevi's death. Maybe his body had floated up from the bottom of the lake. Had anyone told his mother? The thought of her lying ill and dying and learning of the passing of her last child was enough to make me tear up. I'd wanted to find a way to allow them to meet again, to get to know each other again, as I longed to do with my own parents.

As Zavryd flew closer, I told myself to get it together. I didn't even know what the news was yet.

I'll meet you... I almost said out front, since the tourists were ogling the tiny house, now taking turns going inside, but the driver remained inside the bus. Only then did I realize it was a *goblin* driver. He would definitely notice a dragon arriving. *I'll meet you at the side of the property.*

A dragon *harrumph* sounded in my mind. Was that an agreement or refusal?

Leaving my chisel on the door—the carving, appropriately enough, featured a dragon—I grabbed my hammer and headed toward the trees along the property's border. They provided enough privacy that the neighbor's house wasn't in view.

Zavryd landed, breaking branches off a few trees, and his tail knocked over a wheelbarrow that I was positive shouldn't have been in his way. He had camouflaged himself, but that would only make the knocking over of things stranger to anyone who glanced over.

This residence does not have a sufficient landing pad, he announced.

I rubbed the back of my neck. *It's on five acres. I'd think a dragon could find a landing pad on five acres.*

The land is occupied by many dwellings, trees, and clutter. His tail flicked dismissively at the upended wheelbarrow. *You should remedy this for future visitors.*

I doubt the people who buy these houses and move in will invite dragons over for dinner with any regularity. I used telepathy, not wanting anyone to hear us. The tourists appeared suitably distracted, but I hadn't activated my camouflage charm, and they might think it odd if I appeared to be talking to myself.

Freysha slid off Zavryd's back, her face grave as our eyes met. Hell, her news *was* about Sarrlevi. I could tell.

Give me the bad news first, please. I didn't want to know, but I had to know.

I regret to inform you that Meyleera Sarrlevi, despite my father ordering a guard to watch her home day and night, has disappeared from our city.

I rocked back on my heels. That wasn't the bad news I'd expected, but it was also distressing. And infuriating, damn it. My bitch of an aunt was still gunning for Sarrlevi. Didn't she know he might already be dead?

Roaring in frustration, I pounded my hammer into the ground over and over, not caring what the tourists thought when they glanced over.

This is no more acceptable than using me to demolish cabinetry, Sorka spoke into my mind.

I halted mid-swing. *Sorry. You're right. But damn it.* I hastily cleaned the dirt off my hammer with my shirt and turned back to Freysha.

She had her hands up as she regarded me warily. I felt bad about losing my temper, but with Zavryd behind her—still in his dragon form—she couldn't have believed she was in danger. Maybe she'd been defending herself from flying clods of wet dirt. Zavryd eyed a clump that stuck to his shoulder. It slid off, and he gave me a baleful look with his violet eyes.

I was pissing people off left and right today. *Sorry,* I told them. *Does anyone know where she went? Where Princess Barothla took her? I assume she's the one who did it, right? Nobody else would be vile enough to kidnap a sick old elf lady.*

Freysha hesitated. *She* was *in the capital and spoke to my mother —the queen—but the guard watching Meyleera's home fell asleep and didn't see who took her.*

Fell asleep? Was he incompetent or drugged with some chemical? I thought of the floating canister that had sprayed Sarrlevi with knockout juice. Maybe that was a favorite trick for alchemists.

I left before that was deduced, but it was during the middle of the day, so it is unlikely he voluntarily permitted himself to take a nap.

What did Barothla talk to the queen about? Your mother didn't believe *my conniving aunt, did she?*

I was not invited to the meeting. I knew you would wish to know, so I came here immediately.

Yeah. I rubbed my neck again. *Thank you. Do you have any idea how long Sarrlevi's mom can survive without that stuff she was receiving through an IV?* Not sure if Freysha knew English medical terms, I pantomimed a needle sticking into my arm.

Freysha hesitated, but I was fairly certain she understood the question. *I am not certain how long, no. We are hoping that whoever kidnapped her—*

Princess Barothla.

—wishes to keep her alive and has the medical knowledge to do so.

I'm sure she has the knowledge; I'm not sure she'll use it. She might be out for revenge. The thought gutted me. Poor Meyleera didn't deserve such a fate. She didn't deserve any of the awful stuff that had happened to her in her life. *Have you heard anything about Sarrlevi?* My *Sarrlevi?*

Freysha mouthed *my* uncertainly.

Varlesh.

She shook her head. *I have not heard anything regarding him.*

That was weird. I would have expected the elven warriors to have bragged about their victory over him to the king and anyone else who would listen. Or, if they weren't sure they'd gotten him, wouldn't they have at least reported that he was on the planet?

I reminded myself that Freysha was young by elven standards and, by her own admission, not in the loop regarding what went on with her parents and politics. *Where is the village of Menlolee in relation to your capital city?*

More than a thousand miles away on another continent.

Ah. That might explain why word hadn't gotten back to the king.

Freysha looked to the south, frowning for a moment before raising her eyebrows. Zavryd was also looking—no, *glaring*—in that direction.

That ludicrous hippie seeks to use my distraction to beat me in locating the lost dwarf princess. He has found nothing but residues of magic, but he taunts me, as if he is a skilled tracker. Zavryd rose to all fours, his tail going rigid behind him. *He has* no *skills. As all can clearly see.*

You will return to the competition with him? Freysha asked.

I sensed what they'd already sensed. Xilneth was flying this way with Hennehok on his back. He didn't land but sashayed from side to side, inasmuch as a dragon could sashay, as he flew over the property. At least he was camouflaging himself from the tourists. Or so I assumed. None of them reacted when he did a lazy barrel roll above the tiny house. I caught sight of Hennehok's green face as he squinted his eyes shut and used his magic to keep himself affixed to the dragon's back.

Yes, and I will beat him to finding those who are missing. You will obtain a ride back to the lair with my mate or her comrade. Zavryd sprang into the air, leaves stirring on the trees as his wings flapped. His tail brushed but, thankfully, did not destroy the bus as he took off in that direction. Even so, the vehicle shuddered, and the goblin driver blinked and looked around.

Dragons are interesting beings, Freysha said.

Yeah. Now worried about Sarrlevi *and* his mother, I couldn't muster the energy to care about dragon antics. I started back toward the house and my chisel, though I was thinking of pounding something with it instead of working on the carving.

There is other news, Freysha reminded me as she followed me.

I halted. *The good news?*

At this point, I couldn't imagine what *good* could come out of the elven home world, but I hoped for something.

The scientist Hyslara Broadleaf flew to the capital on an evinya. *I was not there for her arrival and meeting with my parents and one of our preeminent healers, but they were all very excited. My father told me Broadleaf believes she was able to replicate the formula that can cure ill elves of* Shiserathi *Disease.*

"She actually did it?" I blurted aloud, no longer caring if the tourists noticed me talking to visitors. An elf wasn't as alarming as a dragon. "I didn't think she would do anything I asked after, well, after she kept me from helping Sarrlevi when the thugs with weapons arrived, and I bashed up her lab to escape."

So I heard. There was vociferous complaining, I understand. She wants you forbidden from returning to Veleshna Var.

"What's new?" I'd probably already been forbidden from returning to Dun Kroth. Unfortunate, but it wasn't as if these places had been accessible to me a month earlier anyway. "Do you know for sure that the formula works?"

Freysha looked curiously toward Tinja's group as we approached, then also switched to speaking aloud. "It will only be through trial with ill elves who volunteer to receive it that its efficacy can be proven, but she followed the recipe that you gave her. My mother is suspicious of the source, but Broadleaf is an expert in her field and knows which substances typically have which effects on the elven body, and she says they were all logical ingredients. She also analyzed the final formula on a microscopic as well as magical level and believes there is promise. Since it is a fatal disease, it is likely she will find people willing to volunteer to be treated. She specifically brought it to the capital since you'd mentioned Meyleera. Had she arrived earlier in the day..." Freysha turned her palm upward.

"Barothla is horrible." I wanted to challenge her to a fight so I could knock her head off. "Why did she take Sarrlevi's mother? She's already *poisoned* him with that awful chemical. He's too crazy to do her bidding now, if he's still alive at all." I closed my eyes and took a breath, willing myself to keep it under control.

"I do not know. As I said, we have no proof that Princess Barothla was the one to kidnap her."

"Because a geriatric elf painter is likely to have so *many* enemies who wish her ill."

Freysha could only turn her palm skyward again. Right, she

didn't have answers. But she'd brought me what information she could. I appreciated that.

"Thank you for coming to tell me about this. Is Broadleaf still in your capital?"

"She may be. I came as soon as I learned about these events."

"Is there any chance... I don't know how much sway you have, but could you ask her if she's able to get rid of the chemical that she and Barothla and other scientists once worked on? Get rid of it in the *brains* of those afflicted?" Unfortunately, I didn't know if that was possible. I didn't even know if Barothla had a cure. She was pissed enough with Sarrlevi—and *me*—that she may have intentionally chosen something that caused effects that couldn't be reversed.

"I can ask, but I must wait for someone capable of creating a portal to send me home." Freysha's expression grew bemused when she looked toward the sky in the direction the dragons had flown off. "Or return to Val's home in time to meet the elf my father will send to retrieve me later. He did not approve of my coming to Earth today, not because he objects to my sharing the news related to Meyleera, but because we don't know who sneaked into the capital and kidnapped her from her home right underneath the palace. He always worries that I will be a target for assassins."

"All the assassins are busy with another gig right now. Trust me." I waved to my chest. "Though you could get taken out by accident because you're standing next to me."

"I was surprised when we arrived at this domicile-in-progress to find it so heavily warded."

"Everywhere I hang out for more than two minutes needs to be warded these days." I kept hoping the assassins would grow tired of targeting me, especially since Sarrlevi and I—mostly Sarrlevi—had killed a number of them. But maybe that made me a more enticing challenge. "I can't believe Val wants to send her kid to work for me." Though I assumed she didn't want Amber's employment to begin until *after* the assassination issue was cleared up. Which I hoped would be soon.

"You will employ Amber in wood carving?" Freysha smiled and rested her hand on the door.

"Probably wood *carrying*. I'm not running an art school here."

The corners of Freysha's eyes crinkled in amusement. "Perhaps one day you will. It is very fine work and already enchanted against..." She ran her hand over the door. "Projectiles?"

"I didn't intend to enchant it, but I *was* thinking it would be nice if magical arrows couldn't pierce it."

"There are also enchantments on the drainage pipes." Freysha looked around the house. "And the chimney. And many items in the interior. This house appears very durable now. Were you selling it to a magical being, this would increase the value, but I do not know if humans are able to sense and appreciate such things."

"Just the carvings. Come on. I'll take you to Val's house." If there was any chance Freysha could sway the alchemist to work on Sarrlevi's brain problem, I didn't want to delay her. I waved and started toward my truck only to realize the bus had blocked the driveway, and the driver didn't seem to be in the seat any longer. "Give me a sec."

After putting away my tools and grabbing my hammer, I jogged toward the tiny house where the photo-taking was wrapping up.

"Matti." Tinja hopped up on the steps so she could see over the heads of the tourists and waved to me. "Do you have a payment processor for your phone so you can swipe human credit cards? I have several people interested in ordering my tiny-home plans for this very model."

"No, I don't sell stuff, so I've never needed that."

"You sell houses!"

"People don't buy houses with credit cards. You've seen me

sign all the paperwork and go through the month-long process of people getting financing approved and having funds wired."

"So slow and inconvenient."

"Just open a Venmo account." I narrowed my eyes at her. "Then you can order slabs of granite for *your* projects with *your* money."

"Yes, I will consider this. Very wise."

"That's me. Wisdom incarnate. Can you get your groupies to move their bus? Where did all these people come from anyway?" I eyed the tour-leader goblin who was speaking with some of the humans while gazing at Tinja in what might have been adoration.

"I have been networking, Matti. With other goblins! Until recently, I hadn't realized how many of my people were entrepreneurs, learning how to survive as civilized city goblins on your world. This is Zatphun, whose family settled in the forests across your great ocean. He brings tourists with magical blood—or humans who are interested in the magical—to see places of interest in America, specifically Seattle. They go to many typical tourist destinations, such as your spire restaurant and fish market, but they also visit the haunted cemetery downtown, Vampire Venue in Queen Anne, Shaman Alley in Ballard, and many other places that are significant to the magical community. Recently, he added the Coffee Dragon to his itinerary."

"I bet Nin and Dimitri love that."

"Yes, certainly. Tourists are good paying customers, Matti. And now Zatphun is bringing them to see my tiny homes as well."

"Because they're naturally of interest to tourists who like seeing magical stuff."

"This one is." Tinja waved to the interior. "They are most impressed with the self-cleaning enchantment you put on the countertops."

I'd done that? Why was it so hard to use my power to defeat my enemies and so easy to enchant construction zones?

Tinja's smile faltered. "I cannot, however, promise that the plans will instruct the buyers on how to add magic to the homes they will build." She touched her lip and brightened with an idea. "Not unless you are willing to start an enchanting factory and can ship self-cleaning granite countertops around the world?"

"No, I am not. Make a note to tell them to look for a local enchanter. Now, the bus?"

Tinja murmured to the other goblin in their native tongue, which involved some pointing and nodding. Freysha chuckled.

"You understand them?" I asked in surprise before remembering Freysha studied goblin engineering as well as elven nature magic. Maybe she'd been to their world.

"I do. I gather the tourists were hoping to get some stuff enchanted, so Zatphun doesn't want to see you go."

One male was waving a tablet in one hand and a key fob in the other as he pointed both at me.

"I don't know how to enchant many things, especially not things I'm not crafting. Unless he wants his keychain to be rust-proof, I'm not the person."

"I believe you are underestimating your skills. You've learned much quickly."

"I also don't *want* to enchant keychains."

Freysha smiled. "Understandable."

Maybe Tinja was trying to save me from such tedious work as well, for she pointed at the bus and said, "He says you can ask the driver to move it, and he will be happy to oblige."

I would have done that to start with, but I didn't *see* the driver. When I checked with my senses, I realized he was still in the bus, but his aura was diminished. Maybe he was on the floor taking a nap.

"Princess Freysha," Tinja said. "Do you know if—"

"*Princess*," one of the tourists blurted in accented English before switching back to her language and pointing vigorously at

Freysha. Several phones and tablets came up, taking pictures of the startled Freysha.

Sorry, I told her, jogging toward the bus. *I'll get the truck and pick you up in a second.*

Freysha, who'd always struck me as shy and probably introverted, smiled painfully at the attention.

The goblin driver still wasn't visible when I walked around the front of the bus toward the door. Once more, I checked the area with my senses. His aura was *definitely* weak. A nap shouldn't be diminishing a goblin's aura.

The bus door was open, and I climbed warily inside.

The goblin lay groaning on the floor of the bus, a dagger sticking out of his gut.

16

A WHISPER OF MAGIC FLOWED THROUGH THE BUS, AND THE DOOR creaked shut behind me.

Though I didn't yet sense anyone inside but the goblin, I spun toward the open aisle, raising my hammer and blurting, "*Hygorotho*."

Light flashed as the tip of a magical sword thrust against the barrier that Sorka had erected even before I voiced the word. The face of the pointy-eared man—*assassin*—with blue-tinted skin came into view as I sensed his aura for the first time. An elf with... troll blood?

He bared his teeth as his attack was deflected but summoned power and used it to rail at my protection as he slashed again.

Letting myself rely on Sorka's barrier, hopefully not unwisely, I resisted the urge to parry and instead swung my hammer in under his sword. The narrowness of the aisle, with high-backed seats crowding me on either side, made it hard to use the weapon. Worse, he had lightning-fast reflexes. He finished his attack and sprang back before my hammer came close to catching him.

Growling, I stalked down the aisle after him, hoping to corner him in the back. His hand dipped into a pocket, and he withdrew a magical sphere. A grenade?

I willed more power into my barrier as I swung, attempting to knock the sphere away before he could hurl it at me. Though I managed to disrupt his throw, the assassin whipped his hand back too quickly, and I didn't succeed in striking it from his grip.

A vision of the bus exploding flashed in my mind. That was *not* how I wanted to clear the driveway.

Using his sword to block me, the assassin turned sideways and drew his other arm back, the grenade in his grip.

I swung over the seats toward his chest, but he parried easily. He smirked, the bastard, as if he knew he had this under control.

The hammer clipped a seat back as I retracted it. My height was *not* my friend in this situation.

Taking advantage, the assassin lunged up the aisle toward me with daunting speed. Only the barrier saved me from being cut.

My elbow struck a seat, and I snarled. Though I launched another attack, one he easily avoided, I glanced back toward the door. Outside, I would have more room to maneuver, but would he follow me out? And, if so, would he blow up the bus anyway?

Before I'd decided to spring for the exit, the glass of the emergency door in the back shattered inward.

Eyebrows flying up, the assassin glanced behind him. This time, *I* took advantage, rushing in and jabbing him in the stomach with my hammer.

It clanked against armor he wore under his shirt, but my frustrated blow landed hard enough to knock him back, almost into the arms of the person who sprang through the broken window, knocking glass everywhere.

Sarrlevi.

Clothing torn, grime matting his short blond hair, and his face utterly savage, he roared as he sprang on the assassin.

I scooted away, certain they would end up bowling me over, but Sarrlevi attacked so rapidly that even the agile half-elf didn't have a chance. The glowing sphere flew from his hand as he had to draw a second weapon in the hope of fending off Sarrlevi with his dual blades.

Swearing, I couldn't decide whether to catch it, try to knock it through a window, or sprint out of the bus. A groan from the goblin reminded me that there was a victim who would be blown up *with* the bus.

Protect me, Sorka, I silently begged as I lunged to the side to catch the sphere, hoping it wouldn't explode on impact with my hand.

The hammer emanated uncertainty but the barrier allowed the sphere through. I caught it as gently as I could, wincing with the fear that it would blow up. It didn't, but once it was in my palm, I sensed it throbbing rapidly, as if building to a detonation.

Though I had no idea how it worked, I attempted to use my enchanting magic on it. I envisioned a sword glowing red as it was forged in a smithy, then being thrust into a barrel of water to quench the heat.

In the back of the bus, the assassin cried out and went down. The sphere's throbbing slowed.

Blades dripping blood, Sarrlevi stepped on the fallen assassin and toward me. His eyes held the same crazy gleam that they had on the kayak-rental dock days earlier. When he looked at me, he saw an enemy, not an ally.

I rested the sphere on a seat, then skittered away from Sarrlevi, wanting to give him a minute to cool down and remember who he was. Who *I* was. But my heel clipped the goblin, eliciting another groan from him, and I teetered before catching my balance on a seat.

Sarrlevi stalked toward me.

"Varlesh," I said aloud and in his mind, terrified he'd

completely lost it and I wouldn't get through. "It's me. Matti. I'm on your side." I swallowed as he kept coming, his swords raised, his face savage. "I want to help you. Like you just helped me. Thank you."

His eyes flickered toward my hammer as he advanced. Did his animal brain, that primitive part of him that was in charge now, see the weapon as a threat?

Though terrified of being defenseless, I set the hammer down and raised my open palms toward him.

He prowled closer, his eyes full of battle rage. Blood lust. The desire to kill everything in his path.

"Varlesh Sarrlevi," I said, making myself hold that terrifying gaze. "I'm your friend, and I want to help you. Put your weapons down."

He was so close that I could see every bead of sweat bathing his face. I shook, afraid I would have no choice but to grab my hammer and defend myself. If I could.

Two feet away from me, he drew a sword back to strike.

"Don't do this," I whispered and licked my lips. "I love you."

I'd wanted to say that in a private, relaxing moment, maybe after we'd made love in his chalet in the mountains, with ice frosting the windows and platters of cheese and glasses of wine nearby. Not here. Not like this.

But the words made him pause.

Matti? came Freysha's concerned voice from the driveway. She and Tinja had realized what was going on and run over. *Do you need help?*

Give me a minute, I told her, never taking my gaze from Sarrlevi's.

"I love you," I repeated, "and I'm pretty sure you don't want to kill me. Put your swords away, please."

Sarrlevi jerked his weapons down and stepped back. As he

tilted his wild eyes toward the ceiling of the bus, a huge shudder went through him.

"I'm sorry," he rasped, his voice almost as animalistic as his face had been. "I didn't see... recognize... My brain isn't working."

"I know." I lifted my arms and stepped forward. Maybe I should have run away, but I wanted so badly to help him, to *fix* him. If only I could.

His swords remained at his side, points down.

I hugged him.

"Not wise," he whispered, tremors coursing through his body. "You shouldn't—" He didn't finish the thought, instead bending to brush his cheek against mine, to inhale deeply, as if my scent was comforting.

"I know, but I thought you were dead. There was nobody to take me back to search for you, and I—"

I was on the verge of apologizing for not helping, not being *able* to help, when he'd called for assistance, but he growled and stiffened, turning his head toward the window.

Not only were Tinja and Freysha out there, but the tourists had swarmed to the area. They were taking photos through the bus windows.

I groaned and would have clasped Sarrlevi's hand, but he still gripped his swords. "Let's go somewhere private." I nodded toward the door.

"Yes," he rasped but first shifted his swords to one hand so he could draw out his magical cleaning cloth. As he had before, he carefully wiped his blades in that ritual he seemed to find calming. It had to be a reminder of his former actions, his former self.

The swords were far cleaner than he, he who was usually tidy and immaculate. Now, he looked like the victim of a crocodile death roll.

When he'd finished and sheathed his weapons, I clasped his

hand and turned around, then winced. I'd forgotten about the poor goblin.

"Can you heal him?" I asked before I could think better of it. With that gash still on his cheek, as well as a number of new bruises, Sarrlevi didn't look like he could even heal *himself*.

He shook his head bleakly. "I barely managed to focus for long enough to create the portal to come here. And I think it was only because I so badly wished to see you again that I succeeded."

I swallowed, touched by that.

"Healing requires more fine magic over an extended time, and I don't think… I haven't been able to—"

"It's okay," I hurried to say and squeezed his hand. He was usually so calm and articulate that it was wrenching to see him like this. "I'll ask Freysha."

A goblin needs a healer, I told her, hoping that was in her repertoire of magic. Sarrlevi always said he wasn't a healer, but he did a fair job of it. *The driver.*

I will come in when…

I'm leading him out, I said, certain that Freysha was afraid of Sarrlevi right now. With good reason.

Thank you.

There's also a body in here, an assassin who attacked me.

I saw.

Can you take care of it? Realizing an elf might interpret that as growing vines over the body to hide it, I added, *If you can levitate it outside and behind a bush, I'll figure out what to do with it later.*

I will.

As we exited, Tinja and Freysha managed to keep the tourists back, though Sarrlevi glared and growled at them. Feeling like someone walking a pit bull along a chain-link fence with barking dogs on the other side, I led him up the driveway toward the house.

But Abbas was still inside working, so I veered toward the trees where Freysha and Zavryd and I had talked earlier.

As soon as we stopped, Sarrlevi slumped against a stout pine, then gripped it for support. I remembered him pressing his face against a tree in Veleshna Var and was sad that Earth trees probably weren't as comforting to an elf.

"I'm super glad to see you," I whispered.

Though tempted to hug him again, I didn't. I didn't want to risk awakening that lust within him. It wasn't as alarming as the battle rage, but it would be better not to do anything that would make it hard for him to keep control. Which he would find even more difficult, I had no doubt, once I told him about his missing mother. I hated that I had to give him that news.

Or did he already know?

"How long have you been here?" Was it possible, he'd been hanging out all day? Watching over me but not wanting to risk getting close? If so, I understood his reasoning, but I would also be frustrated since I'd been worrying for the last three days about whether he'd lived or died.

"Not long." Eyes closed, Sarrlevi leaned his temple against the pine's bark. "I sensed Thorvald's mate leaving as I arrived, but I was confused about all the people here, and I was not certain, regardless, if I should... I thought I should stay away. I came for you, but I'm afraid of... me." He shook his head bleakly.

"I know. I get it. I wish Zoltan could find a way to reverse what's happening to you... I *do* have a little good news. Uhm, and then some bad news. Be ready."

He laughed without humor. "It's all bad news anymore."

"Tell me about it. But Broadleaf made the formula and thinks she has the cure for your mother's disease."

His eyes opened. "She made it? After..."

"The horrible way I charmed her by smashing her laboratory?

Apparently so. I'm guessing she did it not for your sake or mine but for her people's."

"I think I killed one of the elven enforcers," Sarrlevi whispered, his eyes haunted. "I tried not to, but there were so many, and my blood was hot. It was so hard to think, to want to do anything but lash out. I barely even saw them. I—"

Though chilled, I made myself keep my tone even and nonaccusatory. "You should do your best not to develop that disease yourself, because it's possible your people won't use the formula to cure you. Your mother, however, hasn't committed any crimes."

"No," he whispered. "Every crime has been committed against her."

"Yeah." I took a deep breath, struggling to bring up what he needed to know, that she was missing. *Temporarily*, I hoped, but I had no idea how to find her. "How did you get away?" I asked instead, quailing from what I feared would make him lose his tenuous grip on his sanity again.

The tourists were filing into their bus. I hoped Freysha knew how to dispose of that sphere as well as cure the goblin. Once everyone was gone, it wouldn't matter as much if Sarrlevi went wild.

"You aren't the only one who tricks opponents," he said, managing the briefest of smiles.

At first, I didn't know what he meant, but he shared an image of me flying backward during my battle with Barothla. That had been when I'd allowed myself to hit down hard on the driveway, letting her believe she'd bested me so I could pull out a vial of acid.

He also shared imagery of himself on the platform outside Broadleaf's laboratory, the elves trying to keep him busy until the *dashar* arrived. In the aftermath of being drugged, Sarrlevi had struggled to get his body working fully again, and it hadn't been much of a *trick* to let one elf knock him backward through the railing. He'd flailed as he tumbled toward the water, but he'd also taken a deep breath and twisted at the last second to dive in headfirst.

As the creature had darted toward him, he'd swum rapidly underneath it. It had managed to take a chomp out of him, stirring the savage monster within him, and he'd slashed it with his swords, almost killing it before remembering that he had to fool not only it but the elves. He'd stabbed it once more to drive it away, then used his magical camouflage to hide his aura.

Holding his breath to stay deep underwater so he wouldn't cause ripples on the surface, he'd swum as far as he could before rising. He'd found a pebbly beach where he could slip out and cross into the forest without making footprints in case the elves searched for him. Even so, he'd worried about leaving droplets of blood.

Sarrlevi lifted his shirt, peeled back one of the green plant-fiber pads that his people used as bandages, and showed me bite marks in his abdomen and side. They had to have been painful, but at least they were healing well. Unlike the inflamed scratch on his cheek and the back of his hand. Barothla's bite was far worse than that of a huge monster.

I wanted to reach out and touch him, to comfort him. Reluctantly, I stayed back.

"I crawled off into the woods. The elves searched for me and almost found me a couple of times. My magic, as I said, isn't reliable right now." Sarrlevi lowered his shirt—and his head. "I would have come sooner if I could have. I knew you would worry."

"It's not your fault. Varlesh, I'm so sorry that the one time you asked for my help, I wasn't able to give it." I hated knowing he'd been alone and bleeding under a bush while people hunted him. I wished I could have been there with him. Even if I couldn't have done anything to heal him or keep the elves away, I could have at least offered my company. He shouldn't have to endure this descent into madness alone.

"I know she stopped you." Sarrlevi bent forward and gripped his thighs. "I wouldn't have asked for your assistance if I hadn't been—I was struggling to fight with that drug slowing my body and this—" he grasped in the air by his temple, "—*whatever* slowing my mind."

"You can ask me for help with anything anytime, okay? Maybe next time, I'll be able to break free to get to you sooner."

"I don't usually *need* help." He stared glumly at the ground.

"Sucks to realize you sometimes do, huh?" I reached out and touched his arm, just briefly, not wanting to wake his beast. "I've been grappling with that myself these past weeks."

"Yes," he said, that raspy quality back in his voice as he looked at his arm and then to me. "You understand."

His lust monster wasn't creeping into him, was it? I held up a hand, as if I could deter it. "I need to tell you something else, some bad news." I bit my lip, knowing it would be better to rip the bandage off quickly, but it was hard.

"You're out of cheese?" Sarrlevi asked into my long silence.

"No. I'm savoring what you brought last time. I didn't know—" I stopped myself from saying I hadn't known if he was *alive* and hadn't wanted to finish off all I had left from him. "I thought that in your current state, the cheesemonger who supplies you with your orders might refuse your business."

"Really. I am an excellent long-standing customer, and I tip well."

"You smell like a swamp, dude."

The bus trundled away, leaving Freysha and Tinja speaking in the driveway.

Waving for Sarrlevi to follow, I walked farther toward the back of the property. If he lost it, I didn't want them to be endangered. It was bad enough an assassin had shown up looking for me when so many people had been around.

"The bad news is worse than a cheese shortage," Sarrlevi said.

"Yes." I took a deep breath and faced him. "Barothla showed up in the elven capital. They don't have proof she did it, but... your mom went missing."

Sarrlevi's face frosted over as he turned into a statue. I hurried to share everything Freysha had told me, reminding him that once we found his mother, we might have a cure. Whether he heard anything after the word *missing*, I didn't know. He didn't move, didn't even seem to be breathing, but he emanated rage.

Finally, he clenched his fists and spoke, his voice raspy again. Not from lust, I was certain. His words were in Elven. Was he even aware of that?

"English, please," I said, though the part of his brain responsible for language might be as affected as everything else.

Speaking in a slow growl, he said, "I will find her and kill her."

His body shook with anger. Fury.

He jerked a hand up, but it wasn't until magic swelled beside us that I realized he was forming a portal.

"Wait," I blurted, grabbing his arm.

He flung it up and jerked out of my grip. I stumbled backward, catching myself on a tree.

"I *will* kill her." His hands balled into white-knuckled fists, and he threw his head back and roared.

"Varlesh, listen. You can't kill her until we know where your mom is and if the formula works. You have to wait. Do you even know where Barothla is?"

"I will find her."

I was relieved he didn't know since he wasn't capable of reason right now.

"And I will *make* her tell me where my mother is." He looked at the tree above instead of at me.

"I'll gladly help you with that. But listen. Why don't you stay here with me? If she wants you, I think she'll assume you're with me and come here in search of you. Remember, all bad guys eventually come to me. It's a proven fact." I decided not to point out that the trend had started with *him* looking for me. He wasn't in the mood for humor.

His gaze lowered, and he squinted at me. Considering the argument?

"If I wait," he said, "she may kill my mother."

I shook my head. "I don't think so. If Barothla wanted her dead, it would have been easier for her to sneak into her house and put some poison in her IV than sedate her guard and sneak out *with* her. In broad daylight. In the middle of the elven capital and a hundred feet from the palace."

I barely kept from making a disparaging comment about the quality of the security there. It irked me that the elven king and queen hadn't been willing to listen to my warning that my aunt ought to be kept off their world altogether. Though I admitted I didn't know what version of the story had gotten through to them. Just because I'd asked General Grantik to recommend that didn't mean he had. All the dwarves walked on eggshells around Barothla.

"That may be correct," Sarrlevi said.

Relieved he could still reason, I nodded. "She's probably not back in the dwarven capital either. Even though her people look the other way at some of the stuff she does, I highly doubt she could carry an elven noble through the palace and lock her up in one of her cages without anyone saying anything."

It was possible she'd used camouflaging magic to return, but would she risk her people finding out? Surely her *father* would object, even if nobody else did. If there was a way I could have been certain of seeing him and not her, I would have asked

Sarrlevi to take me to Dun Kroth so I could tattle on my aunt to my grandfather.

"Hang out with me." I didn't add, *and let me keep an eye on you*, but that desire was on my mind.

"I don't trust my control enough to be around someone I care about," Sarrlevi said quietly.

"Right. Instead, you should be around strangers who'd be happy to see you dead."

"I wouldn't worry as much about hurting *them*."

"I don't want you hurting anyone." I kept from making that *anyone else,* but the thought that he might have inadvertently killed one of his own people horrified me. "I don't think *you* want that either. Assassins trying to kill me, notwithstanding." I wouldn't shed a tear for that guy's death, but the elven guards had been following orders, I was sure. I didn't want Sarrlevi accidentally killing more innocent people. In his current state, I might be the only one with the power to prevent that.

His gaze shifted over my head, though he didn't seem to be looking at anything. "I couldn't forgive myself, Mataalii, if I hurt you," he rasped, and a shudder went through him. Even when he spoke rationally, almost calmly, he still struggled with himself, struggled for control. "Or worse," he added in a whisper.

"Well, *I'd* forgive you. This isn't your fault. When Barothla inevitably comes, we'll wring her neck until she tells us where your mom is and how to fix you." I didn't bring up the conversation with Zoltan and his uncertainty about whether elven brain damage would heal. I had to believe it could if we removed the chemical compound that was keeping Sarrlevi from healing now...

"Broadleaf didn't know of a cure for this," he said, his eyes locked in the distance, "did she?"

Sarrlevi had been unconscious when I'd spoken to Broadleaf, so he couldn't have overheard our conversation. Maybe he assumed I would have told him about it if she had mentioned a cure.

"No," I admitted.

"I'm not sure..." He met my gaze again, his eyes grave. "There's going to come a point when I can't be useful to you—to anyone."

"I hope you're not going to give me a dagger and ask me to cut your throat or some selfless-sacrifice bullshit like that." I scowled at him.

He opened his mouth, then closed it again. Hell, that *was* what was on his mind.

"Look, Varlesh. Hold it together a while longer, okay? I'm *sure* she'll come here looking for you. She'll make whatever horrible demand she has in mind—she didn't go through all the effort of kidnapping your mother simply to kill her, I'm sure. And we'll grab her and get the cure for you *and* your mother out of her." I snapped my fingers. "I'll get some more of Zoltan's truth drug."

"There may not *be* a cure to this." He jerked a finger toward his temple. "If Broadleaf didn't know of one..."

"She didn't work on it as long as Barothla. And *she* didn't customize it into fingernail paint."

Sarrlevi set his jaw mulishly.

"There's a cure. *Trust me.*" At first, I said it only to try to convince him. After all, I'd been having this very doubt earlier. But, between one eye blink and the next, I realized that Barothla *had* to have a cure. Of course. "Varlesh, she wouldn't be wearing the stuff on her fingernails where she could accidentally scratch herself if she didn't have a cure."

His eyes sharpened. "You're right. I hadn't thought of that."

I nodded, relieved he saw the reasoning, and reassured by it myself. "Because you're being crazy and fatalistic. I blame it on the chemicals in your brain, not you."

"Generous."

"As mongrels are known to be. I need to put a giant toilet decal on my truck. Want to help?"

"That is... for another scheme?" His forehead furrowed as he probably tried to remember what else I was involved in that week. His own issue had to be consuming his thoughts.

"Nah, toilet decals are trendy this year. I want to look good riding around town."

"Lying is not your forte."

"Nope." I offered him a hand before remembering I shouldn't get close. "You'll help?"

He clasped it. "Yes."

17

EVEN THOUGH I DIDN'T *THINK* A PERSON COULD BE ARRESTED FOR putting a flyer in someone's mailbox, I sweated in the driver's seat, as I waited for the street to be completely clear of pedestrians, vehicles, and nosy squirrels.

My truck idled in front of the property next door to Hart's, another home walled off by a brick wall and privacy hedges, though no invisible magical barriers protected it. I'd already confirmed that I could sense metal pipes flowing from the underground water main in the street toward the properties on either side. Given that they weren't magical, I sensed them better than I'd expected, but since I'd started learning enchanting, I found I could often feel the materials I was working on with more than my fingers.

In the passenger seat, Sarrlevi sat with his swords and pack between his legs and his hands on his thighs, clenching and unclenching his fingers. Sweat gleamed on his forehead too.

Though I didn't say anything, I was almost as worried about him now as I'd been when I hadn't known if he was alive. Barothla had better come soon. Hart's party was tomorrow night, and I wanted a cure for Sarrlevi before then. Not because I needed him at the party—Val had promised her assistance already—but because I worried he might not have a lot of time left before he went completely rabid and couldn't be brought back to a rational state of mind.

The night before, he'd sat in the truck, unwilling to come into my house. I'd used my magic to fix the spring in the seat for him, but I doubted it had soothed him. Numerous times, I'd woken and looked outside, and he'd either been sitting and rocking on the seat or pacing around the neighborhood. He wouldn't admit it, but I didn't think he'd slept for a long time.

"Nobody is around to observe you." Sarrlevi glanced at the flyer clenched in my hand. "Do you fear mechanical observation devices?"

I hadn't been thinking about security cameras, and I winced before reminding myself that we weren't doing anything condemning. Obnoxious maybe, but not condemning. "No."

I drove forward, slipped the flyer into the mailbox, then headed to the next property to do the same. I highly doubted the neighbors compared notes on what businesses stuck advertisements in their boxes, but, just in case, I didn't want the Hart property to appear to have been singled out.

The third mailbox had a locking mechanism, probably to keep people from doing exactly what I was doing. I drove to the next one, dropped another flyer in, then headed out of the neighborhood. Tomorrow evening, as the sun was setting and guests started to arrive, I would be waiting nearby with Val to work my magic. And then, when Hart—or, more likely, his staff—called, I would be ready to *un*work my magic.

"What happens if they are familiar with another plumbing service and call *them*?" Sarrlevi hadn't said much about my plan when I'd explained it on the way over, but I didn't take it as a snub. He was distracted.

"Val and I get to tie up and gag the competition as they come into the neighborhood. There's only one street out to this point, so we would see them." I would prefer *not* to jump plumbers attempting to do their job. Willard had made it clear she didn't have any pull to get me out of jail if I was arrested, and I didn't want to get Val in trouble either. But it *was* my backup plan. My hope was that Hart's staff didn't have a go-to plumber, since it was a relatively new house and didn't likely have a lot of issues, and that someone would remember having seen my flyer in the mail. The words *same-day emergency service* in large letters ought to be a selling point. I would make sure they had a legitimate emergency. "You're welcome to come along if you like," I added.

"To plumb? Or to hold your tools while *you* plumb?"

"Val is going to do that, at least to start with, but under her overalls, she's going to wear a slinky dress that her daughter picked out so she can sneak off and blend in."

"Will you?"

"I'm thinking about it. I'm the one who really needs to spy on Hart and his guests. I've got a little black dress that Penina picked out for me for a dinner where she was receiving a reward. She didn't want me to embarrass her with my usual *flair*, if you can imagine. The fact that Zadie *oohed* at it and stroked it in my closet tells me it's socially acceptable."

"Do you like it?"

"It's pretty boring. There aren't any sequins or fringes or tassels. I've got a fringe flapper dress in my closet that would be more to my tastes. It's got sequins and *shimmers*. I think it was inspired by peacocks." I smirked, remembering how horrified Penina had been when I suggested that outfit for her dinner. The discussion had been what prompted her to drag me out to buy the black dress. "Have you been around on Earth often enough to see peacocks?"

"I am familiar with them, yes." Sarrlevi managed a smile, as if my burbling pleased him. At the least, maybe it took his mind off his discomfort. "When I am better, you will show me this dress," he added.

I beamed a smile at him for saying the words *when I am better*. I hoped he now genuinely believed we could find a cure.

"I'll be glad to model it for you. It's not as *easy access* as my robe, but you can see a lot of leg through the fringes."

His gaze drifted to my legs. They were covered in denim so not very interesting, but that was good, I reminded myself. I didn't want him thinking about sex now.

"We'll relax and have a good time when you're better," I said, to make sure he knew that last part was a stipulation.

"Hm." His gaze lingered as I drove out of the neighborhood and headed home.

"I have a confession to make," I admitted.

He shifted his gaze from my legs to my face.

"When I was getting the ingredients for your mom's formula out of your pack, I saw the envelope with my name on it." I glanced at him. While I didn't think he would be irritated, I felt guilty because I'd inadvertently intruded upon his privacy. I'd needed the ingredients and *chanced* upon the letter, and I didn't regret reading it, but I hoped he'd actually meant to give it to me. To be that raw and real. "Being the naturally curious sort, I opened it and read your letter."

Sarrlevi nodded. "Good."

The tension seeped out of my shoulders. "Thanks for writing it. It meant a lot to me."

He nodded again. "I did not know if I would get an opportunity to say those words. Even if I did, it is... difficult for me to voice my feelings."

"To be vulnerable?"

"Perhaps."

"Me too. I get it." I smirked at him. "Especially when you don't know if someone's response is going to be to *tease* you."

"Or call you a haughty elf," he said.

I hesitated, not sure if he was implying that such things stung him or pointing out that I also teased him. In the beginning, it had been more of a curse. He'd driven me nuts with his arrogant superiority. But since then, he'd started using my name and stopped calling me mongrel. "Well, sometimes you *are* haughty."

"Yes."

"But maybe I could start calling you a *handsome* elf instead of a haughty one." That was a meaningless compliment though. He'd been born beautiful; it didn't say anything about his character. "Or a *supportive* elf, one who keeps having my back even though we never should have been... anything."

"Yes."

"It was impressive when you leaped through the back window of the bus to take out that assassin."

"In a saner moment, I would have used my magic to unlock the door and enter without knocking broken glass everywhere."

"That wouldn't have been as epic. Unhinged Varlesh has a flair for the dramatic."

"Unhinged." He sighed. "Leave it to someone with dwarf blood to use adjectives related to building."

"Sorry." I winced. "I meant supportive."

Sarrlevi reached over and rested a hand on my shoulder. "I am not bothered by your teasing. I am simply uncertain of myself and my... capabilities at this time." His voice grew softer as he added, "And my appeal in this state."

He wasn't sure if someone could love him right now?

"I understand. But if someone cares, they care about a person in *all* states." I gripped his hand. "It's a rule."

"Is it?" Maybe that hadn't always been his experience.

"Definitely. Like no swords at the dinner table, it's a completely indisputable rule."

He managed a faint half-smile, one that made my heart ache.

"I love you, Varlesh."

"I hadn't imagined voicing it under these circumstances, but I also love you, Mataalii."

I blinked, not wanting to break down weeping while I was driving. His hand dropped to the seat, but he didn't look away from me.

"I'm glad." I took a deep breath and dashed moisture from my eyes. "What circumstances *were* you imagining for voicing those words?"

"Perhaps I'd envisioned us in my home and speaking after I'd satisfied your wildest desires in bed. Or—" his tone grew more serious, "—after successfully helping you rescue your mother."

I was relieved that he wanted to do the latter now. I was amenable to the former too but especially appreciated the latter. "You can say it again after we do those things. I'd really like it."

"I will," he said softly.

As we headed back to my house, I debated on how I would get to Barothla to extract the cure from her if she *didn't* show up on Earth.

18

"WHEN WILL YOU EMBARK ON YOUR SCHEME?" SARRLEVI ASKED AS I took the freeway exit for Lynnwood.

"Tomorrow night. That's when the party is."

"I will attend to ensure you are safe."

I eyed him sidelong, noting the sweat gleaming on his forehead, his hands clasped tightly against his thighs, fingers digging in as he sought to retain his control. "I appreciate the sentiment, but I don't think you can pass as a plumber right now."

Why I'd said *right now*, I didn't know.

"I will not attempt to do so, but I will be there."

"Lurking in the background in a stalkerly fashion?"

"To protect you from enemies, yes."

I wrestled with being pleased he cared and worried he would screw everything up. In his current state, he might overreact to someone putting a hand on my arm. And, as he'd already proven, he could barely recognize *me* once he got riled up in battle mode.

"There's a powerful barrier around the property, remember." I turned off 196th and toward my neighborhood, passing kids riding bikes and throwing footballs, and wished *my* life were that normal. “That’s why we have to do the ruse, so they’ll lower it to let us in to fix things.”

“I am aware. I will find a way in.”

Sarrlevi sounded confident, but if it were that easy, we could have sneaked in *without* the ruse. I didn’t argue though. Maybe Val and I, once inside, could find whatever device maintained the barrier and turn it off. Then Sarrlevi could slip in more easily.

Though I wasn’t positive I *wanted* him there. If all went according to plan, Val and I would get answers, not a fight.

But—as I admitted with a rueful snort—when did things ever go to plan?

Abruptly, Sarrlevi leaned forward. His eyes pointed in the direction of my house, though we hadn’t yet turned down my street.

“*She* is here,” he growled.

“She who? Barothla?”

“Yes.” Sarrlevi jerked a hand from his thigh to wrap around the hilt of one of his swords.

“She’s not hiding herself?” I couldn’t yet sense anyone magical in the area but didn’t doubt that he did.

“No.”

“Well, that already rings alarm bells in my mind.”

I slowed the truck as we neared the corner where I had, weeks earlier, attacked my aunt. Then I also sensed her, either standing in my yard or in my house. So much for the protective wards. She’d probably flicked a hand and strode right past them.

I didn’t sense Tinja and hoped that meant she was at the work site, not that Barothla had done something to her.

“We will be careful,” Sarrlevi said, his voice raspy with a disturbing mix of hatred, anticipation, and craziness. What if he lost control of himself and killed her before we could get his cure? And learn the location of his mother?

"Do you know how to do that, right now?" I stopped the truck, not yet making the turn onto my street.

Sarrlevi turned fiery eyes toward me. Already, the warmth—and even the recognition—from earlier was fading.

"Continue." He pointed in the direction of my house.

"Do you have a plan? We should have a plan to face her, don't you think?"

Sarrlevi snarled, thrust open the door, and leaped out.

"That is *not* the plan I had in mind," I said as he ran toward the house.

He wasn't camouflaging himself. Did he realize that? Or had he lost the capacity to conjure that magic or even worry about it?

Camouflage, I told him telepathically, in case he would obey, then parked by a bush.

I rubbed my own camouflage charm, something I should have done as soon as we'd driven off the freeway. By now, Barothla knew we were here. But if she didn't know exactly where I was, maybe that would help.

Hammer in hand, I leaped out and ran toward my house.

We might have a fight on our hands, Sorka, I told the weapon.

I am prepared. Do not let her take me.

I'm not planning on it.

Sarrlevi's angry voice arose from the yard, the words in Elven.

Trying not to let my feet pound loudly on the pavement, I ran up the sidewalk until they came into view. Barothla stood in my driveway with her meaty arms crossed over her chest and a powerful barrier around her. As she had the last time I'd seen her, she wore the one-handed hammers in sheaths attached to a belt on her hips, a belt that also held numerous pouches. Alchemical things she could throw at us, no doubt. Was it possible the cure for Sarrlevi's affliction was in one of them?

Once more, Barothla wore that awful red nail polish. Why,

because she wanted to scratch *me*? It wasn't as if she needed to gouge Sarrlevi again.

He prowled around her, then sprang in with his swords and attempted to cut through her barrier. The magic of his aura crackled, as powerful as ever but wild and erratic. I couldn't tell if he was trying to conjure an attack or simply spitting magic like a faulty electrical outlet.

He was definitely spitting curses, or maybe demands. Since he continued to speak in Elven, I couldn't understand him.

Could Barothla? She stood calmly in the face of his attacks, not bothering to turn to keep an eye on him as he circled her in the driveway. In the past, he'd been her equal—or more—in magic and had been able to rip down her barrier to grab her. Now, he couldn't get through, even with his magical weapons. She had a trick up her sleeve.

Better make your demands telepathically so she can understand, I told Sarrlevi as I crept warily toward Barothla.

The wards along the sides and back of my property remained, emanating faint magic that I could sense, but the ones along the sidewalk out front were down. Ripped away by her powerful magic.

At least the front door stood closed, with no obvious damage done to the house. Yet.

With my charm activated, Barothla shouldn't have sensed me, but she looked in my direction. Not vaguely in my direction but straight at me. A few trinkets embedded in her armor glowed. Had she found something to let her see through magical camouflage?

Where's Sarrlevi's mother? I asked her telepathically, though I didn't expect her to answer my questions without a truth drug in her system.

As she stared coolly at me without replying, I groped for a plan. Behind her, Sarrlevi backed up a couple of steps and leveled one of his swords at her. The magical beam I'd seen his weapon conjure before shot out of the tip, aiming for her head.

I opened my mouth to warn him not to launch deadly attacks, but her barrier deflected the beam. It bounced toward a neighbor's yard and sliced through the top of a tree. The trunk broke off and dropped fifty feet, obliterating part of a wood fence.

Varlesh, stop, I said. *That's not working, and I live in this neighborhood. I don't want it destroyed.*

Seething, he didn't look over at me, didn't acknowledge me at all. Again, he yelled at her in Elven. Demanding to know what Barothla had done with his mother, I wagered, but I wasn't sure. There wasn't any sanity in his eyes. He might have been ranting about wanting to kill her.

What do you want? I asked Barothla, thinking she might answer that question. She wouldn't have come to Earth because she wanted to stand in my driveway and be attacked all day.

This. She smirked at me.

I waited for her to show me something or say what *this* was, but she only continued to smirk.

The temptation to rush in and swing my hammer at her face surged through me, but I halted at the head of the driveway. One of Sarrlevi's swords was Sorka's equal. If it couldn't get through her new and enhanced barrier, I doubted my hammer could either.

The haft warmed in my hand, a sense of indignation coming from Sorka but not disagreement.

Can you tell what she's added to her repertoire to make her barrier more powerful? I asked Sorka.

There is dragon magic here.

I swore. *Meaning she got an artifact made by dragons?*

Did dragons even make artifacts? They carried so much power with them, they hardly seemed to need tools or weapons, and I hadn't heard of many things that had been crafted with their magic.

Meaning she got a dragon. *He or she must be nearby. Camouflaged.*

How could she have gotten a dragon to help her? I peered around, as if I might spot one perched on the roof of my house. *And* why?

To protect her presumably.

It had to be more than that. That smug smirk promised Barothla was up to something more conniving.

Why did you take his mother, and what do you want now? I asked her again, willing my modest power to compel her to talk. Not that it would work. I was learning to enchant things, not interrogate people.

Barothla snorted, mentally batting away my attempt at compulsion. *I do not know what you're talking about. I am here on your world doing research for one of my experiments, and this mentally unbalanced assassin is attacking me without provocation.*

Oh, he's been provoked.

Sweat streamed from Sarrlevi's face, and he panted from all the effort he was expending. Before this, I'd never even seen him out of breath. He had to realize his attacks were futile, but he didn't stop. Or maybe he didn't realize anything. Maybe he was beyond rational thought.

She sends her telepathic words wide, Sorka said, *for any in the area to hear.*

At first, I thought that meant she wanted Sarrlevi to hear them, but no. If there was a dragon around, she had to want *it* to hear.

Realization struck, and before Barothla spoke again, I knew what she was up to. Cursing, I pulled my phone from my pocket to text Val.

You see what I was talking about. Barothla looked not toward me but toward the house across the street. Maybe the dragon was perched on the roof over *there*. A new for-sale sign was staked in that yard, promising my neighbors were moving away from my house for some odd reason. *This is what I've endured numerous times now.*

As Barothla continued, I texted Val to please send Zavryd to help with a dragon problem. But if the observing dragon was his sister or mother, I didn't know what he could—what he *would*—do. Even if it was a stranger, he might not care about dragon justice being carried out.

He is not only a conniving heartless killer who snubs his nose at dragon law, Barothla said to our invisible audience, *but he has descended into madness. He should be* killed *if not taken for punishment and rehabilitation by the wise dragons who rule over the Realms.*

"You total kiss ass," I spat, then, not sure if whatever dragon was watching understood English, switched to telepathy. *He's only crazy because you attacked him with a chemical thing that's making him mad. You did this on purpose because he wouldn't* murder *your sister—my* mother*—for you.*

As you say, he attacked me. Barothla flung an arm toward me, though she again looked across the street. *And so did you, mongrel bitch. Because you think if I'm gone and my dear sister is also gone, King Ironhelm will arrange for* you *to inherit the dwarven throne.*

Sarrlevi sprang at her again, trying to keep her from continuing, but she knew she was protected by dragon magic. She didn't even glance at him.

You're as deluded as he is, Barothla continued. *As dangerous and insane as all the vermin on this wild world. As the dragons well know.*

I hefted my hammer, wanting so badly to throw it, but her eyes glinted with triumph. That was what she wanted. To have me also act like a crazed maniac in front of the dragon.

Yanking the weapon down, I spun toward the house across the street. *I volunteered before, and I'll do so again. Mind scour me to learn the truth, to see that Barothla was the one to—*

Watch out, Sorka barked into my mind, wrapping a barrier around me.

Not a second too soon. A blast of Barothla's power struck it.

"No," Sarrlevi snarled, again hacking at Barothla's barrier but again thwarted.

Across the street, the air shimmered, and I abruptly sensed our dragon observer. Not perched on the roof in her native form but standing in the yard and shifted into a young human woman with purple hair and a black leather jacket.

Zondia'qareshi.

19

I didn't know whether to be relieved that we were dealing with a known dragon or not. Though Zondia had the face of a teenager, her eyes glowed with power, and her features were flinty. As she started across the street toward us, she glared icily at me, as if she thought I'd been scheming against her or maybe that I'd tricked her before.

Mind scour me to see the truth in my mind, I told her. *My aunt is the one who's plotting against her sister, and she poisoned Sarrlevi so that—*

Those two scheme together against the dwarves and the dragons, Barothla boomed telepathically, her words drowning out mine. *They should both be taken for punishment by the mighty Dragon Justice Court. Watch out!*

The last words startled me into looking back at her. I caught Barothla mouthing something as she pointed at Sarrlevi. His face twisted, as if he were trying his hardest to fight against the chemical compound addling his mind. Or maybe something else.

With a roar, Sarrlevi raised his swords and strode around Barothla and toward Zondia.

For a second, I could only stare in surprise. He wouldn't *attack* a dragon, would he? That would be suicide.

But as Barothla's smug smile grew, I knew without a doubt that she was manipulating him. Maybe with compulsion magic that he couldn't, in his current state, resist.

"Varlesh, no!" I lifted my hands and faced him.

He didn't even glance at me. Zondia halted in the street, wrapping power around herself, and Sarrlevi charged straight at her.

"No, damn it." Throwing myself at someone with two killer longswords raised was idiotic, but I didn't think, only reacted.

With my arms spread wide, I didn't attack, simply hoping to tackle Sarrlevi. I expected to smack into a defensive barrier and be thwarted, but, in his rage, he wasn't defending himself. I thumped against his side, wrapping my arms around him and trying to knock him to the ground.

But his reflexes were good even if his mind was shot, and he shifted his weight and braced himself, barely taking a step when my body struck his.

"Don't do this," I blurted, tightening my arms around him, barely keeping from clubbing him with the hammer that I wouldn't let go of.

His steps slowed but only for a moment. He roared and flung me aside, one of his blades nicking my arm. Pain lanced through me, and I might have released him even if he hadn't overpowered me.

Don't attack the dragon, I yelled into his mind as I stumbled away, again trying to will my magic to make the words powerful, to override Barothla's manipulation. A blast of power from the side sent me flying. Barothla.

Sorka's barrier had dropped, probably because it had needed to so I could hug Sarrlevi, and the dwarven magic hurled me into the street. Zondia glanced at me as I flew past her but only for a second before returning her focus to Sarrlevi.

He stood a few feet from her with his blades raised, but he'd halted mid-step. Had my words made a difference?

Don't attack the dragon, I repeated, twisting and trying to land on my feet. Sorka restored our barrier. My momentum took me into a parked car, and I bounced off.

You see how he seethes at you and intends to attack, Barothla yelled telepathically. Did she sound the least bit frazzled? Afraid that her plan wasn't working?

Though I knew he would have hated it in a saner moment, I landed in a crouch and again concentrated on influencing Sarrlevi. *The dragon isn't your enemy. Don't let Barothla control you. Get ahold of yourself, please.*

His lips rippled, tendons standing out in his neck, as he attempted to obey. But Barothla yanked her hammers off her belt and ran up behind him.

Look out, I yelled, though he was already turning to meet her, protective magic wrapping around him.

Their respective barriers sparked as they clashed together, power writhing in the air between them. Zondia stood still, eyes slitted as she watched, as if she hadn't yet decided what to do. Her power still wreathed Barothla, however, keeping Sarrlevi's blades from reaching her.

Lady Zondia'qareshi, I said as respectfully as I could. *Please stop helping the princess. She schemes against Sarrlevi, tried to have her own sister killed, and deliberately infected Sarrlevi's mother with a deadly disease. All because she wants to be in line to inherit the throne.*

You speak against an ally of mine, half-dwarf, Zondia said, not glancing at me, instead watching Barothla hammer at Sarrlevi's defenses, trying to use the extra dragon power to her advantage. *I doubt your words, though... the elf* is *oddly unstable.*

Yes. Because of her. I shared the memory of Barothla clawing Sarrlevi with her red nails as he gripped her.

Zondia looked coolly at me. *It looks like she defended herself.*

Hell, I should have picked a different memory. *He's defending his* mother. *Can't you mind scour her and see all the horrible things she's responsible for?*

Even as I asked, I knew the answer might be no. Sarrlevi had said dwarves had mental resistance that could keep even dragons from easily reading their thoughts.

Though compromised, Sarrlevi deflected all of Barothla's attacks and was clearly the superior warrior, but he couldn't get through the dragon barrier to reach her. In addition to swinging her hammers, Barothla started throwing things at the ground—vials that wafted smoky chemicals into the air. Would they get through *Sarrlevi's* beleaguered barrier? Either because he was weary or the chemical ruined his ability to concentrate, it kept wavering.

He coughed, tears leaking from his eyes as he fought. A gem gleamed on Barothla's armor—some protection against the noxious odors?—and she was unaffected.

I strode toward the battle, intending to help. If Zondia could assist Barothla, I could surely assist Sarrlevi.

But the dragon disagreed. With a great blast of power, she knocked me flying again. Even though Sorka's barrier remained around me, it couldn't keep me from sailing across the yard, bouncing off the side of my house, and landing in a flower bed. Thanks to the hammer's protection, the attack didn't hurt, but it left me flummoxed. What more could I do?

Barothla's pouches clinked and jangled as she jumped around, swinging her hammers. I wanted so badly to rummage through the contents and find the cure for Sarrlevi that I hoped she carried.

I eyed the metal clasp of her belt. Everything in the pouches was magical, but *it* wasn't. If she weren't protected by that barrier, I might have used the enchanting magic I'd learned to manipulate it into corroding.

But did the barrier extend into the ground? Or could I, just as I was planning with my plumbing sabotage, come up from below?

Maybe if she stood still…

Where is she? Sarrlevi cried telepathically. *You kidnapped my mother from the elves. Where did you take her?*

Yes, I thought. *Make it clear to the dragon that Barothla is the criminal here.*

Abruptly, the sweating Sarrlevi whirled away from Barothla. I didn't hear whatever mental words she compelled him with, but, once more, he raised his swords and charged toward Zondia.

Barothla lowered her arms. Her chest heaved as she caught her breath; for the moment, she stood still.

Zondia wrapped power around herself, the barrier too much for Sarrlevi's swords to break through. When he'd once dueled with Zavryd in human form, he'd gotten through Zavryd's defenses, but he couldn't do so now. Either Zondia was more powerful or Sarrlevi's powers were diminished.

Though I was terrified for him and how Zondia would lash out in response, I focused on sending my power through the ground toward Barothla, toward her belt buckle.

You dare strike at a dragon, elf? Zondia roared telepathically.

I wanted to defend him, but I dared not call attention to myself. For the moment, nobody was looking in my direction. My power wrapped around Barothla's belt buckle, and, with the same magic I'd used in the vision where I'd freed my mother from a cage, I willed the metal to warp on the molecular level. To lose its strength.

As she'd done against me, Zondia lashed out, and Sarrlevi flew down the street.

You are right, dwarf princess, Zondia told Barothla. *He has lost his sanity. I will take him to the Justice Court, but he may be too far gone to rehabilitate.*

Barothla lifted her chin. *Then he must be killed. For the safety of the Realms.*

Again, I had to fight to concentrate and not yell out a defense.

After twisting in the air, Sarrlevi came down lightly on his feet, facing Zondia. He paused, and magic swelled about him, intense concentration in his eyes. For a few seconds, he managed to focus the power that had been swirling chaotically around him, and he tore at Zondia's defenses.

To my surprise, he ripped away her barrier. It must have surprised her too, for she jerked around, raising her hands and transforming into a dragon. A form in which she would be more powerful.

With a final flick of my magic, I broke Barothla's belt clasp.

Knowing she would sense it loosen right away, I hefted my hammer and threw it at her.

With Zondia distracted, the extra power in Barothla's barrier ought to have disappeared. I willed Sorka to puncture what remained, to smack into her back.

Sarrlevi threw one of his own weapons. The sword hurtled hilt over point through the air and, even as Zondia finished transforming into a huge lilac dragon that took up the street and more, it sank deeply into her shoulder. She screeched in pain as the magical blade cut through scale and lodged in flesh.

Shit. She was going to kill him.

My hammer pierced Barothla's barrier and landed as I'd envisioned, striking her in the back. Unprepared, she went sprawling, her belt falling off as she tumbled across the driveway.

"*Vishgronik!*" I barked as I ran toward my hammer. Telepathically, I told Sarrlevi, *Stop attacking her and get out of here. Please, Varlesh.*

He already had halted. Maybe because I'd knocked out Barothla's concentration—and her compulsion on him—when I'd sent her flying.

Horror flashed in his eyes as Zondia snapped her fanged jaws down to bite his sword and tear it free from her shoulder. As she flung the bloody weapon into the street, he realized what he'd done.

Get out of here! I yelled again at him as my hammer returned to my grip.

Rage twisted Barothla's face as she climbed to her feet. Whether she had noticed she'd lost her belt, I didn't know, but she hurled a wave of power at me. Sorka's barrier protected me, the attack parting around it and instead hitting my house. Siding and shreds of elven repair vines flew.

"Damn it," I snarled.

Barothla reached for her hip, the belt that wasn't there, and her eyes grew round with surprise. But she didn't hesitate for long, reaching into a pocket instead. She pulled out several vials and threw them, not right at me but at the driveway and walkway near me. The glass shattered and spewed smoke and fumes into the air.

I growled, wanting to stalk toward Barothla and club her again, but the haze, quickly billowing to cover the driveway and spreading into the yard, made me pause.

In the street, Sarrlevi risked lunging closer to the dragon to pick up his sword. Roaring, Zondia stalked toward him.

Run, please, I told him. *I can handle this.*

If I could have formed a portal myself, I would have, then thrust him through it. He lifted his weapons and faced Zondia, but she paused and looked toward the sky. Sarrlevi did too.

I sensed Zavryd coming. Though I didn't know if he would be able to stop this, or if he would side with his sister against Sarrlevi, I felt some relief. Maybe he could deescalate the situation.

Then I sensed Barothla running toward the driveway—toward her belt—and my relief disappeared. Maybe she had something valuable in it, and she wanted to get it back. But if the cure was there, I needed it.

Risking the smoke, I also ran toward the belt. At the same time, I hurled my hammer toward Barothla's chest.

This time, she anticipated the blow and shifted her power around to harden the barrier in front of her. When the hammer struck, it didn't get through. But the throw bought me time. I dove, rolling across the cement as acrid fumes tore at my nostrils, eyes, and mouth, and grabbed her belt.

Barothla cursed at me in Dwarven, but Zavryd was flying closer.

As I rolled into the yard, trying to get away from Barothla and that awful smoke, she glanced uneasily toward the sky. She waved an arm, summoning magic, and a portal formed behind her.

Another portal formed in the street. Zondia, head whipping on her long neck, snapped toward Sarrlevi.

Before she reached him, he dove backward, disappearing through the portal he'd made.

Seconds before Zavryd arrived, Barothla jumped through the portal *she'd* made.

Zavryd landed on the roof of my house. In the street, Zondia roared in fury.

I flopped on my back in the grass, Barothla's belt clasped to my chest. With two angry dragons looming, I had no idea if I was safe.

20

THE MAGICAL BARRIER AROUND ME FADED, AND I SAT UP, HOPING that meant I was safe. At the least, Sorka ought to believe I was safe.

A screech of pain and fury from Zondia left me uncertain about that.

Once more, magic swelled nearby. An imminent attack?

Cursing, I marshaled my battered muscles and leaped to my feet. The cut on my arm from Sarrlevi's sword hurt more than the rest of my body, but I didn't blame him for that. I hoped he'd gotten away and was safe.

Zondia wasn't readying an attack; she'd made a portal, a huge one that hovered over the street. In the house opposite mine, the curtains stirred, and I caught the neighbor gaping out. *Hopefully*, the dragons were camouflaged from mundane humans, but even if they were, watching Sarrlevi, Barothla and me fight had to have been odd to witness.

Without any final words that might have warned me what she thought about me, Zondia sprang into the air and flew through the portal.

Only when it disappeared and quiet descended on the neighborhood did I realize that Zavryd wasn't alone on the roof. His long black-scaled neck extended over the yard, and he gazed blandly down at me, but it was Val, who rode on his back, that I looked to.

I love it when he lands on elevated things, she told me, sliding off his back.

At least it's a one-story house. Focusing on him, I asked, *Uhm, Lord Zavryd, where did your sister go?*

She is capable of ascertaining where portals lead, even after they've disappeared. She will continue her mission to capture the assassin and take him before the Dragon Justice Court.

I swore. I wasn't surprised that my words—my pleas—hadn't swayed Zondia, but I hadn't thought she would be able to follow Sarrlevi. What if he'd gone back to his home, the mountain chalet with the cheese cellar, and led her straight to it? What if she *destroyed* it in an effort to capture him?

"Will you take me after her?" I looked from Zavryd to Val and back—*he* was the only one who could, the one I'd have to convince. "You know what's happening to him, right? Val and Zoltan told you? It's not his fault that he's going mad."

He attacked a dragon, Zavryd stated implacably even as Val gave me a sympathetic look and swung down from the roof to land on the walkway. *That is inexcusable under any circumstances and must be punished.*

"It's not his fault. You *know* it's not. My bitch of an aunt poisoned him with that brain stuff. And she compelled him to attack your sister."

"It's true, Zav," Val said. "I told you about it. What's up with your sister showing up here anyway?"

I resisted the urge to demand the same and say Zondia *wouldn't* have been attacked if she hadn't butted in. I had to be calm and reasonable so I didn't piss off Zavryd too. If only that were my forte...

"Yes, she was backing up Barothla in a fight that *Barothla* picked," I told him. "Look at where we are. *My house.* She was waiting here, knowing we would show up, and setting a trap. Barothla had Zondia skulking over there, watching everything as she *goaded* Sarrlevi into attacking. And it only worked because of the chemical compound." I shook out my stinging arm, then held it up to Zavryd. "He attacked *me* too, even though he cares about me. She's making him crazy."

Was that what Barothla had planned all along? Or at least since she'd successfully slashed him with her nails? She must have known he would be too crazy to complete his mission for her, but had she wanted to take the opportunity to get rid of him forever? To see him killed—or punished and mind-wiped—by the dragons? And had she only taken his mother to ensure he would come after her? So she could set everything up with a dragon spying nearby?

I understand there is no cure for the madness that afflicts his brain, Zavryd stated, irritatingly calm. What did *he* care about Sarrlevi? *You are fortunate he did not kill you. If the Dragon Justice Court also cannot thwart the disease, it may be better that he be killed. With madness twisting his mind, he would not be a candidate for rehabilitation.*

"There *is* a cure." I turned to Val and thrust out the purloined belt. "I got her belt, all her pouches and vials."

"There's a remedy in there?" Val asked.

"I'm sure of it."

"But you don't know."

"Barothla wouldn't be traveling around the Cosmic Realms with that horrible nail paint—the delivery mechanism—on her own fingers if she didn't have a cure." I'd been certain when I'd shared that logic with Sarrlevi, and I was still certain, but Val and

Zavryd exchanged long looks, as if they pitied my naivety. Meanwhile, Zondia might be thrashing Sarrlevi on another world.

"Val can take the whole belt to Zoltan so he can figure out which vial has the cure." I waved it, and a couple of items in the pouches clinked faintly, though most sounded insulated. "And Lord Zavryd can take me to stop his sister from ruthlessly slaying an elf who doesn't deserve that fate."

If she catches up to him, she will take him to the Dragon Justice Court, Zavryd said. *She will not slay him.*

After watching her shriek in rage with that sword wound in her shoulder, I didn't believe him. Even if her mission was to capture Sarrlevi, I worried she might arrange an accident. I also didn't know how good he would be at evading her with his mind addled. He'd been lucky to make that portal and escape at all.

"We'll both take her stuff to Zoltan." Val waved at the belt. "He can try to figure out if there's a cure while we finalize our plans for the mission tomorrow."

"But Sarrlevi—"

"Do you know where he went?" Val raised her eyebrows.

"I have an idea. Jiaga."

She looked at Zavryd.

That is the name of a wild world, he said. *An entire planetary body. Unless you know of a more precise location on it, we would not be able to locate him.*

"The mountains. He has a home there."

There are mountains all over the planet.

"Snowy mountains?"

Zavryd gave Val that pitying look again.

"If you can't track him down, can't you communicate with your sister and ask her where she went?"

Even a dragon cannot communicate with another dragon across the stars. We must be on the same world.

"Let's go to Jiaga, and you can chat her up then." I beamed a hopeful smile up at him, though I wanted to grab his scaled neck and shake it and *force* him to take me. "I'll buy you some ribs as a thank-you."

I expected some dragon salivation, but his nostrils flared, and he jerked his head up, looking to the west.

"Let's just get these vials to Zoltan to check out." Val hefted the belt. "Sarrlevi is a tough guy. He can take care of himself."

"Not right now, he can't." I shook my head bleakly. "He needs me."

Xilnethgarish. Zavryd said the name like a curse.

A moment later, I also sensed the dragon flying over the rooftops in this direction. And were those the auras of Artie and Hennehok on his back? Maybe *they* could take me to Jiaga.

Not waiting for them to come into view, I attempted to project telepathic words to them. *Hey, guys. Can I get a ride to Jiaga, please? A friend is in need of help.*

Matti? came Artie's response from the distance. They were still a mile away. *We have found clues that might indicate we're close to finding the base used by the organization that has your parents.*

I rocked back. Normally, I would be delighted by the news, but... Sarrlevi.

That's great, I made myself say. And it was.

Yes, but the area is shrouded in magic and well-protected. Xilnethgarish sensed that another dragon had been there and was responsible for the magic. We're not positive it is the right place, but it's worth investigating. We came to seek help.

Which I'm sure Zavryd and Val will give, and I definitely will too, but can you take me to Jiaga first?

What is on Jiaga? Xilneth boomed into my mind.

My ally Sarrlevi is ill and being unfairly chased by the dragon Zondia.

Zondia'qareshi is there? Xilneth replied, not mentioning

Sarrlevi. *Many moons have passed since I serenaded her with the joyous and beautiful songs of my clan.*

I blinked.

Zavryd, who'd apparently been included in the conversation, stood on all fours, his tail going rigid as his talons dug into my roof. *You worthless lust-filled cracked egg of a dragon,* he called to Xilneth, shingles tumbling free and falling into the grass. *I have forbidden you from courting my sister.*

But she *hasn't forbidden it,* Xilneth replied smugly.

Though I cared nothing for dragon *courting,* I hurried to say, *I'm sure she's on Jiaga. Please, will you take me there? I'll, uh, tell Zondia how handsome you are.* I couldn't imagine that working, but if Xilneth was serenading Zondia, maybe she would be too distracted to raze Sarrlevi's house.

I will take you, mongrel dwarf. Yes, you will speak my praises to her. This will work, will it not? Females are influenced by other females, even diminutive females from lesser species.

Yeah, I've got all kinds of influence. I waved my hammer in invitation since the green dragon had flown into view.

No, Zavryd boomed. *I forbid it.*

More shingles tumbled free as he flexed his talons. My poor house was not having a good year.

As Xilneth landed on the roof across the street, a portal formed in the air several meters off the ground. *Come, mongrel.* He levitated Artie and Hennehok off his back and into the street.

What about the hideout and the other dragon? Artie asked.

Gather allies so that we may assail it, Xilneth said. *In the meantime, I will see if Zondia'qareshi wishes to join us in the battle.*

She does not, Zavryd said. *Friend of my mate, do not go with this fool. He will leave you in another realm at the first distraction.*

"I don't have much of a choice," I muttered and waved at the belt. "Be careful with that, Val. At least some of that stuff is strong enough to burn the beard off a dwarf."

Her eyebrows rose, and she gripped it more gingerly. "That's at least not something I have to worry about."

"You might look funny without eyebrows."

"True. Come back to the house when you're done. If they figured out where the hideout is, maybe we don't have to go through with the party."

"You're not looking forward to being my plumbing assistant?"

"I'm not looking forward to wearing a dress." Her nose crinkled, and she stepped back as Xilneth's power wrapped around me and he levitated me into the air and toward the roof.

"Thanks, Val." I waved to her and did my best to ignore the fuming Zavryd.

Going by the way he and Xilneth were glowering at each other from the rooftops, I wagered they were still throwing telepathic insults.

As I landed astride Xilneth's back, the neighbor crept out of his house. He might not have been able to see the dragons, but I had little doubt he'd seen me float past his window. After glancing left and right—he didn't think to look up—and over at Val, he darted toward the street. No, toward the for-sale sign next to the street. He taped a piece of paper with writing in black marker on it.

Price reduced! All offers considered!

If I ever managed to fix my life and resolve everything, I might still have to move out of my neighborhood.

With me aboard, Xilneth opened his maw and stuck his tongue out before swooping toward the portal. Zavryd hissed like a snake. The neighbor ran back into his house, the door slamming loudly behind him.

We disappeared through the portal, my hammer clutched in my grip as reality blurred and distorted, time turning dreamlike and strange until we arrived on a frigid world that immediately had me tucking my hands under my armpits. Snowy mountains far below made my insides churn, and I squeezed my thighs against Xilneth's scales, willing my magic to keep me secured.

I am calling across the world to Zondia'qareshi, Xilneth informed me after flying a few lazy circles over the peaks. *I do not sense her in the immediate area.*

What happens if you call and she doesn't want to answer? Though I could only speak telepathically to nearby people, I had no idea how it worked for dragons and what limitations they had.

Oh, she always answers when I call.

Because she adores your singing?

She does *adore my singing, but she usually calls me a worthless fool who should learn to contribute more to the Realms.*

So she's playing hard-to-get, huh? Trying not to think about how high we were, and how horrific a death I would experience if I fell, I peered at the mountainsides. There was no way we would have lucked into coming out above Sarrlevi's chalet, but I couldn't help but hope to be that fortunate. By now, wasn't I due some luck?

Precisely. But she is not responding. I do not believe she is on this world.

I slumped. It had taken too long for me to find a ride. What if she'd already come, caught Sarrlevi, and left?

Do you know anywhere else she might have gone? Xilneth also sounded disappointed by her absence. No doubt, he'd already selected a song to croon at her.

I sighed. *Maybe the Dragon Justice Court.*

Or some other world. It was possible Sarrlevi *hadn't* come here.

Oh, distasteful. Something like a shudder went through Xilneth.

You don't like your own dragon court?

Certainly not. Do you *like the Human Justice Court?*

I thought about saying we didn't have such a thing but got his point.

My clan, the Starsingers, have few perches on the Dragon Council, and we are not much involved in the rule of the Cosmic Realms. Our opinions matter little to other dragons.

It would have been better to hold out for a ride from Zavryd, who didn't fear trips to the Dragon Justice Court, not when his mom was in charge of it. But would he have given me that ride? I didn't know. He didn't care about Sarrlevi. None of the others did. I shook my head. It wasn't fair.

It is unpleasantly cold here for dragons, Xilneth said.

Half-dwarves too. A frosty wind had me wondering if I could stuff anything else in my armpits for warmth.

Where do you wish to go, mongrel?

It's Matti, and... back to Earth, I guess. I looked sadly toward the gray sky and white mountain peaks, silently apologizing to Sarrlevi for leaving him on his own again. *To Val's house, if you can.*

The lair of a Stormforge dragon is almost as distasteful as the canyon presided over by the Dragon Justice Court.

Are you sure? He and Val have a hot tub and a sauna.

I have not been invited to partake in the human amenities. Xilneth formed another portal.

As we returned to Earth, I worried I wouldn't see Sarrlevi again.

21

As the sun set, casting shadows from the trees in the Medina neighborhood, Val and I sat in the cab of my truck, the toilet decal firmly affixed to the side. We were tucked in a private driveway two houses away from Hart's, facing the street and watching as luxury cars passed, some heading to the party.

The owners of the home behind us appeared to be gone. I hoped nobody showed up and wondered why a plumber was waiting in their driveway. In a few more minutes, I would attempt my pipe sabotage.

Val's phone buzzed, and my heart sped up as Zoltan's name flashed on the screen.

After Xilneth had returned me to Val's house the night before, Zavryd driving him off before I'd gotten a good explanation about the evidence of a lair that Xilneth, Artie, and Hennehok had found, I'd found Zoltan examining the contents of Barothla's belt. Never had I envisioned a vampire rubbing his hands gleefully together and *ooh*ing and *ahh*ing, at least not over something less than an exotic vein to be sampled.

He hadn't been excited because he knew exactly which vial

was the solution to Sarrlevi's problem—he'd been quick to point out that he didn't know if *any* of them were—but because he had the opportunity to examine the formulas of a master alchemist from another world. The last I'd heard, he'd stayed up all night, which was usual, *and* all day, which was not.

"What's up, Zoltan?" Val answered.

"What's *down*, you should ask, dear robber."

"Uh, okay." Val looked at me and rolled her eyes. "What's down?"

"My prices for your delightful acquaintance who has liberated so many fine formulas for me to examine. Many of these vials contain compounds I've never *seen* before."

"I bet Matti would be delighted if you just gave her samples of your truth drugs for free," Val said.

I nodded, hand straying to two vials of the formula in the pocket of the plumber overalls that I wore over the black dress I'd opted for in case I needed to blend in and mingle—God forbid. I would fit in with these people like a tarantula in a cage of hairless rabbits.

"Free?" Zoltan asked. "Dear robber, I said I would *lower* my prices, not *give* away my valuable wares. After all, the ingredients cannot be acquired for free."

"Twenty bucks says you're the richest person living in the house. You can afford to give away freebies."

"I'm well-monied *because* I don't consider such foolish notions. Do tell your voluptuously veined comrade that I am making progress on determining which formulations cause deleterious effects to the magical compound in my Petri dishes."

"Wouldn't there only be one compound that would do anything?" I asked.

"I have only so many sample dishes," Zoltan said, "and it takes time to assess whether the chemical compound is affected. It is not some laboratory mouse that starts thrashing about when unpleasant reagents are sprinkled on it."

"Thanks for the imagery," Val muttered.

"One who beheads foes should not quail over such minor details," Zoltan said.

"I don't behead people. You're thinking of Sarrlevi. Let us know when you've got a cure."

"Certainly. There is no need for such impatience. *Your* rates, dear robber, remain unaffected."

"Imagine my shock." Val hung up and stuck her phone in her pocket. "We should probably get going before the people who live here come home." She tilted her head toward the house behind us.

"Give me a minute."

Closing my eyes, I used my senses to track the water pipe from the street to the house, attempting to follow it after it branched to the kitchen and various bathrooms inside. I wanted a bathroom near a common area on the main floor, one guests would likely use. There.

I could also sense the barrier around the property, ensuring the wrought-iron gate in the fence would keep out even the strongest of magical strangers, but, as Sarrlevi had suggested, it didn't extend far underground. Much as I'd willed my magic to rise up from below to tinker with my aunt's belt clasp, I could send tendrils of it upward through the pipes and into the bathroom.

First, I manipulated the vent pipe, hoping a few unpleasant sewer odors would waft back into the house. Then, I used my magic to block the drain so the toilet would overflow the next time it flushed. An adjustment to the tank would ensure it *kept* overflowing. Finally, I crimped the shutoff valve so the staff wouldn't be able to turn off the water flowing to the toilet. Someone might think to cut it off to the entire house, but that would likely be a last resort.

I wished I could guarantee that a guest or the staff would do some serious business to make a real mess, but an overflowing toilet alone ought to be cause for mortification at a party full of fancy rich people. Hell, I'd be mortified if my *non*-fancy work buddies were over for a barbecue and bathroom shenanigans happened.

"Okay," I said, drawing my magic back. If any artifact inside had detected my tinkering, I wasn't aware of it. "I'm done. Now we just have to wait for someone to use the facilities. The call afterward should be prompt." I drew my phone out and waved it, the temporary number I'd grabbed forwarded to it.

"Aren't you worried about being recognized when we show up at their door?" Val asked. "This guy probably had a picture of you to give to the assassins."

I took what was formerly a Mariners cap and now read *Dalton's Plumbing* off the dash and plopped it on my head, tugging the bill low to shade my eyes.

"Oh, yeah. You're an entirely different person now."

"The Clark Kent effect." I shrugged. "I doubt Hart will be the one to answer. It'll be his staff, and they probably don't know anything about the people he's hired assassins to kill."

I *was* prepared to be recognized, but as long as we got through the magical barrier first, it didn't matter. If we had to fight, so be it. One way or another, I would find an opportunity to question the guy. I tapped the vials in my pocket to reassure myself the truth drug was still there.

"You think he arranges such things himself?" Val asked.

"Considering it's a heinous crime to have people murdered, probably."

"What if he does open the door?" Val asked. "Weber, the rich guy I had to spy on, did for me."

"Were you there as a plumber or the Ruin Bringer?"

"As myself."

"An important person he invited personally to his home?"

"I don't know about my importance, since I can't even get a discount on alchemy potions, but to be his bodyguard, yes. I do see your point."

"All we need is to get in."

"Just to reiterate what Willard told me, we can't start beating up Hart's guests. Or him. These aren't trolls and orcs at the Warts and Wands Pub."

"Oh, I'm beating up Hart."

"Matti..." Val eyed me. "Just put the drug in his drink and lure him off for a chat."

"A chat with my hands around his neck."

"You've been spending too much time with Sarrlevi."

"Not as much as I'd like." I stared at my phone, willing it to ring.

"Don't do anything criminal. Willard also reminded me that if you get arrested, she doesn't have any pull in the civilian world."

I didn't point out that we were embroiled in a scheme to trespass on someone's property, a criminal activity, and that she'd agreed to help. She might retract her offer.

"I can't believe you're doing this in your own truck," Val added. "Why didn't you get a rental?"

"A rental would still be tied to me." I *had* artfully smeared dirt and oil over the license plates to make them hard to read. We'd been lucky not to be pulled over on the way here.

"You could have stolen something."

"I like how you warn me not to criminally beat people up in one breath, then suggest I should have started the night with larceny in the next."

"*Light* larceny. We could have returned the van afterward."

The phone rang, a number I didn't recognize, and I pounced. Only as I lifted it to say, "Dalton's Plumbing," did I worry that such promptness might be suspicious, especially since it was after regular business hours.

"Uhm, Matti?" a familiar voice asked.

"Zadie? This isn't your number."

"I know. It's been a long day full of calls, and my phone died, so I'm using the other agent's. There's a new house being listed that I wanted to tell you about."

"This isn't a good time, and Abbas and I are going to be busy on the building project for a while anyway. We're not looking for anything else yet."

"I wasn't thinking of it for your *business.*"

Though I was tempted to tell her this could wait until tomorrow, it wasn't as if I had anything else to do until the Hart household called. "Did you find a lakefront property that I can afford?"

"Not exactly. I found a beautiful old Victorian house in Green Lake that you could renovate. It has a *view* of the lake from a number of the rooms."

"Green Lake?" Val mouthed.

Zadie could have been describing *her* house.

"That also doesn't sound like something I could afford," I said.

"It's going to be coming on the market at a reduced price," Zadie said.

"Because it needs a *lot* of remodeling?"

"Yes, and the neighborhood isn't the best."

"A house in Green Lake with a view of the water isn't in a good neighborhood?" I asked skeptically. Oh, I knew the Highway 99 side wasn't as desirable, but the houses over there still went for a fortune if they had views. "Are there werewolves?"

"Well, the house across the street is known to be odd. Werewolves, vampires, zombies, and a weird chick with a sword frequent the place."

Val snorted. "Zombies, right. Try dragons."

"The owner of this property is listing it at a lower than typical price. Apparently, he also tried to sell it last fall, but some kind of battle broke out across the street while the potential buyers were doing the home inspection. Their car was dented and a window broken, and they withdrew their offer. That happened with a *few* offers. Now, he's just trying to sell quickly rather than holding out for top dollar."

"That neighborhood does sound fraught." I eyed Val—and the amused smile flirting with her lips. "Maybe I should wait for something to come up right on the water. Besides, I was thinking more Lake Washington than Green Lake. It's a quieter area. Maybe something by Matthews Beach."

"Those houses are out of your price range and on tiny narrow lots. Where would you and your roommate store all your tools and projects? This Green Lake house is on a big corner lot, and I think we could get the price down even more."

"But it's not on the water."

"Be realistic, Matti. You can't afford waterfront in Seattle."

"Are you supposed to quash my hopes and dreams in one breath and try to sell me a house in the next?"

"That's my job as your real-estate agent, yes. And waterfront isn't all it's cracked up to be. In addition to the tiny lots, you end up with goose poop all over the lawn."

"That does sound awful. Does the Victorian house have a turret?" I might have eyed Val's, and its view of the water, with longing.

"Of course it has a turret. I wouldn't try to sell you a substandard house, Matti."

"Just one located in a bad neighborhood."

"I've got news for you, girl. You're part of a bad neighborhood *now*. Do you know how many people on your street have put their houses up for sale this month?"

I sighed. "I saw the signs."

"For the greater good of Seattle, all you half-blood weirdos who are dating even bigger weirdoes should live on the same street."

That was probably true. Val, who was leaning her elbow against the door, her hand cradling her chin, kept listening to the conversation with vast amusement on her face.

"I'm not in the market this month, but send me the listing, I guess," I said.

"Will do."

I hung up and looked at Val. "Do you and your magical buddies feel bad about lowering property values in your neighborhood?"

"Nah. Seattle is an overpriced housing market. We're doing the people a service."

"The people who don't mind vampires, werewolves, and zombies shambling down the street at night?"

"They're dragons, not zombies, and they don't only come out at night." Val winked and waved at my phone. "No plumbing calls yet?"

"Not yet. I would have ditched Zadie instantly if another call had come in." I eyed the phone, willing it to ring, then looked at the street, remembering that we had to plan for the possibility that another plumber would be called in. If we had to waylay people, tie them up, and steal their van, I truly would be doing something criminal.

"Wearing a dress under overalls isn't that comfortable." Val shifted and stuck her hand through her neckline to make an adjustment.

"I know. My undies are crawling up my butt." I managed a smile for her, though distractions filled my mind. "Thanks for coming along, Val. I keep asking you for help. Someday, I hope I'll be able to help *you* with something."

"Oh, I'm sure Willard will scrounge up a mission for me where it would be useful to have the assistance of a half-dwarf enchanter.

And you're always welcome to come along to battle hydras with me. You're good in a fight."

"I'm not sure how good I'd be against nine heads attacking simultaneously."

"The secret is to get them tangled up with each other."

"I'll keep that in mind. I really do mean it. If you ever want help, let me know."

Val smirked. "You could help by moving in across the street and keeping some innocent *normal* person from being afflicted by my housemates and houseguests. *You* wouldn't bat an eye if a fairy ring activated in the middle of the night."

"Probably not. Would Zavryd crush my mailbox with his tail when he lands?" I wagered that was what had happened to the damaged car of the home buyer Zadie had mentioned.

"You might have to enchant it to resist mangling by dragon tails."

"Santiago hasn't taught me that enchantment yet."

"You'd think that would be Lesson One."

"In the Pacific Northwest, rust is a more frequent visitor than dragons. For *most* people."

That earned me another smirk.

Then my phone rang, another unfamiliar number, and I forgot the conversation. "Dalton's Plumbing."

"We have an incident with an overflowing toilet," a woman said—not Hart. Good. "Can you get someone out right away?"

Though I wanted to blurt a decisive, "*Yes!*" I reminded myself not to raise suspicion with overeagerness. "Yes, we have someone on call. We do charge a fifty-dollar after-hours fee in addition to our hourly rate."

"That's fine." She gave me her name, rather than Hart's, but it was the correct address.

"I'll dispatch someone right away."

"Can you give me the name, please?" she asked.

It was a perfectly normal question, and I knew many service businesses sent the name and face of the worker for security purposes, but I hadn't anticipated it and almost gave her a fake name. But someone might check IDs before letting us through the gate—and the magical barrier.

Val mouthed her own name. Right, she was further removed from all this. Val's photo wasn't likely on the wall in Hart's office with darts in it.

"Val Thorvald," I said. Since Val was more commonly known as the Ruin Bringer, I hoped nobody would recognize her surname. I also hoped the woman didn't also ask for a license number. Even though I *had* one, I'd never worked for anyone but my grandfather and didn't have it memorized.

"Thank you."

I hung up before she could ask anything else I wasn't prepared to answer.

"Guess I'm driving." Val waved for me to get out and change places with her.

Before, I'd been thinking of asking her to use her camouflage charm so that only I had to pass muster as a plumber, but that wouldn't work now.

"Yes." I handed her the other company cap I'd made. "But wait a few minutes. If we show up in thirty seconds, that'll be suspicious."

"Where's the business located?"

"Bellevue. We don't have to wait long." I switched sides with her, which involved rotating my hammer and her sword so they remained within our reach. I'd tossed a drop cloth over the weapons in case anyone peered in. My wrench-filled toolbox rested on the seat between us.

"Just so you know, in case the shit hits the fan," Val said, "Zav is over on the Olympic Peninsula, looking for the supposed lair that

Xilneth and your dwarf buddies found evidence of. It wouldn't take him long to get here, but it's not as close as Green Lake."

"I didn't expect his help at all, but thanks."

"While you're drugging the homeowner, I thought I'd try to find the artifact that maintains the barrier and knock it out. It's possible Zav is powerful enough to rip the barrier to shreds on his own, but if it's another tool that your mother made, it's possible he's not." Val tucked the end of her braid under her cap and adjusted her overalls again, making sure none of her dress showed through.

"Good plan." I also double-checked my outfit. "I would be tempted to wait and see if they find the hideout without the need for all this, but this might be our only chance to get to the world-traveling Hart anytime soon."

"Yeah, and our dragon allies might not be able to get in even if they *do* find it. In addition to whatever your mom can make, Xilneth sensed that another dragon had been in the area. That's going to make everything more complicated—and might explain why this organization has been so hard to find." She nodded in the direction of Hart's house. "This guy ought to have information on security systems—and security enchantments."

A dog walker who had passed going the other direction after we'd parked came back, eyeing our truck curiously. Because we'd been in the same driveway for a while? Or because we were sitting in the cab twiddling our thumbs?

The woman didn't stop, but I waved at Val, figuring we had better go. Things could fall apart once we were inside the barrier but not before. These people had been messing with me for months and imprisoning my mother for decades. It was time to get to the bottom of things, one way or another.

22

My heart skipped a few beats when we pulled up to the gate in Hart's driveway, and a guard with magical blood stood at a station tucked inside. A burly half-troll in a short-sleeve, button-down shirt, he gazed balefully at us. Or maybe... suspiciously?

I didn't know why, but I had assumed Hart's staff would be mundane humans. Neither Val nor I was camouflaged, since our ruse depended on actual plumbers showing up, which meant he could sense *our* magical blood as easily as we could his.

"Stay calm," Val murmured, rolling down her window. "Plumbers," she told the man.

I hoped he was bored. Since guests had already arrived, he must have passed numerous cars through already.

A camera leering from the guard shack made me want to pull my cap lower over my eyes.

"Name?" The man peered at her, then across at me, his brow furrowed.

He'd definitely noticed that we had magical blood. It wasn't that unusual to encounter those with elf or dwarf—or troll—

ancestry in the Seattle area, but it wasn't common either. And two such individuals working together might pluck at his Spidey senses.

"Val." She showed him her driver's license.

"Don't you have a work ID?" The guard frowned as he leaned against the side of the truck to look more thoroughly at us.

"I'm part-time and got called in last minute." Val rested a hand on his bare arm and smiled. "I understand this is an emergency."

"Uhm, yes." He looked at her hand on his arm, then to her face. In seconds, the suspicion in his eyes turned into speculation, if not outright lust. "Maybe it won't take long, and you can stop by on the way out."

I would have rolled my eyes, amazed that Val's sex appeal could come through even under the hat and unflattering overalls, but she was using her elven beauty for the good of my mission, so I had to cheer it on. I did wonder if her mate got jealous when she flirted with other guys. Maybe it was good that he was on the other side of Puget Sound tonight.

"Since this is a gated house," Val said, "I think that's a requirement."

"Uh, yeah. Are you really a plumber? You're really, uhm— You look good for a plumber."

"Part-time."

"What do you do the other part?"

She patted his arm. "Dancer."

Sword dancer, maybe.

"Come by the Lucky Strike tonight, and maybe I'll be there." Val trailed her fingers up his arm.

He licked his lips. "Like late? There's a party here tonight, so I gotta stay 'til midnight."

I scratched my jaw, wondering if Val could bat her eyelashes at him and he would spill all of his boss's secrets. Sadly, Hart probably didn't confide his megalomaniacal plans to take over the world—and kidnap dwarves—to his gate guard.

"Late." Val withdrew her hand.

His fingers lifted, as if to recapture it and put it back on his arm —or on something else—but a Bentley pulled up behind us. The guard leaned into the station and rested his hand on something magical on the wall. I couldn't see it, but I could sense it, and a faint pulse of orange light brightened his face momentarily. Val and I exchanged significant looks as we sensed the barrier lowering.

Clearing his throat, the guard said, "Go ahead. Service door is beside the garage."

"Thanks."

"The Lucky Strike, right?" he called after us as Val pulled through the gate.

"Yup."

"That's a bowling alley, isn't it?" I surveyed a manicured lawn with elaborate hedges and topiaries.

"There's a dance floor," Val said. "And they're open late on the weekends."

"I know bowling a few frames gets me in the mood to wiggle my bottom."

"I'll let Sarrlevi know in case he's looking for ideas for date night. Damn." Val was peering around too as she drove slowly up the wide driveway. "There's a ton of magic in this place."

"I noticed."

The barrier went back up, and I tried not to feel like we were trapped inside. Val and I were capable fighters, after all. We could handle whatever this place threw at us. And now we could get a better idea of what we were dealing with.

The grounds and the house emanated a lot of magic, enough that I would struggle to determine what individual items did.

Finding the artifact that powered the barrier wouldn't be easy. I was positive the doodad in the guard station, a magical item with a minimal aura, was only a switch. If we could sneak back out to the gate later, we might be able to turn *off* that switch, but it also might be keyed to the guard. It would be better to take out the artifact itself.

We passed an attendant waving cars toward parking spots between the detached garage and the six-bay main garage attached to the sprawling three-story marble and white brick house. He pursed his lips in disapproval at my truck meandering past the luxury cars and pointed sternly toward the far bay in the attached garage, one with a large RV door. It rolled up as we approached.

"Hm," Val said, eyeing the interior.

Well-lit, the garage gleamed with built-in cabinets lining the walls above a fancy stamped-concrete floor that would probably crack if anyone actually drove an RV on it. A couple of vintage cars occupied two of the spots inside, but the large bay in front of us was empty.

"Plumbers don't usually get invited to park inside." I pointed at the driveway to suggest we stop before entering; I didn't want my truck to be trapped here any more than myself.

Another man wearing slacks and a short-sleeve, button-down shirt stepped into view, waving for us to go inside. Maybe that was the security uniform. At least this guard didn't have magical blood, though someone else on the far side of the garage did. Not troll blood but dwarf blood. I supposed it was too much to hope to run into a potential ally.

"They probably don't want their guests to have to look at our ugly plumbing truck," Val said when the guard waved again, more insistently pointing for us to park in the garage.

"This is my personal vehicle, you know. It's not ugly; it's well-used."

"There's a cartoon toilet on the door." Val pulled into the garage.

"Not an *ugly* cartoon toilet. Tinja hand-drew that." I peered about for whoever had the dwarven blood, but my senses said he was behind a Hummer on the other side of the garage, the tall vehicle blocking my view.

The guard who'd directed us inside came in behind us and pressed his thumb to a fingerprint reader on a fancier garage-door opener than I'd ever seen. It included a camera mounted on the wall above it. That feeling of having my truck—and myself—trapped returned.

"Showtime." Val reached for her sword but hesitated. "Mundane humans can't see Storm when it's on my back, but there's someone with magical blood in here."

"I know. He's going to sense my hammer. I'll try saying it's a magical sledgehammer in case I need to break through walls to get to pipes." I had no idea how to explain Val's sword. "Do you want to stay in the truck? You're just the driver after all."

"No." Val scowled at me.

I grabbed Sorka, the dual heads stuffed into a tote so that only the haft stuck out. It was a remarkable haft with a few Dwarven runes running down it, but it shared the bag with a plunger, so I hoped most people would be deterred from looking closer. I also grabbed my toolbox.

"I suppose I could leave my sword in the truck." A twist to Val's lips suggested how she felt about that idea.

"Let's talk to these guys, and maybe you'll have an opportunity to lean back in and grab it." I hopped out.

The guard pointed us toward a door leading into the house. It was on the other side of the garage, near the Hummer—and the hidden half-dwarf. Though it was hard to tell from auras, I believed the mixed-blood was male, so he couldn't be the woman who'd called me. Was it odd that she hadn't come out to greet us? Maybe she waited inside.

Taking the lead, I headed toward the door with Val. She carried only a bag of tools, but her finger kept straying toward the tiger charm on her neck thong. Even unarmed, she wasn't without weapons.

As we neared the door, the half-dwarf stepped into view, a man a few inches taller than me. Like the other guards, he wore a button-down shirt, but armor—or maybe a bulletproof vest?—was visible at his neckline. He carried a spiked mace and a shield that looked like it had come off a medieval set of armor in a castle. The old-school weapons surprised me more than the fact that he was armed.

"Trouble," Val murmured as three more men stepped into view behind him. They carried police truncheons but also had pistols in hip holsters.

A battle is imminent, Sorka spoke into my mind.

I think you're right.

"Uhm, hi." I tried a smile and wave while hoping they had instructions not to shoot unless they had to. Didn't the sound of gunfire tend to alarm one's guests? "We're the plumbers."

"*That* one—" the half-dwarf pointed his mace at Val, "—is the Ruin Bringer."

I blinked. *Val* wasn't the one I had worried would be recognized.

"I'm not sure what she does for her day job," I said, groping for a way to salvage the situation, "but she's my driver and plumbing assistant at night. I understand you have an overflowing toilet? Is it that way?" I pulled out a wrench, not missing the way the men crouched, ready for something more deadly, and pointed it at the door.

"*You* have dwarf blood."

"You do too." I smiled at them again, but these guys weren't buying anything I was selling. The guard who'd waved us in grabbed a crowbar and moved to stand behind Val. "Dwarf blood is handy, isn't it?" I added to distract them as she rubbed her tiger charm. "Mine makes me short. I can get into crawlspaces and wriggle around in spots where the big guys can't."

"Kill them," the half-dwarf said to his buddies. "The boss doesn't want any trouble at his party."

"Uh." I held up the wrench as silver mist formed at Val's side. "Doesn't *the boss* want his toilet fixed?"

"Tiger," one man blurted.

"Get them!"

I dropped my tools and pulled out my hammer. The guard behind Val swung the crowbar at her head, but she whirled in time to block it. Sindari sprang past me, leaping over the half-dwarf's head to land among the trio of men behind him. He snarled and lashed out with multiple paws, and I hoped that would alarm them so much that they couldn't pull their guns.

The half-dwarf hefted his shield and charged me.

"*Hygorotho*," I barked to erect a shield of my own, then stepped forward and swung my hammer.

With the wall on one side and the Hummer on the other, there wasn't a lot of room to maneuver. The half-dwarf's shield kept me from swinging at a vital target, but I connected with it hard enough that he should have reeled back. A normal human would have. But he was as strong as I—stronger—and merely braced himself and kept coming.

Shifting the shield to the side, he lunged and swung at me with his mace. I raised my hammer to defend, but his spiked weapon struck my barrier and bounced off.

Growls and shouts came from behind him as Sindari sprang about, avoiding blows and slashing with his claws. A gun clattered under the vehicle. Behind me, Val knocked her opponent into a wall with a punch that struck like a battering ram.

The half-dwarf scowled at me. “Where’d you get that hammer?”

“Garage sale.” I swept it toward his head, but he was fast and raised the shield to deflect the blow.

The movement left his legs open, and I spun to deliver a roundhouse kick to the side of his knee. Though he tried to jerk his shield down to block it, he wasn’t quick enough. When I connected, he gasped in pain and stumbled to the side.

I hammered his shield out of the way, then kicked him again. He flailed with his mace but didn’t come close to me. Stepping in, I smashed my hammer down on his shoulder.

Bone crunched, and he yelled.

“How much soundproofing do you think these walls have?” Val asked calmly, sliding past my battle to help Sindari with the others. She’d run back to the truck and grabbed her sword.

The half-dwarf crumpled to the floor, and I kicked his mace out of his hand. It skidded under the Hummer with the gun.

Stepping past my downed opponent, I clubbed one of the three remaining men. Another rolled away from Sindari, grasping at slashes in his abdomen that wept blood. Val cracked another on the side of the head with the hilt of her sword.

One of the men scrambled to his feet and ran toward the door. I intercepted him, swinging with my hammer. It slammed into his gut. When he pitched forward, I kicked him. He flew backward, tumbling across the floor to flop down in front of a water heater twice the normal size. Either a lot of people here bathed at once or Hart had a soaking tub the size of a swimming pool.

“I’ll look for something to tie these guys up.” Val jogged toward textured metal cabinets and a workbench on a side wall, though I doubted Hart was the kind of person to own many tools and supplies for DIY projects.

I ran to the others, checking for firearms, but Sindari had done a good job disarming people. Impressive considering his lack of fingers and thumbs.

"Call off your cat," the man bleeding on the floor demanded, an arm lifted toward Sindari, though the tiger was only standing there, ensuring the guard couldn't flee.

Cat? Sindari asked. *The indignity. Val, inform this man that I am an apex predator.*

"I think he's learned that already." She rummaged in cabinets as our enemies groaned.

Glancing at the camera—and the door leading into the house—I grabbed my toolbox.

"Heavy-duty climbing rope and carabiners?" Val asked dubiously. "I suppose we can cut this and tie them."

"I've got my own rope." I pulled out a roll of duct tape. "Works good for gagging people too."

"Handy."

"For all situations." I bound and gagged the half-dwarf first, glad he looked woozy. He was the one I worried most about. Not only might he be strong enough to break free from rope—or duct tape—but he might be able to communicate telepathically with the staff inside the house. "When I envisioned having to tie people up this evening, these weren't the guys I imagined."

"I would be alarmed that you were envisioning such activities," Val said, "but I was too. And these *were* the guys."

As I worked, I glanced toward the door to the house, surprised nobody had charged out yet. Wasn't someone inside monitoring those cameras? Not that I would complain if there wasn't. I couldn't help but hope that we would still be able to get in and snoop around unnoticed.

As we bound the last of the men, the barrier around the property went down.

"More guests arriving," I assumed.

But Val frowned and looked toward one of the windowless

walls. I was about to ask what she sensed when I sensed it too. A dragon.

It wasn't Zavryd, Zondia, Xilneth, or any other dragon I'd encountered before. Whoever he was, he was flying in over the lake—heading straight for this house—and I realized the barrier had been lowered for him.

"Well, that's unexpected," Val said.

23

After dragging the men we'd defeated and duct-taped into an alcove by the water heater, I took my tools toward the door, but I hesitated to open it. The dragon flew closer, his powerful aura preceding him, and landed on the roof of the house. If anyone shouted in alarm, I couldn't hear it, but the fact that someone had lowered the barrier meant he had been expected. Invited?

Why would a dragon from another realm want to come to an art party on Earth? Or come to Earth at all? Zavryd always implied it was a deplorable world overrun with verminous humans.

"That's not a dragon I'm familiar with." Val jerked her chin in the direction of the roof, though he'd landed on the other side of the house. "Sindari?"

I have not encountered that dragon before, her tiger companion replied.

"It could be a Silverclaw here to stir up trouble," Val said. "Those are political enemies of the Stormforges, Zav's clan."

"Maybe it's the dragon whose presence they picked up over on the Olympic Peninsula. I'm crossing my fingers its arrival is distracting the staff, and we haven't been noticed."

That was a lot to hope for. Before grabbing their weapons and heading to the garage, the guards had to have reported that someone had recognized the Ruin Bringer coming in. And another guard had to be monitoring the security cameras around the premises. I asked Sorka to wrap her protection around me again.

As Val stepped up behind me, her sword in its scabbard across her back, the barrier over the property reengaged.

She grimaced. "So much for my thought to call Zav over to help."

"Are you communicating with him now?"

"No. He's out of my range, but sometimes when I shout in my mind loudly enough, he hears me anyway, even when he's on the other side of the world. We have a link."

"Some people have phones."

"He's not into Earth techno baubles, as he calls them." Val waved to the door and glanced at my tools. "Still going to try the plumbing ruse?"

"Yeah. Will you stay here and make sure those guys don't free themselves?"

Val blinked. "Stay... here?"

"The people here recognize you."

"Other than the dragon, I don't sense more magical beings inside. Just a lot of magical *stuff*."

"Some mundane humans can recognize you too." I was about to point out that the dragon was outside, not inside, but his aura had altered—because he shifted into a human?—and he'd come down from the roof. He hadn't yet entered the house but had jumped down to what might have been a deck. I could only tell so much with my senses.

Fortunately, he was on the far side of the house from the service door and up a level from the garage. "Just stay for a minute.

I'll holler if I need help or the plumbing scheme doesn't work and someone tries to kill me."

Val's lips pressed together. She looked like she wanted to say the plumbing scheme was already out the door, but she shrugged and said, "It's your mission. Sindari and I love sitting uselessly around in garages while others walk into danger."

The silver tiger tilted his head in what did *not* look like agreement.

"Good," I said, ignoring her sarcasm. "Camouflage yourselves too, please. I'm here to *learn* things, not start fights."

Val propped her fists on her hips. Why did I have a feeling she would do her own thing?

Maybe it was vain to hope that I could find Hart, get him alone, and force him to swill the truth drug, but that would be far more likely if the house didn't erupt in chaos first.

Leaving Val in the garage, I opened the door and stepped into a huge mud room with slate floor tiles, a dog-washing station, and wooden benches, cabinets, and hooks for hanging gear. Two kayaks were mounted on one wall.

Frantic voices speaking in strained whispers came from a wide hall beyond. One sounded like the woman who'd called me. She was giving orders to someone else in Spanish, and I caught and recognized the word *baño*. And was that the faintest sewer scent that wafted toward me?

Since the mission had started out poorly, I couldn't bring myself to feel smug.

Resisting the urge to activate my stealth charm and camouflage myself, I cheerfully called, "Hello? It's the plumber."

Hopefully, they were so concerned with the toilet problem that they hadn't paid attention to the men marching out to the garage with weapons.

Two frazzled women with mops appeared, waving for me to

come. They started out speaking in Spanish, then shifted to English.

"This way. Hurry, hurry."

We passed the fanciest laundry room I'd ever seen, with two sets of fire-engine-red washers and dryers, and a marble counter with a large hammered-copper sink. Who bought a specialty sink for the *laundry* room? A woman was currently using it to dump the contents of a mop bucket.

Next was a security room with monitors showing images from all over the house, but the door was open with nobody sitting at the station. One of the guards in short sleeves strode past with another bucket full of water and emptied it in the laundry room. Maybe he was the one who usually watched the monitors.

My guide led me past a double-doored rec room that looked out toward the lake. Couches, pool tables, and a bar complete with numerous taps were ready for entertaining. All the guests, however, had to be on the floor above. Possibly because of the puddles dotting the hallway floor.

Voices came from stairs that led upward, not the frantic voices of the staff but the calm voices of people mingling. It didn't sound like anyone was alarmed by the arrival of a dragon. Or the toilet mishap.

When we reached the stairs, water was flowing down them from above. Hah. Lovely.

I did feel bad for the men and women with mops, frantically trying to staunch the flow of the waterfall. Even though I'd been the one responsible for the sabotage, I almost suggested cutting off the water to the house, but this excellent distraction was good for me.

My guide led me up the stairs and turned left into a hall. To the right lay an open living area with huge windows overlooking an expansive deck and the water beyond, including the dock and a yacht and boathouse that hadn't been visible from the lake. I sensed two substantial magical items in the high-ceilinged room. One was a towering golden man-shaped statue along a wall opposite a huge fireplace. The other was in a corner and too small for me to see through the people inside.

Guests mingled as servers with silver platters brought out drinks and appetizers. Numerous people glanced toward the hallway—and the stream of water flowing across the marble tiles and down the stairs—so it was clear the staff hadn't managed to hide my incident.

Good.

Other guests looked toward the open glass doors that led to the deck. The dragon was out there in human form. A solid reason to scurry after my guide and get out of sight. And I was about to do that when someone moved, and I spotted Hart.

He looked exactly as he did online, with short gray hair and glasses, and dressed in slacks and a sweater with a collared shirt. Talk about a geek vibe. It was hard to imagine the guy hiring assassins. Hart had confidence for a geek, though, and smiled at people and spread his arms in invitation to his shape-shifted visitor.

Appearing human, the dragon had long silver hair that hung around his tan-skinned handsome face. He wore elven clothes that could have come out of Sarrlevi's wardrobe, but something about his look and amble made it easy to envision him with a surfboard, heading for the waves. When he glanced into the house, captivating green eyes scanning the crowd, I hurried down the hall and out of his view.

I might not be as notorious as Val, but that didn't mean I wanted a strange dragon noticing me. Nor did I want to try to kidnap and drug Hart when he was near a strange dragon. I *did*, however, wish I could hear what they were talking about.

"In here." My guide waved me to a closed door with water flowing out underneath it, despite a soaked towel pressed against the gap. A hastily written sign taped to the wood read *Out of order.* She opened the door for me, revealing the toilet with the lid down, as if *that* would stem the tide flowing from the bowl. "Hurry, please. This is such an embarrassment to my employer and his guests."

"I'll get right on it."

I set my toolbox on the counter and my plunger-hammer bag on the toilet tank—the only spots free of water in the relatively small powder room. It would be a simple matter to fix my sabotage but not with someone watching, and I groped for a way to get the woman to disappear, but she stepped into the hall and closed the door firmly.

"Tell Thomas that the bathroom will be under control shortly," she told someone, her voice coming through the door. She switched to Spanish again to call to someone else, then walked out of earshot.

Well, I'd made it in. For the moment, I was stuck in the powder room, but as soon as I fixed the toilet, I could camouflage myself and explore.

Since I was familiar with the sabotage, it didn't take me long to reverse it. I was careful with my enchanting, however, aware of the proximity of the dragon. Such a powerful being would sense magic being used nearby. Hopefully, he wouldn't think anything of a random half-dwarf casting enchantments in the powder room. As Val had pointed out, Hart and the rest of the guests seemed to be fully human.

Val? I whispered telepathically and as pinpoint as I could, not wanting the dragon to overhear. *I fixed the problem. I'm going to camouflage, sneak out, shut the door, and hope nobody notices the bathroom has already been repaired.*

Okay.

I frowned. Her voice hadn't come from the garage. *Where are you?*

Nowhere.

Nowhere doing what?

Trying to find the artifact responsible for the barrier so I can get it down in case Zav arrives.

Though I worried about the guys in the garage escaping, or someone coming to check on them, I couldn't blame her for not wanting to stay there.

Sindari is guarding the garage crew, she added.

Oh, good. Thanks. I think the barrier artifact might be in the living room. Do you think a dragon will be able to see through our camouflage magic? As I asked, I rubbed my charm and debated grabbing my tools. Though reluctant to leave them behind, I decided I had better. If someone looked in the bathroom, they would think I was still working and had gone to shut off the water or something.

I've evaded them successfully before when they've been hunting me, Val replied, *but I wouldn't get close.*

Close isn't what I'm planning. Trust me.

I gripped the knob, but before opening the door, I pressed my ear against it. If one of the staff was right outside, they would notice a door opening of its own accord.

Footsteps sounded as someone in heels strode down the hall. I waited for them to fade. The susurrus of voices from the living room came through, but I didn't hear anyone speaking near the door.

Problem, Val told me, sounding like she was on the main level with me now. *Sindari says more guards came into the garage and are looking around.*

Is there any chance you used your elven magic to cleverly hide the tied-up guys?

Uh, no. What was I supposed to do? Grow vines over the water heater and that alcove?

Sarrlevi might have.

That would have been more *suspicious, not less. Sindari says the tied guys have been spotted. You better move fast, Matti.*

I'll try.

Frustrated with how quickly everything had fallen apart, I opened the door. The hall wasn't empty, but there wasn't anyone in front of the bathroom. I headed for the living room, hoping Hart had parted company with the dragon, who I sensed was on the move, and I could get a chance to tug him off for a private meeting. A private interrogation.

If the dragon hadn't been present, I might have taken a more direct approach, simply jumping Hart and trusting I could fight off the well-dressed partygoers. None of them looked like the type to spring into a brawl to help an acquaintance.

Before I reached the living room, two guards in their short-sleeved shirts jogged up the stairs from below. Their grim faces suggested they'd come from the garage—and knew about the trouble. One looked into the living room while the other headed down the hall in my direction.

I scooted back into the bathroom, knowing the guard would see me if he got within five or six feet. He glanced toward the door—noticing it had opened by itself?—but kept walking as he pulled out a phone. To warn the head of security of the problem?

When I stepped back out, the other guard had moved into the living room. He wasn't raising an alarm, rather wandering past guests and looking around. He probably had orders not to disturb anyone.

I sensed the dragon climbing an open staircase against the wall opposite the big windows and was in time to see him follow the sweatered Hart across a balcony and into a wood-paneled hallway upstairs. The rest of the guests remained below, sipping wine and champagne as they waved toward artwork on easels, drop cloths hiding the pieces from view. I didn't care about the paintings; if Hart was having a private meeting with a dragon, I wanted to spy on it.

Though I felt vulnerable out in the open, I trusted my camouflage charm and headed for the stairs. Several times, I had to stop or take a wide berth around groups of chattering people, lest I draw too close and they see me. Presumably, plumbers weren't supposed to wander out of the bathroom and into the party.

Had I removed the overalls, the dress underneath might have allowed me to fit in, but it wasn't such a huge gathering that I could count on strangers being able to slip in unnoticed. The guests interacted as if they all knew each other, the Richie-Riches of the greater Seattle area.

An older couple with linked arms made it to the stairs ahead of me and, after depositing empty glasses on the tray of a waiting server, headed up. As if they'd been there before and knew the place well, they strode toward the same hallway Hart and the dragon had gone down. Maybe it wasn't a private meeting but a gathering of select colleagues? Or—my heart thumped noticeably in my chest—maybe a meeting for members of the organization?

When the server with the tray looked away, I darted past and up the stairs. Halfway up, an orange-glowing cylinder in the corner of the living room caught my eye. The artifact I'd sensed earlier. It rested on a wooden stand, and a fig tree sprouted from soil inside it. One of the powerful artifacts I'd sensed was... a pot?

That didn't seem right. It was emanating power, and two of the bare-armed security men stood near it. Watching over the party? Or guarding it because it was valuable?

When I brushed it with my senses, trying to determine the enchantment, I realized I'd been right before. Pot or not, its magic powered the barrier protecting the house.

Val? I reached out as I crossed the balcony. *I know where the artifact you're looking for is.*

It's not the one next to the golem in the living room, is it?

Uh, golem?

That statue thing. I think it comes to life.

A neat party trick. It is in that room. It looks like a planter. Before creeping into the hallway, I shared an image of it with her.

Hell. That's not going to be easy to get to. Where are you?

Trying to spy on a meeting with a dragon.

Healthy.

Like a strict diet of only cheese and salami.

You live on the edge in all aspects of your life.

Numerous doors were closed along the wood-paneled hallway, but one at the end stood open, the backs or shoulders of a few people visible inside. Beyond them, walls filled with built-in bookcases rose to either side of tall windows overlooking the lake. The dragon stood near one.

I would have trotted right into the room, but a guard was stationed in the hall by the doorway. More problematic, a band around the inside of the doorframe emanated magic. It reminded me of a metal detector, and I envisioned it beeping—or possibly incinerating me—if I tried to walk through it with my hammer.

If the guard hadn't been there, I might have run up and poked it with a finger to test it.

A new couple came up the stairs behind me, their strides intentional, their outfits more appropriate to a Fortune 500 boardroom than a cocktail party. They murmured to each other in a language I didn't understand, but it made me think of the Dubai hotel where the half-orc assassins might have been hired. Once again, the thought that Hart's guests might be part of the organization—the far-flung *global* organization—came to mind. Hell, if a dragon was involved, it was *more* than global.

I had to get into that meeting.

Knowing the approaching couple would see through my camouflage if they got close, I darted through the only other open door along the hallway and into a marble-tiled bathroom with a vessel sink that looked like something out of the Chihuly museum.

The lights came on automatically, and an air freshener in a socket puffed two sprays of lavender over the vanity. I almost cursed, afraid the guard would notice. Apparently, camouflaging magic worked fine on people but *not* on motion sensors or whatever activated the smart-bathroom amenities.

Fortunately, nobody shouted, "Who's in there?" or anything like that.

The female half of the power couple that walked past only glanced into the bathroom. Something on her emitted magic. A weapon? A charm?

After they passed, I peeked back into the hallway. The guard nodded politely to them and stepped aside. The man walked through the doorway without trouble, but the magical metal detector flashed and buzzed when the woman drew even with it. She gasped, as if she'd been jolted, and skittered back.

"Do you have any magical weapons, tools, or artifacts, ma'am?" The guard spoke politely, but his hand dropped to a pistol at his belt.

"Just my letter opener." She touched the lapel of her jacket.

I grimaced, realizing the implications. Not only would the thing detect my hammer, but it would detect and probably knock *out* the camouflaging magic of my charm. There was no way I could get in.

24

WHILE THE WOMAN DREW HER SUPPOSED LETTER OPENER OUT TO debate with the guard whether it was a weapon, I stood in the bathroom and wracked my mind for a way to get in. Run outside, climb up the side of the house, and go through a window? Unfortunately, I still sensed the dragon standing near the windows. I could also sense magic coming from them, magic similar to that of the detector on the door. Though the overpowering aura of the dragon made it hard to pick out individual items in the room, I could tell there was other magical stuff in there too.

The only sure way to go in was through that door. It crossed my mind to claim the pipes that ran to the downstairs toilet went through the library, and I needed access, but who would believe that? Besides, if some *servant* had to intrude upon the room, Hart would simply move his meeting.

Maybe if I set my magical items aside and looked like one of the guests, I could walk in with someone. The guard had called that woman *ma'am* instead of using her name. He, at least, might not be that familiar with the people invited to the meeting. Hart would be another story, but maybe there were some aisles of books in addition to the cases built against the walls, and I could slip in and stand out of sight.

Fat chance, but I had to try.

If I leave you in the bathroom, I silently asked Sorka as I removed my overalls, *you can float around the corner to come to me when I call the power word, right?*

The idea of being parted from my hammer did not appeal, especially when a dragon was waiting, but the library wasn't that far away.

A bathroom? Sorka asked. *Your mother never left me in such a lowly place.*

She didn't take you into bathrooms to keep her company? Girls like to chat with other girls while they pee.

I have not observed that custom.

Maybe it's an Earth thing. I carefully leaned the hammer behind the door, then smoothed my dress. Hopefully, nobody would look that closely at the black Keds I'd chosen for footwear, not wanting anything that would be unbelievable for a plumber to wear—or hard to fight in.

The hammer-shaped charm was the only other magical item on me. Once I removed it, I would be visible to everyone.

Biting my lip with uncertainty, I peered back into the hallway. Maybe it would be better to reunite with Val, break that artifact, and wait until Zavryd and Xilneth could come help us.

But Hart might get away, and I wouldn't learn anything. A *battle* wasn't what I needed.

"What do you mean the mongrel daughter isn't dead yet?" a stiff haughty voice spoke loudly from the library.

I stared. The mongrel daughter. That had to be me.

And was that the dragon speaking? His accented voice radiated arrogance and power.

"Thank you," the guard said, accepting the woman's weapon—

it looked like more of a dagger than a letter opener—and peering into the room.

The woman hesitated, then walked in to join her partner.

The guard tapped an earbud and said, "Yes?" quietly to himself.

Someone answered the dragon, but I couldn't hear the words. I needed to get closer. Maybe if I sneaked to within five feet of the door—

Hart came into view but only for long enough to tell the guard, "Let Nakamura in but nobody else."

Nakamura? That was the real-estate mogul, the only guest I'd recognized on the list, and the man Willard had thought I should proposition to try to get a date to this party.

"Yes, Mr. Hart," the guard said, though he seemed to be focused on whoever was speaking to him through the earpiece. The rest of security might be discussing the presence of the Ruin Bringer and her tiger in the house.

The door closed, denying any chance I'd had of hearing the meeting.

"Nobody but the invited guests have been up here," the guard replied.

And one half-dwarf hiding out in the bathroom…

The guard walked down the hall, and I skittered back from the doorway, worried he would start checking the side rooms. I still gripped my charm and was camouflaged, but would the automatic light being on tip him off to someone inside?

He passed the bathroom with only a glance inside—one that gave no indication that he saw me—and continued to the balcony, reaching the railing and looking down. If not for that magic detector, I could have sneaked into the meeting right then.

"Mr. Nakamura," the guard said, his voice barely audible now. "You can go right in. Mr. Hart is expecting you."

I peeked out. Nakamura was cresting the stairs, and the guard, after nodding politely to him, headed down. It was probably to check on something that *Val* was doing, so I shouldn't have been delighted, but... here was my chance. Maybe.

I found a Band-Aid in a drawer and used it to stick my charm to the hammer haft. *Bring this with you when you come.*

This is not *dignified,* Sorka told me.

Mom made the charm. It's great.

I refer to the beige tape you've plastered to me.

Just be glad you don't have arm hair. Oh, and try to camouflage yourself in the meantime. Maybe rub the charm.

Sorka *harrumphed* into my mind as I walked out. My heart raced and every pore broke out in sweat as I fluffed my hair and attempted to look like an invited guest who'd just used the facilities. I couldn't help glancing toward the door, worried the dragon would sense my hammer now that I wasn't holding it with the camouflage magic activated. I highly doubted Sorka could rub the charm herself.

Nakamura looked at me, nodding without suspicion, and his glance took in my chest. If I hadn't been halfway to a panic attack, I might have laughed. Maybe Willard's date idea would have worked.

"Nice to see you, Mr. Nakamura," I said.

He paused. "Have we met?"

"Briefly at a benefit for the REIA last year, I think," I said, having no idea if he'd attended that but certain he at least knew of the organization. "I'm in real estate and a huge fan of your books." I smiled, doing my best to suck up without appearing to suck up. "I'm in renovations mostly, but if I were smarter, I would start keeping the properties and build an empire, like you have."

His eyebrows rose infinitesimally, and he didn't appear that impressed by my sucking up. Aware that Hart and the dragon might be discussing my life—or death—at that very moment, I wanted to end the conversation. But I also wanted him to invite me to walk in with him. Possibly behind him so the others wouldn't notice me.

"Hart invited a house flipper to one of his shindigs?" Nakamura asked.

"I usually get invited to parties because of my art. Sometimes my boobs, but that depends on who's doing the asking and what kind of party it is."

He blinked and glanced down again. That probably hadn't been the kind of tactful thing that people usually discussed with him, but he *had* looked at my chest, so I'd assumed some interest.

"I'll bet." Nakamura smiled for the first time. "Hart's parties don't usually get interesting until later when everyone's clothes come off and the hot tub is fired up. What kind of art do you make?"

"Lots of things. Wood carving especially. I do custom doors and stair bannisters and such." Realizing that wasn't the kind of *art* that ended up in galleries and gained one notoriety, I thought about embellishing—lying—but I knew little about the real art world. Instead, I took out my phone to show him pictures, holding them up as I glanced toward the balcony. That security guard might return at any moment.

I expected scoffing, but Nakamura took my phone to look more closely.

"Very good work," he said, flipping to the next picture—I was glad there weren't any naked photos of me with a lover in the lineup. "It's almost magical."

Not *almost* since I apparently had been enchanting things I'd been working on for longer than I'd realized...

"I'd love to see it in person," Nakamura added, smiling at me again.

"Sure. I'm working on a door for a house right now. You know, when I'm not at parties hanging out in the bathroom because I'm socially awkward and have no idea what to talk about to those people downstairs."

"The stock market, the minutes of the last Federal Reserve meeting, and what interest rates will do this year."

"Scintillating."

"Not really." Nakamura returned my phone and offered his arm. "Coming to the meeting?"

"Sure."

His eyelids drooped. "Coming to the hot tub afterward?"

Was he *flirting* with me? Flattering. If Sarrlevi chewed up my heart and spat it out before leaving Earth forever, I would have to remember that showing guys my wood carvings was a turn on. Or maybe it was the black dress, for his gaze strayed to my chest again.

"Absolutely," I said, though I was positive I would end up dead or fleeing for my life long before that hot tub was fired up.

Security is looking for me, Val informed me telepathically as Nakamura and I walked toward the door.

I gathered. You haven't done anything to the artifact yet, though, right?

No, but my tiger chewed on someone's shin, and they know I'm in here somewhere. They're trying not to alarm the guests, but I heard them say they're getting a magical gizmo to detect invisible people. I'm not sure they know you're here or who you are.

I'm going to choose not to be offended.

Uhm... Why can I sense you, Matti?

A real-estate mogul is taking me to the secret meeting in the library.

Nakamura opened the door without knocking and led the way past the glowing detector. It didn't beep and buzz for him, but I held my breath as I stepped inside, afraid even my magical blood might set it off.

It didn't, but the conversation halted, and several people

including Hart and the dragon looked at us. Hart nodded at Nakamura but frowned at me and lifted a hand.

This had been a dumb idea. It was only one room, there were only a dozen people inside. Even though there *were* aisles one could duck into, that would only have worked if everyone hadn't seen us come in.

"What are *they* doing here?" the dragon demanded, whirling not toward us but toward the window.

Those who'd been looking at me also turned toward the window. Under the guise of getting drinks—near the door, there was a bar with several full glasses of wine set on top—I unlinked my arm from Nakamura's. I plucked up a glass for each of us, though I was certain Hart had been on the verge of saying guests weren't invited to his powwow. I offered wine to Nakamura though he didn't glance at me as he accepted it, instead also looking toward the window.

Abruptly, I sensed Zavryd. Zavryd *and* Xilneth.

They were flying over Lake Washington. Coming here?

I winced. Even if Val could get the barrier down to allow in dragon backup, that wasn't what I wanted. The idea was to spy on the meeting without being discovered, not make a forward assault on a key member of the organization.

"It is irritating enough," the dragon said, "that I must constantly dodge that sanctimonious Stormforge twit now that he's spending so much time on this world, but now he brings my sister's idiot offspring as an ally? To what end?"

"I'm certain they won't disturb us, Lord Varlatastiva." Hart waved upward—to indicate the barrier?

"Stormforge can tell the queen about me. My kind don't know that I'm here—they *didn't*—and it will be simpler to bring my plans to their culmination if other dragons continue to be ignorant of them."

Since nobody was looking at me, including my newfound date,

I said, "Oops, I forgot my purse," quietly enough that only Nakamura should hear, then eased behind a bookcase. What were the odds that everyone would forget I'd walked in with him and continue their meeting?

Unfortunately, the alcove made by two rows of bookcases wasn't *that* hidden. Anyone standing in front of the door or the bar would be able to see me.

Sorka? I reached out telepathically. *We may need to find out soon if you're powerful enough to break through a magic detector. I don't know if it keeps people—and weapons—from entering or is mostly to alert the guards about magical threats.*

Whatever its power, I am certain that I can breach it.

Subtly?

I am a hammer, and I was made by a dwarf.

That's a no, right?

Correct.

"Dwarven-enchanted or not, this barrier is unlikely to be sufficient to stand up against two of my kind," the dragon—Varlat-whatever—said.

Dwarven? Something else my mother had made? If only *she* were here.

"You've said in the past that there's no reason the dragons should care what you do here on Earth," Hart said.

"That was before the Stormforge queen's offspring took up residence across the lake." Varlat spat.

A pounding at the door made me jump. The security guard?

The door opened before Hart reached it. I froze, certain he would look over, see me, and remember I'd wandered in uninvited.

He still carried a drink in his hand and appeared more peeved that his meeting was being disrupted than concerned about his life. Maybe it wouldn't be so bad if Zavryd and Xilneth got through the barrier and chomped him to pieces. Though that wouldn't help me find the organization's hidden base.

"What is it?" Hart asked the guard, not glancing at me.

I pretended to study a shelf of stuffy classics with gilded trim on the faded hardbacks.

"The Ruin Bringer is here, Mr. Hart. We've tried to handle it on our own so as not to alarm your guests, but we can't find her and believe she's hidden by magic. The plumber is missing too."

I'd been afraid someone would remember me.

"Well, they can't get in here." Hart pointed his glass at the doorframe. "As to the rest..." He wandered out of my view but only for a moment before returning with a small magical artifact, an oval-shaped stone. "*Breyute.*" It glowed, and he handed it to the guard. "This should reveal anyone hidden in a room. Find her and interrogate her. I don't know why *she* would be here, but you will find out. She must have something to do with those dragons flying over the lake."

"She works for the Army office in Seattle," the guard said. "They may want that power device."

"I have no doubt. Go." Hart shooed the man away.

I willed myself to melt into the bookcase and be invisible. Or at least extremely uninteresting and unnoticeable.

Hart turned and paused, facing me. There still wasn't any recognition in his eyes—strange that a man could hire an assassin to kill someone and not know what she looked like—but he frowned and took a step in my direction.

"It would be less than ideal if Stormforge forced his way in and questioned your weak-minded guests," Varlat announced as a gust of wind entered the room—from a window being opened? "Hart, attend me. I will leave, but you will first know what I wish you to do."

The words had a magical compulsion to them, and Hart

jerked, almost spilling his wine, as he turned from me to stride toward the dragon.

"I thought *we* were in charge," someone murmured, the words barely audible from my spot, "and the dragon was assisting *us*."

I scowled at the bookcase. The addition of a dragon made everything more complicated. How long had he been working with—or *over?*—the organization? If he'd been a part of things all along, it might explain why my mother hadn't been able to get away and was stuck working with these people. She might be a powerful enchanter, but no dwarf was the equivalent in power to a dragon.

Another gust of wind swirled in, smelling of the lake. Varlat must have delivered his orders to Hart telepathically. Damn. I needed to know what the dragon wanted Hart to do.

The barrier around the property went down.

A few guests murmured in surprise. The humans couldn't have sensed the barrier being deactivated, could they?

Varlat climbed onto the windowsill, then jumped out. In the air, he shifted into his dragon form and flew away. The barrier reactivated.

At the edge of my senses, Zavryd shifted from flying idly over the lake to arrowing toward Varlat. But the other dragon took off at top speed, heading south. If all he wanted to do was leave, he could have made a portal. Maybe he wanted to lead Zavryd out of the area? So there was no one left to help me and Val?

My senses told me Xilneth was stationary off to the north—probably sitting on the 520 bridge. He wasn't giving chase, but he didn't have as powerful an aura as Zavryd, and I doubted he could tear down the barrier by himself.

"We may have to reschedule this meeting," Hart said from the window. A soft clink sounded as he closed it.

"And the party?" Nakamura rumbled. "I was looking forward to the hot tub. Ah, where did the buxom girl go?"

I swore silently. Without further distractions, they would find me.

Even without my hammer, I could probably fight my way out of the room, but to what end? I hadn't learned what I wanted to know, and as long as that barrier was up, Val and I wouldn't be able to escape the compound.

Matti, Val spoke into my mind.

Val, I need help.

Uh, I was about to ask you *for help. I'm in the room with the artifact that generates the barrier, and I've managed to get a good look at it, but I don't know how to turn it off. The guards standing by it aren't the ones activating and deactivating it. Can you and your enchanting magic come take a look?*

I don't know.

I could smash it with my sword, but... I've done that to artifacts before to bad results. And this thing is more powerful than the fae doohickey I tangled with last year. It could blow me up. It could blow the house or even the city *up.*

I'll try to get down there, Val, but I'm stuck at the moment.

Very stuck.

Zav took off after that other dragon, but Xilneth said he preferred to leave the hunting for others. Not very helpful, but he did say he'll come question Hart if we can get the barrier down. As much as I'd like to, we can't start beating the crap out of these people. Oh, hell.

What?

It had grown quiet in the library, and I heard footsteps approaching my nook.

One of the guards activated the golem, Val said.

"She's over here," Hart said, "but *who* is she?"

Several people stepped into view, all staring at me. I was trapped.

25

VISHGRONIK! I CRIED TELEPATHICALLY AS HART PULLED A MAGICAL item out of his pocket—a weapon?—and stepped toward me. Subtlety no longer mattered.

"Look out," the guard in the doorway shouted.

Sensing my hammer coming, I lifted a hand, hoping Sorka would fly right past the magic detector. But when she reached the doorway, buzzing, beeping, *and* flashing filled the air.

Startled guests skittered away, spilling their glasses of wine. The hammer hung in the doorway, and I groaned, afraid Sorka's magic couldn't overcome the security device—was it something else that had been made by my mother?

Silver-blue lightning streaked from the hammer, striking the bands in the frame. Some of the lightning escaped into the library. More guests gasped, and footsteps thundered as people ducked behind the bar and bookcases.

A branch of lightning lanced toward a ceiling fixture, struck, and blew it to pieces. Shards of glass flew everywhere, tinkling against the floor and bookcases. Another branch of lightning blasted wine glasses off the bar.

You weren't joking about not being able to do subtle, I thought and stepped forward, thinking of trying to grab Sorka and pull her through.

A sense of smugness came from her. Before I'd stepped out of my alcove, the hammer burst through the barrier, flew past my bookcase, and hurtled into the room. I gaped as my weapon smashed into the far wall, hitting hard enough to shatter glass in the windows next to it.

About to sprint across the room to grab Sorka, I paused when something small and lightweight skidded across the floor toward me. The hammer-shaped camouflaging charm with the scorched remains of the Band-Aid sticking to it.

I pounced on it faster than I would a block of rare Pule cheese. With a quick rub, I activated the charm, immense relief flooding over me as its camouflaging magic took hold.

But I wasn't out of the woods yet. I needed to get Sorka, then cross my fingers that she'd *destroyed* the door artifact, not simply burst through. Given the smoke and acrid scent wafting from it, that seemed a reasonable hope.

When I crept out of the alcove, I found Hart and the rest of the meeting attendants in a circle, staring down at my hammer, shattered glass littering the floor all around it.

Can you float away from them? I held out my hand.

But, as if he'd heard my question, Hart stepped on the haft and squeezed something in his hand. That device, whatever it was, that he'd pulled out when he'd meant to grab me. I couldn't tell what it did, but it flared with power, and Sorka didn't rise up.

I set my jaw. No problem. I would get her myself. At this point, I no longer cared how much trouble I would get in if I clubbed people to knock them out of the way.

But as I crept forward, one of the men blurted, "I think that's the hammer we've been looking for."

I rolled my eyes. Duh.

"That the daughter had all these years and we didn't realize, yes," a woman said.

"We didn't *realize*," Hart said, sounding irritated, "because we didn't care about it. We didn't know it was the key to getting the damn power reactors to work."

"If *it's* here, *she's* here, right?" Nakamura turned and looked straight toward me.

I'd stopped ten feet away to listen to them, hoping they would keep revealing information, but now I completely froze. Was he looking at me or the door? My charm should still be working...

Hart's head swiveled toward the bookcase alcove where I'd lurked. "That was her. You invited her in here, you idiot."

Hart jogged away from the group, and I shifted to the side, reminding myself not to move too quickly or the camouflaging magic wouldn't hold. He ran past, not seeing me, and lunged around the corner of the bookcase.

"She's gone." Hart swore.

"She could be in here but hidden, right?" One of the women grabbed pearls around her neck, as if I were here to steal from them.

"Not with the magic detector up..." Hart pointed to the door but seemed to realize his device may have been broken.

The light fixture that had been damaged crackled and spat sparks.

"Damn it," Hart said.

"I thought you hired every assassin in the world to hunt her down and *kill* her," one of the women said.

"Every assassin in the *Realms*," Hart said. "But she's got some damn elf bodyguard protecting her, and they haven't been able to get through."

A jolt of heartache struck me as I thought of poor Sarrlevi, who kept showing up to protect me even though he was a mess.

"Can't you get your *dragon* ally to get rid of her?" the woman asked. "He's way more powerful than an elf, isn't he?"

"That dragon thinks he's calling the shots. You have to Tom-Sawyer his arrogant ass to get him to do anything."

Forcing my mind away from thoughts of Sarrlevi, I telepathically asked, *Sorka? Can you start a small fire in this room?*

If everyone ran out, afraid for their lives, maybe I could yet grab Hart and pull him off alone to question. I was tempted to wrap a hand around his throat and question him whether he was alone or not. It wasn't as if any of his guests looked like trained pugilists.

But the security guard remained in the doorway, and he had a gun in hand now. Hart had at least one magical device that did who knew what, too. I had to catch him by surprise.

Subtly? Sorka asked.

No.

"Someone, grab that hammer." Hart turned back to the group, squeezing the device in his hand. Magic pulsed from it, and the air around him shimmered. Hell, had it made a barrier? "She'll come back for it."

A crash came from the living room, and I remembered Val's comment about the golem. Uh-oh.

Lightning streaked out of Sorka's dual hammer heads, one branch blasting through a window and another striking the remaining light fixture in the ceiling. People dove away from the weapon. Several scrambled toward the door, pushing the security guard out into the hall in their haste to escape.

No fires had started, but the lightning alone was alarming people.

Nakamura charged past, muttering about the hot tub not being enough of a draw for Hart's parties.

Hart ran to the hammer. A couple of men remained in the

room, having ducked behind bookcases and the bar instead of fleeing. That might be as good as it got for me.

I hurried to the door, then closed and locked it. The solid wood —was that mahogany?—ought to stand up to people trying to knock it down.

Hart reached for my hammer, but Sorka shot out lightning. It struck his barrier, light flashing in his eyes. Though his defensive magic kept the attack from getting through, he shrieked and scrambled back, almost tripping over his shoes.

"*Vishgronik*," I barked and charged toward him, not caring if he saw me now.

Sorka flew into my grip, and I swung at Hart as he recovered his balance and spun toward me. Willing the hammer to puncture the barrier, I aimed for his ribs.

"It's her!" the man at the bar yelled.

Sorka's head pierced Hart's barrier and slammed into his side. He cried out as his feet left the ground and he flew into a bookcase. He struck hard enough to shatter wood—and crack ribs—and screamed as he landed. The heavy and pompous classics tumbled free and smashed him on the head and shoulders.

Feeling no remorse, I strode toward him.

"Mr. Hart!" The security guard in the hallway banged on the door.

"We're locked in with a madwoman," the man at the bar called. "And you took all our weapons!"

I tried to grab Hart and haul him to his feet, but his device was still working. It had re-formed the barrier around him.

I ought to be able to smash through again if I swung hard with Sorka, but I wanted information, not to kill him. He didn't need to know that. Raising my hammer overhead, I waved it threateningly.

"Where are you keeping my parents?" I tried to make my eyes look crazy, like those of the *madwoman* the other man had called me. It wasn't that hard.

Thumps sounded against the door, and the knob rattled.

"Get back," the guard shouted from the hall.

Hell, was he going to shoot the lock?

Wincing in pain, but showing more chutzpah than expected, Hart pushed himself to his feet. "You'll not cow me, girl."

"I'm going to *kill* you, not cow you." I shook my hammer menacingly and hoped there wasn't a camera recording this somewhere. "Tell me where they are." My eyes bored into him, and I wished I could read his mind, see his thoughts.

A flash of dense green forest came to me but disappeared. Was that something from his mind?

"What are you going to do?" Hart glanced toward the door, and I knew he was buying time. "Charge in there by yourself?"

Another crash sounded in the living room.

"Not by myself, no," I growled, tempted to clobber him again.

I sensed that the statue artifact—the golem—had left the wall and was stomping about. Trying to smash Val to pieces? Would she and Sindari be able to handle such a creation? I couldn't imagine a sword doing much against magical metal.

A flare of magic came from downstairs, preceding a boom. Grenades? Or had Val struck the barrier artifact?

The magical protection was still up around the house, so I didn't think so, though it was possible she'd hit it—and it hadn't been enough.

"We're going to change the world for the better," Hart said. "I'd tell you not to get in the way, but it's too late. If those assassins don't get you, the dragon will."

Gunshots fired in the hallway, and bullets thudded into the door, one clanging against metal.

The other people in the room ducked behind cover again. Hart, believing his barrier would protect him, lifted his chin defiantly and didn't flinch from the gunfire *or* my hammer.

Xilneth flew past over the lake, his green scales visible through the window, but with the barrier up, he couldn't come to help.

"My dragon ally returns," Hart said smugly as more shots fired in the hallway. The guard must have kicked the door, for wood splintered, the locking mechanism giving. "He's defeated yours," Hart added.

Defeated Zavryd? I hoped not, or Val would kill me. They shouldn't have even been wrapped up in this.

Snarling, I swung again. Hart's brows flew up as he lifted an arm. As if *that* would do anything. Sorka's power, or maybe my sheer anger and frustration, pierced his barrier, and my hammer smashed into his shoulder. This time, he flew toward the window. Glass and wood shattered as he tumbled through it.

The door banged open, and the guard charged in.

"Over there!" One of the men pointed at me.

"Barrier, Sorka," I blurted, then, as the guard raised his gun, remembered the Dwarven word. "*Hygorotho!*"

It rose an instant before the bullets struck it. Trusting Sorka to protect me, I charged to the window and used the hammer to knock out the rest of the glass.

Hart was on his hands and knees on the grass below, pushing himself to his feet. His barrier must have re-formed again and protected him from the fall, but he gripped the shoulder I'd hit. My blows had to have hurt. I was surprised he was getting up at all.

Another boom came from the living room below, and glass blew from those windows too. Hart looked up at me with pure rage in his eyes.

I stepped onto the windowsill, intending to leap out after him, but a warning from Val made me pause.

Brace yourself. That other dragon insulted Zav, used mind compulsion strong enough to keep Xilneth from following and helping, and tried to trick Zav to his death. It didn't work, and the dragon opened a portal and got away, but I'm going to lay waste to this place. Nobody tries to kill my mate without repercussions.

Is laying waste to the home of a powerful rich guy a good idea? I replied.

No. I'm going to tell Willard the golem did it.

A huge blast of magic came from below. Val must have struck the barrier artifact with her sword. A shockwave rippled through the house. Part of the library floor collapsed, and one of the living room walls blew outward. People screamed. Glass shattered all over the house. The frame of the window I stood in warped and snapped underfoot. Pieces of the ceiling tumbled to the floor behind me.

When I looked down again, Hart was gone. Rubble and glass filled the yard, but he was nowhere in sight. Damn it.

I jumped from the window, frustrated that I'd paused, and landed in the grass in a deep crouch. Magic surged scant feet away, and an explosion ripped through the air. Its power tore holes in Sorka's barrier and sent me flying.

Idiot, I cursed myself. Hart had dropped some booby trap, and I hadn't seen it.

Though I tried to twist in the air to land on my feet, a jagged beam that jutted through the wall of the house caught me, gouging into my shoulder. Pain lanced from the wound, and I flailed, almost losing my grip on the hammer. I landed hard on my back, my head striking a chunk of cement. More pain blasted me, and, for a stunned moment, I couldn't move, couldn't see anything but stars and blackness dancing in my vision.

Struggling to fight off the threatening unconsciousness, it took me a moment to roll to my hands and knees. Nausea swept over me, and pain pulsed through my body. Blacking out would have been more appealing than trying to stand, but this wasn't a safe place for that.

More magic swelled, and I swore, afraid another explosion

would go off. But it was a portal opening. Only then did I realize that Val had succeeded in destroying the barrier around the property.

That ought to mean Xilneth could fly in and help, but it also meant people could portal in. My first thought was to wonder who would bother. Who had been waiting for that barrier to come down so they could come here? And why?

Then a familiar dwarf, a very *angry* dwarf, jumped out. Barothla.

Two armored dwarven warriors with huge axes landed at her side. And would Zondia be on her way to help her again too? The sounds of fighting from the living area promised Val and Sindari were still busy with the golem.

Injured and half-concussed, I was on my own to face Barothla.

26

My hands were bleeding, thanks to glass and who knew what else I'd landed in, but I still had Sorka. I tightened my grip on the haft as I pushed myself to my feet, my shoulder and head pulsing with pain.

The fury in Barothla's eyes promised she blamed *me* for the result of our earlier encounter, as if it was my fault she kept messing with Sarrlevi. What sane person screwed with a deadly assassin?

Where is my lukobar? she demanded.

Uh? Is that the belt?

It's in *the belt, you dolt. Don't you even know what you stole?*

The cure to Sarrlevi's madness. I hoped.

Snarling, Barothla stalked toward me with her pair of one-handed hammers raised, magic crackling about her. I recognized one of the male dwarves at her side—General Grantik. For a second, I was relieved, thinking he might turn out to be an ally, but his eyes were glazed. The other warrior's were too. Barothla had them under her control.

"*Hygorotho*," I whispered, hoping Sorka had recovered from the blast and could wrap her barrier around me.

It flashed twice, as if she were struggling to form it, and triumph glinted in Barothla's eyes. She rushed at me, leading with a blast of energy.

After a third flash of light, Sorka's barrier formed. But it wavered and shrank under the assault of my aunt's power. I crouched, hammer raised, and willed my own power into the barrier, trying to help Sorka maintain it.

Before Barothla reached me, outpacing her dwarven allies, movement in a row of hedges to the left of the house caught my eye. I dared not focus on it with my aunt swinging her hammers at me, but my peripheral vision registered someone rising from the bushes.

Hart. And he'd found a gun.

With a crack, it fired. Straight at me.

My heart pounded as I lifted Sorka's haft to defend against Barothla's attacks even as I ducked, afraid the combined might of my enemies would shred my barrier. The bullet skipped off the top of it, but Sorka's magic wavered. Why was the whole world against me?

Barothla had tracked me through my hammer, I was sure, but had she also known to wait until I was injured to show up? My body produced pain with each movement.

Her weapons broke through the barrier, and dwarven metal clanged against dwarven metal as I whipped Sorka left and right to parry both. More gunshots fired, Hart aiming at my head. The bullets weren't magical and, though tattered, Sorka's barrier deflected them. That didn't keep them from rattling me.

Val? I hate to ask again, but— I grunted as I parried twice more, resisting the urge to attack back since the other two dwarves were coming in from my right, also swinging. With Hart off to the left, I dared not leave myself open. *I really need help,* I finished.

I'll try. The roof and the stairs fell on the golem, but they also fell on me.

Sorry. Uhm, I'd take Sindari's help too.

I'll let him know.

The roar of a male voice came from the hedges, followed by a scream of pain.

Even as I deflected two hammer blows aimed at my head, I risked glancing over. That had almost sounded like—

Hart crumpled, his neck broken, the gun tumbling to the grass. Sarrlevi stood over him, rage twisting his face.

He had his swords but hadn't drawn them. He'd killed the man with his bare hands. Now, he stepped on Hart's back as he strode from the hedges and drew his blades. His gaze locked on Barothla.

Her attack paused; she'd noticed him. The glazy-eyed dwarf warriors hadn't, or had been programmed to ignore distractions, for they swung at my head.

Cursing, I got Sorka up in time to defend, but the axes weren't as magical—as powerful—as Barothla's hammers, and the blades bounced off my barrier.

Sarrlevi broke into a sprint.

Barothla barked an order at her brainwashed dwarves. They broke off their attack on me, sprinted around her, and rushed over to cut off Sarrlevi.

I winced, afraid he would mow down Grantik, the one dwarf who'd been something of an ally to me.

How do you keep pulling him out of your pocket? Barothla, apparently confident the dwarves would keep Sarrlevi busy, focused on me. Again, she swung her hammers and hurled power at me. *The dragon is looking all over the Realms for him.*

Why do you keep messing with him and attacking me? I snarled at her, enraged as much by her relentless harassment as the pain hindering my movements.

Sorka's barrier deflected her magical attack, but, once again,

Barothla's hammers were strong enough to get through. I knocked one aside but had to duck to keep the other from knocking off my head. With my hammer, I had greater reach, but she still had two weapons to my one.

You're a mongrel bitch who doesn't know her place. Barothla swung for my head again.

I ducked again, her weapon tugging strands of my hair out as it swept past, then lunged at her with my hammer *and* my body. Since she was armored, it was like tackling a cement pylon, but my greater height and weight were enough to make her stumble back. I smashed a knee against her unprotected inner thigh, and she pitched to the ground. I went down with her, hoping to pin her.

She jerked her head up in an attempt to headbutt me. Or maybe bite my nose off, for her teeth snapped like a Doberman's.

And you won't leave things alone that you have no business getting into. I'm making sure she *doesn't come back.* With a powerful magic-assisted thrust, Barothla shoved me off her.

People trying to kill my mother is *my business,* I shouted telepathically and aloud as I tumbled away, hurrying to get my feet under me.

But Barothla, harnessing her magic to add to her power, sprang at me before I could get off my knees. With both hammers raised, she swung toward my head.

I hefted Sorka, using the haft to block the blows, though the impact rocked my joints and evoked fresh stabs of pain from my injuries. Our weapons met and held in the air above my head. Our arms shook as we pressed, each trying to overpower the other. From my knees, I lacked leverage, but I refused to yield to her bullying strength.

A startled grunt sounded behind Barothla. General Grantik went flying, smashing into the side of the house. The other dwarf was already down and not moving.

With Barothla's face scant inches from mine, I jerked my head forward. She pulled back but didn't manage to avoid my forehead smashing into her chin. I struck hard enough to daze her, and the force pressing against Sorka lessened. Again, I smashed my head into Barothla's face, then shoved her back.

Where's Sarrlevi's mother? I asked as she tumbled away.

Gritting my teeth against the battering my body had taken, I used my hammer as a crutch to help me to my feet. Though dazed, Barothla still had her hammers. She lifted them as if to come back at me, then whirled.

Swords raised, Sarrlevi rushed her from behind.

"No!" I blurted aloud and into his mind. "She hasn't told me where your mother is."

His enraged features didn't change, nor did he glance at me or give any indication that he'd heard me.

A crash came from behind. Some random piece of the half-destroyed house falling off, I thought, but Val flew out of a fresh hole in the wall. The great golden golem broke the wall further as it strode out after her. Sindari was riding on its shoulders, slashing at its metal hide with his claws.

Barothla screeched. *You fool. If you kill me, you'll never find her.*

Sarrlevi swung at her with both blades, his movements too fast to track. Only her magical barrier kept him from lopping off her head, but it flashed, and I sensed it faltering. I also sensed Sarrlevi summoning his own power. He was going to kill her.

And I won't cure you! Barothla added, backing away from him now, throwing everything she had into her defensive barrier. Raw fear contorted her face, her eyes full of the realization that she'd made a mistake.

Sarrlevi sprang after her like a rabid wolf.

Varlesh, no. I risked charging up to the fight, trying to come in from the side to avoid the blades, hammers, and spitting magic. It might have been the most dangerous thing I'd done. *We need her. Varlesh, listen to me. Please. I know you're in there!*

But I didn't know that. He didn't so much as glance at me.

With his power enhancing his swing, Sarrlevi destroyed Barothla's barrier and sliced toward her head.

She ducked, but hair and part of her scalp sheared off. Screaming, she dropped her hammers and backpedaled, hands raised imploringly.

But Sarrlevi was like a machine, a machine programmed to kill her, with no hint of his humanity—his elfness—left. I grabbed his arm as he started to swing. He pulled up so hard that he lifted me from my feet and thrust me away. I wasn't light, but his strength was too much, and I flew back.

Though I managed to land on my feet, I couldn't return to him in time. Even as Barothla cried out in Dwarven and telepathically, begging for her life, promising his mother's health, Sarrlevi sliced through her neck and beheaded her.

"No," I rasped, horrified.

We could have forced her to speak, used the truth drug on her again, gotten the answers we needed. But there would be no answers now.

Worse, as I sensed Xilneth flying toward the property, I realized the entire Dragon Council would come after Sarrlevi for killing a princess. It had been bad enough when he'd attacked Zondia. This might not be forgivable. Even if it hadn't been his fault.

"Varlesh," I whispered, tears stinging my eyes.

He spun toward me, his bloody swords raised. There was no recognition in his eyes.

How had he found the mental wherewithal to come here? He must have arrived earlier, intending to protect me, and bided his time until the barrier came down. But with his battle lust engaged, he couldn't remember anything now. Not who he was, not who *I* was.

And that battle lust still burned in his eyes as he stalked toward me.

Hell. Keeping my hammer at my side, I backed away.

A great thump came from Val's battle, the earth shaking as the golem pitched down.

"It's me, Varlesh." I licked my lips, realizing I'd made a mistake in backing toward the house. After a few steps, I ran out of room.

"*Hygorotho,*" I whispered, but he'd torn away Barothla's barrier, and I feared he could destroy mine too.

Growling like an animal, not a man, Sarrlevi sprang for me.

27

As Sarrlevi's blades swept toward my head, I threw Sorka at him, then dove to get away from his deadly swords. Fresh tears sprang to my eyes as my injured shoulder hit the ground, but I made myself roll and roll, putting distance between us. If I could buy time, Xilneth could help. And I sensed Val running toward us.

I didn't see if the hammer hit Sarrlevi, but I doubted it, for he spun and ran after me.

"What is he doing?" Val yelled.

Sorka thudded to the ground. I jumped up, calling for the hammer, but Sarrlevi had already caught up to me. He was too damn fast.

Without my hammer, all I could do was dodge and run. Trying to punch or kick him would have been suicidal.

A blade sliced through the back of my dress as I skittered away.

Sarrlevi paused and ducked into a low crouch. I didn't see Sindari until the silver tiger soared through the air where Sarrlevi's head had been.

"Don't hurt him," I yelled as Sindari's claws flashed.

Somehow, even in his low crouch, Sarrlevi twisted and avoided all four sets of slashing claws.

Val gave me an incredulous look as I ran to stand by her side. Sorka caught up with me, landing in my grasp. I crouched to defend another attack, but Sarrlevi whirled and leaped after Sindari, responding to the most recent threat. Had he even grasped who Barothla was when he'd killed her?

"Oh, no, you don't." Val started after him to defend her furred ally.

"No, you can't," I blurted, grabbing her arm.

"You get him off Sindari or I *will*."

Greetings, humans, Xilneth spoke into our minds. *Zavryd'nok-quetal allowed himself to be lured away, but I am here and can assist you.*

Lured away! Zavryd boomed from the distance. *You allowed that rogue to mind-control you and force you to cower on the bridge instead of chasing after him. Had we both attacked him, he wouldn't have escaped.*

Hold Sarrlevi. I pointed at him, caring nothing for the dragons' squabbles. *Please, Xilneth. Don't let him hurt anyone else, but don't hurt him either. He's an ally.*

Xilneth's power preceded him as he glided in for a landing. It wrapped around Sarrlevi and slowed him down but didn't halt him completely. His face twisted, tendons in his neck standing out, and he kept trying to reach Sindari. The tiger, whom he'd last been attacking, snarled and raised a paw as if to strike back.

"Val," I said.

"That's enough, Sindari." Val raised a hand, though she glanced at Xilneth and said, "We need more power, please."

Ah, I am working on it. He is a powerful elf.

"Tell me about it." I pulled up the drooping shoulder of my dress, the fabric loosened from the slash in the back.

I sensed Zavryd flying back. Though still a mile or more away, he was able to send power ahead to assist Xilneth. Maybe it was my imagination, but a sense of smugness seemed to accompany it, because Xilneth *needed* the help and Zavryd was able to provide it.

However it worked, their combined magic finally halted Sarrlevi, leaving him standing mid-step with his swords raised. I breathed out a sigh of relief.

Xilneth landed on the dock, his tail smashing down on Hart's yacht. Wood splintered as pieces flew everywhere.

Val rubbed her face. "We are going to get in so much trouble for this."

"For dragons and elves destroying Hart's house?"

"I'm sure any number of security cameras caught *us* illegally trespassing in there tonight," she said.

What are security cameras? Xilneth swished his tail several more times to completely obliterate that yacht—and looked to be having a grand time doing so.

Devices that capture recordings of things that happen, Val replied. *They're all over the house.*

That house that is almost destroyed?

She looked toward the devastated structure. *I'm sure some of the cameras have survived the damage.*

The attached garage was still standing. I hoped that meant my truck had also survived.

It would probably take a huge fire to destroy them, Val added.

Did you say fire? I am excellent with fire. Xilneth cackled, summoned magic, and sent an inferno of flames roiling toward the house.

"My truck!" I yelled. "Stop!"

The garage that had previously been standing burst into flame. With thoughts of rescuing my truck in mind, I started in that direction, but before I'd gone three steps, a great boom came from within, and the ground quaked underneath me.

Had that been one of the vehicles blowing up? *All* of the vehicles blowing up?

Something huge burst through the flaming roof. The Hummer. With its tires on fire, it flew over our heads, even over *Xilneth's* head, and splashed down in the lake.

The dragon cackled again as the rest of the roof caved in. Glass heated and exploded. Wood burned. Smoke roiled into the air.

I groaned, grabbing my head with both hands.

"I wasn't kidding when I said Xilneth wasn't the best ally your dwarf friends could have found." Val patted me on the shoulder. "But there's good news. A truck burning in a house fire is kind of a normal thing. Your insurance will probably cover it, unlike a Jeep hurled into the branches of a tree by a dragon."

I stared bleakly around at the burning house, the dead people on the lawn, and the dragon cackling on the dock. "There's nothing normal about any of this."

"At least the cameras have probably been destroyed. Maybe we'll get lucky, and there won't end up being any evidence to condemn us."

Somehow, I doubted I would be that lucky.

"Shit." I dropped my arms.

Val raised her eyebrows.

"I realized my toolbox was in the house too." Again, I groaned and grabbed my head in distress. The tools meant more to me than the truck. Some of them had been gifts from Grandpa, tools he'd used before he retired. I'd had them forever.

"Sorry. It and the truck were innocent bystanders." Val brightened and looked south over the lake. "There's Zav."

"Great. This place needs *another* dragon." I reminded myself that Zavryd was the reason we'd been able to restrain Sarrlevi. *He* was helpful.

"Maybe we can swap Xilneth for him."

Feeling far more defeated than victorious, I walked slowly

toward Sarrlevi. Still clasped in the dragons' powerful magical grip, he was quivering, knuckles white as he clenched his weapons.

I prayed the battle rage would leave him and I could get through to him somehow. "Val, is there any chance Zoltan has figured out a cure yet?"

"I've been a little too busy to ask for updates." She pointed her sword at the unmoving golem.

Sirens rang out in the distance. The neighbors, or maybe the fleeing guests, must have called the police about the flaming house. We would have to leave soon.

I stopped a few feet away from Sarrlevi. With his mad gaze locked on Xilneth, he didn't look at me, didn't even seem to notice me.

That ache returned to my heart. What if the cure hadn't been in Barothla's pouches? What if the secret of how to make it had died with her?

"Thank you for coming, Varlesh," I whispered, hoping for some recognition. Some hint that he knew I was there and cared. "I was in a bind and might have died if you hadn't helped."

He seethed and shook as he continued to glare at his dragon captor. Though I was distraught about my truck—and my *tools,* damn it—I was relieved that the dragons had come. If Val and I had been alone and trying to keep Sarrlevi pinned down, I doubted we could have managed.

A groan came from the side of the house, one of the dwarves crawling away from the flames. Grantik.

Though clearly injured, he made his way toward Barothla's body. I grimaced. Even though I hadn't wanted him to be killed, he was a witness, one who would return to Dun Kroth and tell King Ironhelm exactly who had killed his daughter.

"We're going to have to disappear," Val said as the sirens grew louder. Her phone was to her ear.

Hoping she was calling Zoltan, I only said, “I know.”

Zavryd flew into view, the other dragon long gone. It not only bothered me that Varlat had gotten away but that he had apparently been powerful enough or *clever* enough to escape Zavryd.

Can you guys carry Sarrlevi to Val’s house while keeping him restrained? I telepathically asked the dragons.

What? Zavryd boomed. *The mad elf assassin is not welcome at our lair, even when he is the sane elf assassin.*

“He needs to see Zoltan.” I was about to say Xilneth could take him to my house, but Val stepped forward and gripped my arm again.

“You’re sure?” she asked into the phone.

“Certainly, dear robber,” Zoltan said. “The chemical compound in my Petri dish has dissolved and is no longer affecting the brain material or giving off a magical signature.”

“I’ll tell Matti. She’ll be relieved.” Val eyed the flaming remains of the house—and the garage. “She’s had a bad night.” She raised her voice so Zavryd could hear—he’d landed on a neighboring dock, not deigning to share the closer one with Xilneth—and added, “I’m certain that my mate will agree to alter the wards and defenses around our house to allow Sarrlevi onto the property.”

Hm. Zavryd eyed Sarrlevi, and I worried he would keep objecting. *This elf is uninteresting when he’s incapable of verbally sparring with a dragon. I will allow a* temporary *abeyance so that he may be treated for his madness in the laboratory of the vampire.*

I bent double, gripping my knees. For the third time, tears sprang to my eyes. This time, they had nothing to do with my pain.

Xilneth and Zavryd flew to Green Lake with Val and me riding on their backs and Sarrlevi clutched in Zavryd’s talons. The dragons’ power still restrained him. I’d kept hoping he would come out of his battle rage, as he had before, but when we landed at Val's house and they levitated him into Zoltan's basement laboratory, Sarrlevi was still struggling to free himself, his eyes wild instead of sane.

Seeing him like that tore me up, and I was terrified that we were too late, that the formula Zoltan had identified wouldn't be enough to fix him. It might stop the progress of the destruction of his brain, but if the damage couldn't be healed...

Dabbing at my eyes, I followed Sarrlevi into the basement, Val coming behind me. The dragons remained outside, Zavryd perched on his own roof and Xilneth on the one across the street. From their continuing sniping at each other, I gathered Xilneth wasn't permitted to cross through the wards. At least Zavryd had altered them so that Sarrlevi could.

"Ah," Zoltan said, regarding the red-faced and magically bound Sarrlevi as we entered, "I was wise to arrange a restraining system."

He waved toward a stainless-steel exam table—my mind wanted to call it an *experimentation* table—with magically reinforced cuffs.

"Just the piece of furniture you needed to bring the creepiness factor of this place up to a ten," Val said.

"Really, dear robber. I do not critique your home-improvement purchases, though the addition of a sauna, hot tub, *and* steam room to my front porch has ridiculously cluttered the area."

"That's our back patio, not your front porch."

"I beg to differ. Put him there, please." Zoltan pointed to the table as Sarrlevi hung suspended in the air.

Zavryd must have been monitoring, for a whisper of power swirled down from the roof, and Sarrlevi rotated onto his back and landed on the table. Still fighting, he bucked and thrashed as much as he could with dragon magic restraining him.

I rushed over, hoping vainly that my presence would calm

him. And that he wouldn't lash out at me. Val had disarmed him before we'd left the Hart compound, taking to the air seconds before police cars roared through the front gate, but that didn't mean he wasn't dangerous.

Zavryd, however, kept him still, and I was able to rest a hand on his tense shoulder. Zoltan hurried forward to strap his ankles and wrists to the table. The piece of *furniture*, as Val had called it, looked like something out of an early-1900s insane asylum. The kind of thing a person might have been strapped to before receiving a lobotomy.

"We won't let that happen," I told Sarrlevi gently, trying to make my voice soothing, though I was almost as tense as he. I stroked his sweat-dampened hair, wishing he would relax, that he *could* relax. After days like this, his body had to be exhausted. *He* had to be exhausted.

Sarrlevi bared his teeth and growled. More at Zoltan, who was strapping his last limb down, than me, I thought, but there still wasn't any recognition in his eyes.

"I have good news for you, my muscled half-dwarf." Zoltan turned from the table and toward his workspace, his counters full of books and racks of vials.

Barothla's belt lay to one side, the contents of the pouches emptied. I wondered which vial was what she had called the *lukobar*. The cure? Something else? It had sounded like she might have come back solely for it.

"Yes?" I asked when Zoltan didn't continue.

"I've been reading books on elven physiology. *In* Elven, mind you." Zoltan glanced back. "You're welcome to express awe, since I've been teaching myself the language with little outside aid."

"Didn't Freysha give you some lessons?" Val asked.

"I hardly think those flashcards count. There were cartoon flowers and leaves on them."

"*Most* elven things have flowers and leaves."

"But not cartoon versions."

"I'm awed," I said to pull Zoltan back to the more important matter. "Now, could you help him, please? Maybe a sedative so he stops struggling?"

"Hm, that might be a good idea, though I'm about to inject him with not one but two formulas. I am concerned about adding a third, lest they interact poorly with each other in his body."

"You're injecting him with the cure and what else?" I asked, worried that even *two* formulas might be problematic.

"As I am attempting to tell you, if you'll stop interrupting, I have learned that elven brains *can* regenerate. They're capable of recovering from a great deal of damage. Most of the texts were speaking in the context of injuries from traumatic wounds, but I believe his magical blood may have what it needs to repair his brain."

"I'm relieved." I squeezed Sarrlevi's shoulder, wanting to be encouraging, even if I was afraid to get my hopes up.

"I've made a formula to aid in the healing process and also replace the nutrients that the magical compound broke down and stole from him." With a syringe of yellowish liquid in hand, Zoltan reached for Sarrlevi's arm.

The dragons were in a debate about the chase over the lake and had released their hold on Sarrlevi. They must have assumed he was restrained by the table, and he was, but he bucked when the needle drew close to him. The enhanced bindings succeeded in keeping his wrists and ankles trapped, but they did nothing to stop him from using his own magic. I wouldn't have expected him sane enough to concentrate on summoning his power, but it lashed out at Zoltan, knocking him back.

Val lunged and caught him before he would have struck the counter.

"Ack, what a vile patient," Zoltan said.

"Varlesh, stop," I ordered, flattening an arm over his chest, though it wasn't as if that would do anything to stop magic. "This is for your own good. I promise."

Though I had no experience attempting to heal anyone, or do anything except enchant my projects, I tried to soothe him with my magic. At the same time, I stroked the side of his head, remembering when I'd rubbed his ears and aroused him with magic. I didn't want to do that now, but I wanted to do *something*. I willed calmness and love to trickle into him.

Not much longer, Varlesh, I whispered into his mind. *You've suffered for a long time, but you'll be able to rest soon.*

"Perhaps a sedative isn't a bad idea, after all," Zoltan grumbled, opening a cabinet for another concoction.

"What about the possibility of drug interactions?" I asked as I kept trickling my magic into Sarrlevi.

"We'll take the risk."

I frowned over at him.

"If the alchemist is fatally mangled by his patient, there will be no recovery."

Varlesh, I whispered. *Relax, please. If you can relax for a few minutes, you'll get better.*

For the first time, his head turned toward me. His brows drew down in confusion. *Mataalii?*

Yes. I smiled at him. *I'm here for you. We have the cure. I need you to let Zoltan inject it.*

Mataalii, he said again, eyes locking onto mine.

I didn't know if he'd grasped the rest, but at least he recognized me. And some of the tension ebbed from his body as I kept stroking the side of his head.

A determined Zoltan approached with a new syringe.

I held up a hand to stop him. Without taking my gaze from Sarrlevi, I said, "You don't need the sedative. He won't attack again."

Zoltan looked not at me but to Val.

She shrugged. "He seems slightly less crazy than he was a minute ago."

"Says the person who was *not* knocked across the room," Zoltan muttered.

After eyeing Sarrlevi warily for another moment, Zoltan switched syringes again, plucking up the original concoction.

How is it that you did not recognize a Starsinger dragon, Zavryd asked from the roof, *when you are yourself a Starsinger?*

I've never seen him before, Xilneth replied.

Neither have I, but I am positive he is of your clan. He had that flippant and utterly useless quality about him, as all Starsingers do.

You are an odious and arrogant toadstool.

But not a useless one.

Though I cared little about the dragons, not at that moment, I spoke telepathically to them in case they didn't already know what I'd overheard. *He said his name is Varlatastiva and called Xilneth his sister's idiot offspring.*

Idiot! Xilneth protested.

That's a quote. Though I was focused on soothing Sarrlevi—my magic did seem to be helping—I had the wherewithal to be careful the grumpy dragons didn't think *I* would use such words to insult them.

When Zoltan touched Sarrlevi's arm, Sarrlevi's face twisted, and he glanced toward the syringe.

It's all right, I hurried to tell him. *It's medicine that will make you better.*

I do not trust the vampire, Sarrlevi said, the cogent words encouraging, even if I still worried he would attack Zoltan.

You don't have to. I touched his jaw, turning his face back toward me, relieved when he allowed that. *Just trust me.*

As the icy bite of the needle slid into Sarrlevi's vein, he held my gaze. *I do.*

Good. I kissed him on the cheek.

Zoltan reached for the second syringe. "The first was the cure. This will help him heal the damage."

"Go ahead," I said, not looking away from Sarrlevi.

The fingers nearest me twitched as he tried to lift his hand, but the restraint held it down. *I can't touch you.*

The second needle slid into his other arm.

You'll be able to soon, I promised. *All you want.*

All? The barest hint of a smile touched his lips.

Yup.

More of the tension eased out of Sarrlevi's body. Probably thanks to Zoltan's formulas, but I chose to think that I was helping a little.

He is your uncle, and you do not know him? Zavryd asked.

I have three uncles, and I have never met this Varlatastiva, Xilneth said. *I will return to my clan's home world and speak to my mother.*

Do so. Do not rush back.

Xilneth harrumphed into our minds, reminded us how pivotal he'd been that night, then formed a portal and left.

He is young, Zavryd said. *It is possible this uncle of his has been gone from the Cosmic Realms since before he was born. I had not encountered him before.*

Gone? Val replied, more interested in the dragon conversation than I. *Or here on Earth scheming with ambitious humans?*

That is possible.

Sarrlevi's eyelids drooped, then closed. I leaned forward, resting my forehead on his shoulder.

"Huh," Zoltan said. "I did not need the sedative after all."

"Just a cute girl rubbing his head," Val said.

"I have heard such things can be an effective palliative among the living."

"Definitely."

28

THE SUN CAME IN THE WINDOW AS I ALTERNATED READING AND dozing on the bed next to Sarrlevi, using his arm for a pillow. Since it was the guest room in Val's house, it wasn't a large bed, and he was a tall elf with long arms and legs. I didn't mind squeezing in, though, and doubted he would object to my presence.

I'd slept across the way in the other guest room, and, after having coffee and breakfast, I'd come back upstairs to check on him. And to stay. After the last week's stressors, a morning in bed had been pleasant, though I wouldn't stop worrying about Sarrlevi until he woke up and I knew for certain that Zoltan had chosen the correct formula from Barothla's collection.

I turned my head so I could see Sarrlevi's face. Was the fingernail scrape on his cheek finally healing, or was it my imagination?

The barest hint of beard stubble grew along his jaw, but it was as blond as his hair so barely noticeable. Either he'd been shaving while he'd been crazy or elves grew facial hair very slowly. With my dwarven ancestry, I couldn't imagine what that would be like.

Had I not kept them plucked and shaped, my eyebrows would have taken over my forehead like kudzu creeping over a car parked too long.

I glanced at the clock on my phone. It was after noon, and Sarrlevi had been out a long time. I wasn't as worried as I had been earlier though. Sometime around dawn, his stiff muscles had loosened fully, the last of the tension flowing out of them. Now, I was fairly certain he was *asleep* instead of unconscious.

A thought that was verified when he shifted for the first time, his arm wrapping around my shoulders and his hand drifting to my chest.

"Really, dude?" I asked, though I didn't know if he'd woken. It wouldn't surprise me at all if he was the type to cup a woman's breast in his sleep. I didn't mind, especially since I might have been stroking his chest earlier while cuddling against him, but it deserved a comment. "That's how you greet a woman first thing in the morning?"

Though his eyes didn't open, a lazy smile curved his lips. "I *try*. I've never woken in bed beside a fully clothed female."

That wasn't quite what I'd asked, but he sounded groggy, so I forgave him. And when he absently stroked me through my dress, I might have shifted closer to him.

"You were unconscious, so you probably don't remember, but we came here straight from the battle." I didn't mention that he'd attacked me during it; I hoped he didn't remember that. "We both needed healing." Fortunately, Zavryd had been able to take care of my wounds without trouble. He'd also levitated Sarrlevi up to the guest room. As frustrating as dragons were, they could be handy at times. "You needed *brain* healing," I added. "There wasn't time for me to stop by my house for sexy lingerie and a lacy nightie."

"Thorvald could not lend you a robe?"

"We're the kind of friends that go into battle together, not share clothing." Besides, the height difference would make such an attempt ludicrous.

Since his clothes had been bloody after the battle, I'd manhandled Sarrlevi into a spare pair of Dimitri's pajamas the night before. He and Sarrlevi were closer in height than Val and I were.

"Disappointing." His blue eyes finally opened partway, and he regarded me through his lashes. "Your current garment does not allow easy access."

I swallowed, my body heating from his absent fondling, and those were the precise definition of bedroom eyes looking at me. But I wasn't about to suggest sex when we were in Val's house with her roommates downstairs, and I could sense her and her *dragon* at the other end of the hall. It had been a small miracle that Zavryd had adjusted the wards so I could bring Sarrlevi onto the property to see Zoltan. He would probably throw us out if Sarrlevi presumed to have sex in his house. In his *lair*, as he called it.

"You hadn't slept for days, so I figured you'd need rest," I said. "I assumed you wouldn't have the stamina for anything else for a while."

"My stamina has great reserves."

"Oh, I think it got pretty depleted. You've been asleep for almost eighteen hours. Admittedly, during the first part of that, you were scarily crazy with a vampire experimenting on you."

His brows drifted upward. "I believe you intended to say that I was crazy with a vampire *scarily* experimenting on me."

"That word could be sprinkled all over the sentence."

"Yes."

"I was worried." I watched his face, relieved I didn't see any sign of the monster he'd been. "Like I said, I care about you."

I'd said I *loved* him. And I did. Would he remember? Or had the last couple of weeks been a chemical-induced haze for him?

"Yes." His familiar cocky smile appeared.

Even though I'd missed it, I rolled my eyes. "You must be better. Your haughtiness is coming back. And your hand is still on my boob."

His smile widened. "You like it there."

Yeah. I did. And his smile and bedroom eyes were hot as hell. I shifted closer to kiss him, my hand slipping under his shirt to rest on his abdomen. Well, maybe not so much *rest* on as trace the nicely delineated muscles there.

Mataalii, he whispered into my mind, returning my kiss and bringing his other arm over to wrap around me, pulling me closer. Despite his talk of stamina, and his ability to get my body humming with a look, it wasn't the most impassioned kiss, and I suspected he was also aware of, and perhaps somewhat inhibited by, the nearby dragon.

Yeah?

I am grateful to you.

For allowing you to fondle my chest?

No. Sarrlevi smiled against my mouth. *That is expected behavior from a female.*

Is that so, I said, though I'd seen enough women fling themselves at him to know it was a statement of fact.

Yes. What is unexpected is someone caring for and helping an elf even when he is descending into madness. Even when he is dangerous to others. To her. His grip tightened. *I was afraid I would hurt you.*

I know. I didn't think you would. I hadn't *thought* so, but a couple of times I hadn't been sure. And last night... I swallowed, pushing the battle from my mind. *I'm glad you're better now.*

Yes. Because you helped me. Warm magic trickled from his fingers, curling through my body as it aroused my nerves.

Maybe we could have sex quietly, without anyone else in the house knowing. Though something told me sex with Sarrlevi wouldn't be *quiet*.

No, he agreed, reading my mind. Smiling again, he sent

another tingle through me, straight to my core, and the jolt of sheer pleasure made me gasp and arch against him. *But I do not care if the dragon hears. Or those in the abodes adjacent to this one.*

I might care a little, I replied but kissed him again, tempted to see how much his vaunted elven stamina had truly recovered.

Before we'd gone far in our exploration of each other's bodies, a voice boomed telepathically in our minds. *If the unwanted vile elf assassin has recovered, he must leave the premises.*

Sarrlevi growled, sounding far more like a werewolf than an elegant and regal elf, and broke our kiss. "Does the scaled behemoth not have his own mate to keep him preoccupied?"

"They were preoccupying themselves last night. Trust me." Had I not been worried about Sarrlevi, I might have returned to my house to avoid hearing all the evidence of that.

"Distasteful."

"Because Zavryd is a dragon or because you don't like him?"

"*He* is the one who insults me every time we meet."

I thought about pointing out that Sarrlevi had called him a scaled behemoth—accurate, perhaps, for a dragon, but not that complimentary—but I was so happy to see him feeling better, haughty sneer and all, that I hugged him.

The wards will be recalibrated, Zavryd added when we didn't respond, *in ten minutes, and any intruders will be incinerated.*

"Do you think he's monitoring us and knows we're, uhm, hugging?" I was fairly certain *incineration* wasn't truly programmed into the wards—the goblin and human package deliverers would have objected vehemently to that—but I did draw back.

"If he does, it is because he's a prying pursuant."

"If that means nosy stalker, you do the same to me, you know."

"I do not watch you entwined with lovers."

"You showed up on my coffee date, dude."

"Because of a greater mission."

"And you've peeped in my windows."

"To ensure an assassin hadn't slain you."

"Are you ever going to admit to being a snooping stalker?"

Sarrlevi lifted his chin. "I am an assassin."

"Uh huh. You're lucky I like you." I swung my legs over the side of the bed, deciding it would be wise to get out of Zavryd's hair—scales. "I thump *most* stalkers on the head with my hammer."

"In what manner would I need to encourage you for you to thump a prying dragon on the head?"

I almost mentioned that my cheese stash was running low, but there wasn't a fromage in the world—the *Realms*—that would prompt me to swing at Zavryd. "They've got laws about attacking them, don't they? Which you found out when you stabbed Zondia." I grimaced. "Do you remember that?"

"Barely. But I do have an image in my mind of my sword sinking into her shoulder." He raised his eyebrows toward me, as if to ask if his memory was accurate.

I nodded. "That happened, yes. How did you get away from her? She made a portal and left right after you, and Zavryd said she could track you down."

"I assumed that would be possible and portal hopped—traveled from world to world to lose the trail. In the condition I was in, it was exhausting." Sarrlevi eased out of the bed, briefly resting a hand on the side table. After only one night of sleep, his stamina likely wasn't as recovered as he'd claimed.

"Is she still after you?"

He sighed, fingered the baggy heavy-metal T-shirt that comprised the top half of Dimitri's pajamas, and looked around for his clothes. "Possibly. In a saner moment, I wouldn't have stabbed her, though it was tediously irritating that she was assisting Barothla."

"Who you got in the end anyway." I peered into his eyes. Did he remember *that*?

A troubled furrow crossed his brow, and a long moment passed before he grimaced in acknowledgment. "Yes."

"I don't suppose you got the location of your mother from her before, uhm—" I made a cutting motion across my throat.

His eyes grew grim. "No."

I'd been afraid of that.

Sarrlevi spotted his clothes, which I'd laundered that morning and stacked on a dresser for him, and reached for them. "I barely remember ending her life. My mind and body weren't my own. Had I been able to, I would have attempted to force her to give me that information, but I was so enraged, I couldn't think. I even..." The troubled furrow returned. "I tried to hurt you."

"It's okay."

"It is not."

"You weren't in control of your body—or your mind. I get it."

He closed his eyes and tilted his face toward the ceiling. Long seconds passed, and I didn't know if I should hug him or leave him be to work through things. I didn't want him feeling guilty about anything though. It hadn't been his fault. None of this had been.

Finally, he took a deep breath and looked at me. "If you had not acquired a cure to her insidious chemical, I do not believe I would have lived much longer."

Given that a dragon was after him—once the word got out about my aunt's death, they might *all* be after him—I worried he still wouldn't live much longer. And what would happen to his mother then?

"I will find her," Sarrlevi said with determination. In a softer tone, he added, "I *have* to find her. With Barothla dead, there may not be anyone to care for her."

"I'm going to hope for her sake that Barothla hired a nurse, because I can't imagine her *caring* for anyone regardless." The caged creatures in her laboratory came to mind, and I shuddered at her idea of caring. Even they, I suspected, had been tended by some servant.

"Yes." Sarrlevi removed the heavy-metal T-shirt, folded it, and set it aside. He also stripped out of the plaid pajama bottoms, soon standing naked scant feet from me.

The seriousness of the conversation and our current predicament meant I *shouldn't* have ogled him and enjoyed the show, but I couldn't help myself. I did resist the urge to reach out and touch him. Instead, I smiled in bemusement as he sniffed his folded clothes before putting them on.

"These have a strong scent." He wrinkled his nose.

"We call it laundry detergent."

"It smells of chemicals."

"According to the container, the scent is *botanical rain*."

Never had someone presented with clean laundry issued such a scathing look.

"The proper response," I said, "to someone washing your clothing while you sleep is an expression of gratitude, not haughty distaste for all things Earthen."

"You did not express gratitude when my laundry device took your clothing to clean. As I recall, you tried to destroy it with your hammer. And the soap dispenser—"

I lifted my hand. "Yeah, yeah, I haven't forgotten about the one crime I've committed that you'll never forgive."

"Hm." Sarrlevi glanced at my chest, and I was sure he remembered me naked and *jiggling* as I grappled with his loathsome laundry device.

I folded my arms over my chest and glared at him.

He shook out his shirt—he looked like he was *aerating* it more than unfolding it—and grimaced as he tugged it over his head. Once it was on, he looked down at himself. "I will not be able to properly stalk my prey while doused in such an odor."

"Is this really the most pressing concern in your life right now?"

"No." That didn't keep him from grimacing in distaste as he finished dressing. His nose twitched more often than that of a rabbit foraging in a garden.

"I'll promise to get the hypoallergenic unscented stuff if you stay over at my house. For those with sensitive skin. And noses."

"If I stay at your house, I will bring you a *nashyella*."

"Is that something besides cheese?"

"A magical laundry device."

"You could have any woman on Earth if you brought such gifts."

He looked smugly over at me, as if to say the *gifts* wouldn't be necessary. His smug expression was somewhat diminished by the continuing nose wrinkling over the *botanical rain* scent wafting up from his shirt.

I put my socks and shoes on, the movements accompanied by a haughty dragon giving us a one-minute warning about the wards. Maybe it was my imagination, but I thought I caught *vroom*ing noises coming from the perimeter, like NASCAR engines revving up for a race.

"Do you want me to come with you to look for your mother?" I asked as we headed for the stairs.

"Did you make progress in your quest and learn the location of your parents?"

"A possible location, yeah. Thanks to the help of Xilneth, Artie, and Hennehok." I hadn't gotten a chance to learn the details from them, but I trusted the dwarves would show up again soon.

Sarrlevi's lips thinned. He was probably peeved that he'd been too busy going crazy and being chased by a dragon to help. I squeezed his hand as we descended the stairs, wanting him to know I appreciated all he'd done for me.

He squeezed my hand back. "You must stay and finish your

quest. With luck, I will find my mother swiftly, ensure she has access to the curative formula, and return to help you."

Since the elves had that formula, I didn't know how we would get it. After he'd killed one of their people outside Broadleaf's house, they had to want him dead as badly as the dragons and dwarves. I didn't bring up the concern. The next time I saw Freysha, I would see if she could get ahold of some.

Zavryd stood in the living room, his arms over his chest and a glare on his face as we walked through on our way to the front door. He eyed our clasped hands and looked as dyspeptic as a grandma chaperoning the prom.

"We're leaving," I told him. "Thank you for your gracious hospitality. I'll have some meat delivered."

Sarrlevi might have snorted at the word *gracious*. He spotted his swords leaning by the door and picked them up.

"It is acceptable to share my abode with the friend of my mate." Zavryd nodded curtly at me. "You will not enter the premises again, assassin."

"He was unconscious when we brought him here," I pointed out, "and it was to see Zoltan, not drink all your beer and scratch his balls on your couch."

Zavryd's jaw descended. Either he wasn't used to mongrels speaking so bluntly to him or Val's houseguests didn't presume to do such things. What did it say about me that I'd spent a lot of years working with men who did? Not Abbas. His mother had taught him good manners, but when I'd worked with my grandfather… Well, getting the guys on the job to even put the seat down after using the toilet had been a vain quest.

While Zavryd was temporarily speechless, I hurried past, leading Sarrlevi out the front door and onto the covered porch. I wished we could have sat on the bench swing together and enjoyed the sunny day and each other's company, but his determined face suggested he would head straight off to look for his mother. Probably a good idea. Zondia and everyone else hunting Sarrlevi would think to look for him here. Maybe *my* house before Zavryd's, but I couldn't count on Zavryd not ratting him out if his family asked him where Sarrlevi was.

"Before you go," I said, reluctant to let him leave, "what do you think of that house across the street?"

Even if Zadie hadn't given me the address of the home she'd called about, I had no doubt which Victorian on the street had been listed. The corner lot had not one or two or three but *four* for-sale signs staked in the yard. No matter which way a car came from, the driver would be sure to see them.

"I have no opinion on the human domiciles here." His nose twitched. Either the botanical rain was still bothering him or he *had* an opinion that he wasn't sharing.

"It's for sale. Apparently, it's quite the deal since the neighborhood, this particular street anyway, has grown somewhat questionable since Val moved in."

Sarrlevi nodded without surprise. "Because of the dragon."

"That's part of it, I'm sure." I didn't point out that the last battle that had taken place on the lawn had been due to assassins from *his* guild—former guild—coming after me.

His gaze drifted to the recently regrown dragon topiaries, smoke wafting from their nostrils.

"Zadie and Val pointed out that I could buy it," I said.

Sarrlevi's jaw descended, much as Zavryd's had inside. "You wish to purchase a domicile adjacent to a dragon lair?"

"Well, it has a turret. And a view of the lake. I'm told the yard is free of goose droppings too."

He growled low in his throat. He was definitely developing a werewolf streak. Maybe it was a lingering side effect from his affliction.

"Would you still visit me if I moved here? Look, it's two stories. There might even be a basement. Lots of privacy for people who might be inhibited by having goblin roommates right across the hall." I waved to the house, though I was only musing at this point, not truly considering it. I hadn't even seen the inside. Zadie had promised it needed a lot of work, and the moss-blanketed shingles half-falling off the turret supported that notion.

"Little inhibits an assassin."

"Just scented laundry detergents."

Sarrlevi squinted at me. "You are teasing me."

"Yeah." I grinned. "We decided that doesn't bother you, didn't we? As long as I acknowledge occasionally that you're supportive? Tell me, would you be able to fulfill a mission if your target were wearing clothing scented with *botanical rain*?"

"From a distance. Will *you* not be inhibited by knowing a preternaturally powerful dragon who *snoops* on lovers is perched in his lair across the street?"

"Nope. Maybe the four of us could become good friends. We could tailgate for games and start going on double dates together."

The porch is within the confines of the wards, Zavryd announced into our minds. *Prepare for incineration.*

"Maybe you could move into one of *my* homes," Sarrlevi said, walking without haste down the steps. "Homes that are light years away from that dragon."

I blinked, almost tripping on a step. He was joking, right? Not seriously inviting me to move in with him.

Sarrlevi reached out a hand to steady me. There *was* a twinkle to his eyes. Good. I couldn't move to another planet. My family and my business were here. Even moving to another neighborhood would be a lot of work.

Not wanting to refuse him outright, especially if the idea of living with me appealed to him on any level, I said, "I am looking forward to visiting you in your mountain chalet. The one with the cheese cellar."

After passing under the disapproving eyes of the dragon topiaries and stepping onto the sidewalk, Sarrlevi faced me. "Is it *me* you wish to visit? Or my collection of properly aged and perfectly stored cheeses?"

"We've discussed that before." I grinned. "I believe you said it was okay if I wanted to romance you *and* your cheese."

"The latter I do not believe you would find as stimulating." He clasped my hands and gazed through his lashes at me.

My insides fluttered, and I wondered if Zavryd would complain about kissing done in front of his house.

"Stimulating?" I asked casually, though my gaze wouldn't leave his lips. "Maybe not, but the cheese also wouldn't grope me upon waking."

"Much to your disappointment." He bent as I rose up on tiptoes for a kiss.

It was probably my imagination that the topiaries sighed. *Probably.*

Long before I was ready to let him go, magic swelled in the intersection, a portal forming.

Sarrlevi released me, stepped back, and looked warily in that direction.

"You'd better go," I whispered.

With all the people—and dragons—after him, it was hard to imagine anyone coming through the portal who *wouldn't* shoot first and ask questions later.

"Find your mother," I added.

"Yes." As the portal appeared, Sarrlevi took another step back, wreathed himself in his camouflaging magic, and disappeared from my sight and my senses.

None too soon. A lilac dragon flew through the portal—Zondia—and she was followed by another, a great black-scaled female that I hadn't seen before. As if Zondia hadn't been bad enough, the other female's powerful aura made me want to run behind the house, down to Zoltan's lab, and hide in his coffin.

Zondia perched atop Val's house, her tail wrapping around the chimney. The other dragon landed on the roof of the house across the street, *her* long tail drooping down to come to rest between two of the for-sale signs. If I ended up being interested in that home and made an offer, I would make sure to wait a while. The asking price ought to plummet with each passing week—each progressive visit from a dragon.

I am Queen Zynesshara, ruler of the Dragon Council, the female boomed, her aura radiating sternness as well as raw power. *Where is the assassin Varlesh Sarrlevi?*

Hell. They really *were* after him.

The criminal attacked my daughter, the queen added, tail slapping at the ground in indignation. One sign flattened under it.

"Uhm," I said, wishing I weren't alone in front of the yard.

The queen's eyes narrowed as she focused on me. The door opened behind me, and I sensed Val and Zavryd coming out, but the queen's irritated gaze didn't leave me.

He just left, I replied telepathically. *He's recovered from the terrible poison that Princess Barothla gave him to turn him into a crazy elf who would attack dragons and be someone your Dragon Justice Court would want to punish and rehabilitate. You know Barothla was responsible for that, right? When Sarrlevi refused to assassinate her sister, Princess Rodarska, she got super pissy and vengeful.*

Claws raked through my mind as the queen continued to stare unblinking at me. Abruptly, I was relieved that Sarrlevi hadn't told me where he would go next, just that he would look for his mother. That meant I couldn't inadvertently betray him.

Is it not the way of your kind to refrain from speaking ill of the dead? the queen asked me.

Yeah, but less so if the dead was a total bitch who sent assassins after your mother.

Val made a strangled noise. Maybe she was more circumspect with the dragon queen.

My son informs me that Princess Rodarska may live, she said, still looking only at me. *Since the other dwarf princess is now dead, she must be found. Else we will be forced to intercede in dwarven politics to ensure a proper heir is selected for King Ironhelm.*

I wagered the dwarves and other intelligent races *loved* it when dragons interceded, but I didn't voice the thought, even in my mind. *I am looking for her. I plan to find her.*

Good. Continue to seek. And you, my daughter. The queen's gaze shifted to Zondia on the roof as she completely ignored Val and Zavryd. *You will find the assassin and bring him to the Dragon Justice Court.*

Yes, my queen, Zondia replied.

My queen, Zavryd started to say.

But her eyes flared with light and she said, *You will not address me when you are in that ridiculous inferior form.*

Worried there was room for many more dragons in the area, I backed up to where Val stood by the steps.

Yes, my queen, Zavryd said, more contrite and polite than I'd ever heard him. He took a few steps into the yard and transformed into a dragon. As huge and powerful as he was, he kept his head down and didn't hold his mother's gaze.

You should have brought the criminal to me, she said, *not permitted him to sleep in your lair.*

He was recovering from wounds that altered his mind, Zavryd surprised me by saying. It was almost as if he was standing up for Sarrlevi. *As the mongrel said, he was afflicted due to the conniving of the dwarven princess. She was not a proper heir.*

Zondia growled, reminding me that she might have been a friend of Barothla's, and her tail thumped on the roof. Fortunately, I'd enchanted that roof not long ago and the shingles stood up against such a small show of dragon ire.

When he is brought before the Dragon Justice Court, we will mind scour him and learn all the truths, the queen said. *And then mete out appropriate justice.*

I grimaced, not believing that would go well for Sarrlevi.

Find him, Zondia'qareshi, the queen repeated, then formed another portal. Before leaving, she looked at Val. *Valmeyjar.*

I expected the queen to say something vitriolic toward her or at least call her an inferior mongrel.

Yes, Queen Zynesshara? Val bowed politely.

You may correct my son when he is foolish about who he invites into the lair.

Correct, my queen?

With your sword if need be. The queen sprang off the roof, dislodging a few mossy shingles—*those* had never seen an enchanter's touch—and flew through the portal.

Zondia also left, not making a portal of her own but heading off to scout the neighborhood. If she and her mother had seen into my mind, they knew Sarrlevi had left recently and not through a portal.

Zavryd shifted back into his human form and shook his head. "Nothing good comes of inviting assassins into one's home."

As I gazed in the direction I'd last seen Sarrlevi, all I could hope was that he would successfully avoid Zondia, because I dearly wanted to invite him into mine.

She will not find me, Sarrlevi spoke into my mind from a distance. *As a practiced stalker, I am also good at hiding from others. No matter* what *I smell like.*

You're never going to let me do your laundry again, are you?

Not on Earth, no.

Be safe, I whispered to him, then added, *I love you.*

I know.

I almost teased him for being aloof—he'd been much more open with his feelings when he'd been worried about going mad and dying.

You have my letter, still? Sarrlevi added softly, as if to remind me that his words were in there.

Yes. I'll keep it forever.

Good.

THE END

Printed in Great Britain
by Amazon